INSTAGONER

INSTAGONER

A BARK AND BLOG MYSTERY

SYDNEY LEIGH

LEVEL
BEST BOOKS

First published by Level Best Books 2024

This novel is entirely a work of fiction. The names, characters and incidents portrayed in it are the work of the author's imagination. Any resemblance to actual persons, living or dead, events or localities is entirely coincidental.

Sydney Leigh asserts the moral right to be identified as the author of this work.

Author Photo Credit: Troy Cusolle

First edition

ISBN: 978-1-68512-716-9

Cover art by Level Best Designs

This book was professionally typeset on Reedsy.
Find out more at reedsy.com

To my mother, Rita. You are the best mom I could ever wish for. Thank you for everything you do. I love you.

Chapter One

F itz cycled ahead of me—whistling! The show-off. Why had I agreed to this torturous sport? Isn't this why cars were invented? Sounds of howling coyotes from the nearby mountains filled the darkness, like a warning to me from Mother Nature to check my bad attitude. Locally known as the Enchanted Mountains, I wasn't so sure they fit that description right now. I glanced at the stars above as a shiver escaped from under my thin jacket. Our town was a little less cozy at five a.m.

Through huffs and puffs and clouds of white breath, I dropped my head. Time to blow off this doubt. No more self-defeating rhetoric. This hill would not win. I was in control and would conquer this curve. So what if a heart attack seemed more probable with every spasmic gasp? I should die courageously—an honorable death, some might say.

Ha. "Surprisingly out of shape"—that's what people would actually say. Even my mother would join the bandwagon, telling anyone who'd listen she'd warned me against spending too much time in front of a screen. Mom rarely acknowledged my success as a blogger. Then again, this was probably a good thing. It took her even longer than it took me to get over the viral moment my career kicked off.

Was the utter humiliation worth it? At this point, three years later, I'd have to say yes. She might even agree since the local TV station proposed our upcoming show, bringing her back on the air after her much-loved stint as the local weather girl ended twenty-eight years ago, the day she found out she was pregnant with me.

A lock of hair fell forward as my head began to sag. Corkscrew blond

1

strands bounced up and down in my peripheral vision. *Why are you so perky?* Since Mom and Dad had become snowbirds, spending the coldest months in Florida, I'd noticed a decisive softening in my hair over the winter. Fitz argued it was the lack of humidity. I wasn't convinced. There was less than a week before Mom would be back, and I'd awoken to ringlets. Coincidence? I had my doubts.

Fitz waited halfway up the hill, not a hint of exertion on his handsome mug. I stopped next to him, straddling my bike. He leaned toward me and scrunched up his nose. "You okay?"

Curls stuck to my neck as sweat dripped down my face. I wiped the back of my hand across my cheek, ignoring the black smudges of mascara that had entered into the mix. "Do I flipping look okay?"

He raised his eyebrows. *"Flipping?"*

"Mom saw last week's rant." I took a minute to catch my breath. "All she noticed was the number of f-bombs I used."

"Uh-oh."

Uh-oh was right. My mother wasn't only opinionated. She was also a southern belle with distinct dos and don'ts. Things had modernized since she'd left and moved to the foothills of the Allegheny Mountains in the State of New York, but in her mind, the south hadn't changed since the Carringtons ruled prime time. "You can take the woman out of the south, but you can't take the south out of the woman," she'd told me. One of the cardinal rules? Never curse in public.

I wiped my clammy palms on the front of my pants. "I promised her I wouldn't swear for a week."

He grinned. "You're on a profanity diet? No more shiitake. Got it."

"Shut up and lead the way," I said. "Let's finish this mothertucker."

Fitz bit his lip and mounted his bike.

It wasn't long before he was back to being a blip. I tried to keep up, but in first gear, there wasn't much chance. My legs spun like a hamster's on a wheel. *At this rate, I'll be peddling into last week.* I cranked the gear up and carried on. If nothing else, I wasn't a quitter. Besides, I was doing this for Fitz. I promised him I'd give it a go, and I meant it. He was like a brother

2

from another mother. I was like a sister from another mister.

Fitz was the only one I'd get up for at this obnoxious hour. Although I was beginning to wonder—why were we up this early? Did people not ride their bikes in daylight anymore?

My drifting thoughts slowed. The light up ahead vanished as a dense fog came out of nowhere. It enveloped the dark, quiet road. My eyes shifted left, then right. Had I rolled onto the set of a bad horror movie?

I swallowed. *Don't freak out—go to your happy place.* I took a deep breath and conjured up a rugged lawman with tight pants and a sheriff's hat. *Hello handsome.* A flush of warmth whipped through my body, and my feet pressed through the pain. My pace sped up. Ah ha! Was this how Fitz did it? He was probably up ahead, envisioning some hot surfer dude with long hair and a six-pack. *Yoo-hoo.* Who was that? The luscious lawman was back, front and center, demanding my attention. He winked at me. *Cheeky devil.* I pedaled hard, feeling the burn.

The sheen of two small eyes popped up from nowhere. The lawman vanished, replaced by an oversized raccoon frozen on the spot directly in front of me. His beady eyes stared into the bright light attached to the stem of my bike. His little face, so cute, so helpless, was about to be rolled into oblivion at my hand.

I veered to the side. Loose gravel kicked up under the tires, and I lost control, careening off the shoulder. I hit a snag, and the bike came to an abrupt stop. Unfortunately, I didn't. Cold wind whipped across my face as I passed over the handlebars, and my heartbeat surged into warp speed. My vision morphed into a fish-eye lens, and the ground approached at an alarming rate. I clamped my eyes shut and braced for contact.

I landed with a thud.

Everything was still. And silent. *Am I dead?*

I unclenched one eye at a time. It was pitch black, with only a single white light visible. Was it *The* white light?

Breathe. I exhaled and watched a tiny cloud of smoke dissipate into the air. Okay, not dead. I wiggled my toes and flapped my arms, ensuring I was still intact. Relief set in, and my body relaxed. I remembered the breathing technique Fitz showed me to meditate, and I imitated the long, deep nasal breath.

Time to move. I rolled over and propped myself up on my elbows. The bright light from my bike lay a few feet away. It shone directly into my line of sight, and I winced, bringing my hand up to rub my eyes.

A sense of unease came over me. Goosebumps crept up my arms, and my heart began to thump hard all over again. There'd been a flash of something next to me. *What is that?* My breathing sped up. What had snagged my bike?

I pulled my hand away and eased myself up onto all fours.

That's when I came face to face with morning talk show host and frenemy, Jackie Hunter. Our eyes met, and I got the fright of my life. She didn't. She was already dead.

Chapter Two

J ackie stared at me—no, through me, as my face hovered inches above hers. The lifelessness in her eyes made it impossible for them to focus. One of her eyelash extensions had begun to droop and partially covered her left socket like a dangling spider.

I scrambled back from the twisted body in front of me, my legs and feet slipping in the dewy, cold ground surrounding us.

My heart beat so hard it felt like someone was punching me from the inside, trying to get out. A sense of alertness took over. I was on guard, my senses working overtime in case danger was nearby. All I could see was darkness except for the bike light illuminating Jackie's broken body. She looked almost inhuman, more like a mannequin who wasn't quite ready to be put on display, bent unnaturally to make it easier to dress before prepping her final pose.

My stomach twisted, and I ran out onto the road. Doubled over, I padded the outside of my pockets for a phone. Slick with sweat, I wiped my hands off on my jacket and then grabbed it out of my inside pocket. I called 9-1-1.

By the time I answered all the questions from the operator, sirens fired up somewhere in the distance. Confident help was almost here; the dispatcher ended the call. I tucked my phone in my pocket and looked around. Up the road, a small single light got closer by the second—Fitz's bike.

"Em!" he shouted.

I opened my mouth to call back to him, but a wave of nausea hit, and I pressed my lips together. *Don't you dare.*

Jackie's distorted body remained in the spotlight of my bike. A tingle of fear spiked as I stared at her.

Fitz vaulted off his bike, eyes wide with panic, as the sound of the ambulance drew closer.

"Emily!" His hands latched onto my shoulders, and he inspected me from the top down. "Are you hurt? Did you fall?"

I shook my head. "It's not me."

His eyes narrowed. "What happened?"

I pointed toward the light. Fitz wrenched his gaze away from me long enough to see the outline of Jackie's body in the light.

His body stilled as he took in the gruesome site. I had just enough time to explain the basics when the screaming sirens drowned out any further chance for us to talk. The ambulance arrived, followed by a police car and a fire truck.

Fifteen minutes later, the street was lit up with uniformed professionals in every direction.

I remained motionless as a buzz of energy filled the air. I didn't know what to do or what to think, so I retreated inside myself and tried to stay out of the way.

Before Fitz got pulled into the action, he paused to ask, "You good?"

I forced a smile. "I'll save my damsel in distress bit 'til you're free."

He nodded before rushing off. As a volunteer firefighter, he could be of service. There'd be lots of time for my emotional meltdown later on.

I watched him go as questions began to take shape in my mind. How could this have happened? What were people going to say?

The second answer was easy. *The Queen of Mean is dead.*

Jackie had been the host of a local TV gossip show, *The Morning Dish*. She relished her reputation as someone who tells-it-like-it-is. Chances were, a collective sigh of relief would soon be felt all over town. Especially by her favorite targets.

A prime example was Mayor Andrew Furlong—*Randy Andy*—as Jackie liked to call him. Without her around to remind locals of the deer-caught-in-the-headlights photo she'd shared of him exiting the adults-only shop two towns over, maybe he'd go back to being plain old Mayor Furlong again.

The earthy smell of moss wafted up my nose, twisting my stomach into knots. The sun would be up soon. How long had Jackie been lying there? Mayor Furlong's bestie, Dr. Don Winslow, was with her now. Crouched down, it would be his job to make the official declaration of death. Would Randy Andy be his first call?

Light blue cuffed pajama pants peeked out of his big black boots. He must've been tipped off about who laid here dead. No way he would've shown up in flannels if the body had belonged to anyone else.

Three years ago, I may have even cheered him on. Patted him on the back for the brazen show of disrespect. Jackie was a powerhouse who wielded her influence like a loaded gun. When she'd turned her attention on me, it blew up my world. It took me a long time to claw back from the humiliation I suffered on her show. But I'd done it and came out on top, turning my weakness into strength. Part of the healing process was learning to forgive.

Where was that courage now? I crossed my arms and pushed my fists into my ribs to stop myself from shaking. *Get a grip.*

A six-inch silver stiletto still adorned Jackie's left foot. It remained unsoiled, even against the grisly surroundings, as if above the notion of being dirtied. It shimmered in a way that reminded me of Jackie, like a last act of rebellion from a woman who refused to follow the rules. A gruesome mic drop she would've loved.

Why had Jackie worn those shoes in the first place? The signature red soles gave away the fact she'd chosen Louboutins for a midnight stroll. *Really Jackie?* If it had been me in those sky-high heels, there was no doubt the cause of death would've been a rolled ankle followed by a broken neck. But it was fitting. Few people had ever seen Jackie in anything else. According to rumor, even her hot-pink feathered slippers had some sort of lift.

Doc Winslow finished his exam and stood up. He peeled off rubber gloves, then tossed them aside. Jackie lay there unmoved. Had someone done the same to her? *Stop. Don't go there. I'm not ready for that yet.*

I rubbed my hands over my face and took another look around. Still busy.

What would Jackie think of the scene unfolding now, barely an hour after her body was found? It wasn't hard to imagine. She was a creature of habit.

I could hear the crass tone of her screechy voice with a full list of complaints and demands.

"Where are the news trucks? The cameras? Move people; this isn't a cattle run. Let's see a little energy. If I wasn't dead, you'd all get an earful from me. Get make-up here now. I look as pale as a frozen fish!"

At least the lights would've impressed her. The dark stretch of road was more like the Vegas strip, with bright flashes coming from every direction.

A nearby noise made me jump. A door click. Two paramedics emerged from the ambulance parked next to me. They waited their turn. One of the two switched the lights off, and I was left in the shadows.

I shivered. Worse than the panic was the calm that replaced it. The emergency was over. Jackie was dead.

The back doors of the ambulance swung open. A short, stocky woman with cropped dark hair and a crisp navy uniform hopped off the truck. She took a moment to stretch her thick arms up to the sky. Her partner, a tall, lanky man with tufts of red hair and freckles, emerged behind her.

The two of them pulled out the gurney without exchanging a word. I stood up straighter as they approached as if they were part of an official procession. They brushed by me without making eye contact. I was invisible to them. They had one purpose, and I didn't matter. Getting on with another death on another day.

They reached Jackie and got to work. Their efficiency mesmerized me. Protocol perfected. The pair looked nothing like each other, with the exception of their shared facial expression, almost robotic in its neutrality. There was no delay to ponder the identity of the victim, or to consider what happened. The practiced movements were second nature. No wonder this noble profession had such a high rate of PTSD. There was no allowance for emotion. Everyday heroes expected to leave their humanity at home.

Once Jackie was prepped, she was transferred into a black body bag and lifted onto the stretcher. The added weight made the thirsty wheels squeak. A beeping sound began to ping from inside the bag. It was the same chime my Apple watch made. A look was exchanged between the attendants, and they stopped. The female gestured with her thumb toward the bag. The guy pressed his lips together and unzipped the bag. He peeked inside and nodded to his partner, then reached his hand into the bag and felt around until the sound stopped. Once his hand was out, he zipped the bag back up, and they continued on. He glanced at me this time as they passed by. "I'm sorry about your friend. No one should die like that."

Our eyes met, and my mouth went dry. Did he recognize Jackie? Me? Our relationship was often speculated on since I'd gone from victim to collaborator on her show. Some people assumed we'd become friends, while others saw us more as life-long adversaries. I hadn't quite figured it out myself. Either way, right now, all I felt was exposed, like I'd been caught shoplifting by my next-door neighbor. I didn't respond to the comment, shifting my gaze to the ground.

A minute later, Jackie was lifted into the ambulance, and the doors were slammed shut. The siren was switched back on as it headed out. A sense of relief set in as I watched the ambulance shrink into oblivion. When it was gone, I began to scan the area. Now what?

Chapter Three

It was high time to find Fitz. He'd fill me in on what to expect. I looked for him in the small crowd of busy bees. It didn't take long to spot him. He was talking to his brother, Noah, also known as Sheriff Warner. The pair were taller than most and obviously related, although Fitz wore a hoodie and had sun-bleached tousled hair, like a vintage California beach bum, while Noah was clean-cut with a tidy side part and a pressed uniform.

After a minute, Fitz caught my eye. Noah peered up from their conversation and followed his brother's gaze. I couldn't read his expression but watched as he leaned into Fitz to say something. Fitz nodded in response, and the two of them made their way towards me.

Fitz looked me up and down as they approached. "You holding up alright?"

"Of course," I said, looking away. If I wanted to remain calm, I needed to keep my guard up. There was no way I could handle his way-too-sympathetic baby blues right now.

The brothers exchanged a look. My cool-as-a-cucumber exterior may have had a few cracks.

"Emily," Noah said. "I'm sorry to have to ask, but I need a statement from you."

Something about the formality of his tone fired up my nerves. After ten years of crushing on him, the least he could offer was a little warmth.

"Sure," I said. "This is really awful, and I want to go home."

He met my gaze, and the corners of his mouth lifted. "Not exactly what I had in mind. But I appreciate your candor."

"My candor?" I shot back.

Fitz recognized the direction I was headed and stepped in. "Why don't you tell Noah how you found Jackie's body?"

Noah clicked his pen. "That would be a good start. I'm trying to wrap my head around how Fitz rode right by the victim without noticing anything unusual."

Fitz tapped Noah's notebook. "Em fell off her bike. That's when she found Jackie."

"A raccoon came out of nowhere," I explained. "To avoid it, I steered off the road and lost my balance."

Noah looked at Fitz. He nodded.

"You just happened to land near her body?" Noah asked.

Her body. I shivered. The words sounded so cold. As if it was no more than a shell, separate from the rest of her, like a purse or a shoe.

"I hit a bump and lost control." I spoke slowly. "My guess is the bump was Jackie. It was so dark and foggy, I can't say for sure. Either way, I don't think I would've seen her if I hadn't been so close."

Another click of the pen. "That must've been a terrible shock."

I folded my arms across my chest, and I nodded.

When I didn't offer any more details, Noah pressed me further. "What did you think when you first saw her?"

A surge of dread rushed through me like a shot of whiskey on an empty stomach. I closed my eyes and was transported back.

Noah and Fitz listened as I told them everything I could remember, starting with the moment I saw Jackie's face.

When I was done, Fitz put his arm around me while Noah took notes.

"So what do you think?" Fitz asked Noah.

Noah gave him a look I couldn't read. "Hard to say."

"She couldn't have been dead for long," Fitz pressed.

"With her being outside, it's unlikely we'll get an exact time of death," Noah said.

Fitz nodded. "True. Maybe a hit and run?"

"Probably. But this is a police matter, so keep that between us."

It was weird listening to them talk. So matter-of-fact and void of emotion, as if trying to decide how high to install a new window on a house renovation project or which breakfast food contained the most protein.

I cast my eyes around. Signs of a new day had begun. Light hovered at the edges of the horizon. The sun teased a fresh reveal—the first day Jackie would no longer exist, at least in the here and now. How could something like this happen to her? A pounding headache set in as if I'd partied all night, which triggered the thought: had alcohol played a part in this tragedy? In our town, it certainly wouldn't be the first time.

Eliot Hill was a small place with a big reputation. While the full-time population hovered around the one-thousand mark, it regularly ballooned on weekends and holidays, especially in the winter months, although it was expanding every year.

Traditionally, Eliot Hill was known for its great ski slopes. But it was the après ski delights that really put it on the map. The currency here was fun, and our town did it right. Trendsetting bars, gastropubs, and regular street festivals caught the attention of revelers near and far.

The revolving door of big-name celebrities didn't hurt either. That was thanks to recent leadership from the mayor's office, whose goal it was to sell Eliot Hill as an ideal and affordable location for big-budget movie productions. The town was one of the few remaining ski towns that hadn't been bought up by corporations. And it was just as pretty in the summer months, too. While some of the state-run incentives had been curtailed, town council continued to offer catering discounts, accommodation subsidies, and even dry-cleaning perks. What made it work so well in Eliot Hill was the inclusion of the affected business owners in the meetings to help calculate costs and a collective agreement on the allocation of funds.

Of course, not everyone loved a pleasure-centered economy, and we had more than our share of trouble. Streets littered with after-party garbage, late-night noise pollution, and drunken debauchery were common issues. Luckily, the money brought in from the film crews and tourists meant a robust town budget, even after the subsidies were paid. We had both a fully staffed police force and EMS services to deal with the problems that arose.

Perhaps the most troubling issue? Drunk driving. No matter how hard the community came together to try to eradicate it, the problem persisted. It was possible Jackie had become another heart-wrenching statistic.

Here on Mountaintop Lane however, traffic was usually quiet. It was a residential road tucked away from the raucous crowds. There were only a handful of luxury homes, with long, winding driveways feeding off it. Although it had become part of a busy cycling route, there was only parking for two cars where the road dead-ended.

"You two should go home," Noah said, drawing my attention back. He gave his pen a final click, then tucked it into his shirt pocket. "Do you want a lift? An officer could drive you home and drop your bikes off later."

Fitz looked at me. *Was I up for the ride? Could I manage the short sprint back?*

I shook my head. "It's only a few minutes away. A cool breeze might do us some good."

"Are you sure?" Noah asked.

I nodded, and Fitz agreed.

"All right then," Noah said. "Be careful. I'll be in touch later with a few follow-up questions."

We said goodbye and headed to our bikes. Once it had been okayed, an officer had carried my bike over to where Fitz's lay.

I rubbed my hand over my eyes. It had been a long day already, and it wasn't even seven a.m. Without another word, I mounted my bike and peddled hard. We rode to the end of the street, where we hopped over the curb and followed a gravel path, disappearing into the forest.

We joined the bike route that led back to town. It wasn't long before the dark woods enveloped us, and the horror was left behind. Tears soaked my cheeks as the rich scent of pine comforted me along the narrow, well-trodden trail. A mile ahead, we took an off-shoot that brought us to the Main Street exit. I picked up my pace, desperate to reach the Longbourn Café, AKA home sweet home.

Chapter Four

I breathed in the pungent aroma of yeasty, fresh bread a block before we hit the strip. Janey's Bakery had its door propped open, and the familiar scent flooded the street, leaving no room for any competition. I took a deep breath. *Why hadn't Sara Seabody infused her yoga studio classes with this smell?* The Yoga Den would have a lot more appeal if the odors coming off hot bodies could be replaced with the scent of hot bread. Striped awnings were rolled out above quaint shops, and blackboards were placed outside doors with cheery greetings. The local cheese shop owner, Harold Kim, gave me a thumbs up as I passed by, a fresh chalk handprint visible on his crisp red apron. *Cheese is like a good marriage—it gets better with time,* his board read. Curious. Harold was on his third wife.

The Longbourn Café was already open by the time we arrived. Fitz must've called ahead and asked one of the baristas to cover for him. We pulled our bikes onto the curb outside. I balanced my bike against my hip and pressed my hand against the window to shield the glare from the morning sun. I peeked inside.

The coffee shop was already busy. Bright and airy, Fitz had chosen a mixture of light wood and white brick to give the place a modern, airy feel. The walls were lined with a combination of booths and open tables, and in the middle ran a long granite slab countertop with accompanying stools that divided the workstation and accompanying staff from the customers. Like most businesses that lined the street, the café was much deeper than it was wide. To add to the modern flair, faux greenery was placed in corners, and white dome pendant lamps were lit throughout.

"Busy?" Fitz asked from behind me.

I nodded without turning away. Two people waited in line while a young woman with a crop of bright blue hair took the order of a third. The cool air against my shallow breaths formed a circle of condensation on the window, blurring my view. I rubbed it away before looking back inside. A woman sitting in a nearby booth began to gesticulate wildly with her hands, leaning in as she spoke to the person across from her, a wide-eyed expression accompanying her dramatic explanation. A crop of goosebumps formed up my arms. Then, her face broke out into a laugh. I felt my shoulders relax. I wasn't ready to talk about what I'd seen. I needed more time to process what had happened.

"C'mon," Fitz said. "Let's get inside."

I leaned in for one more glance at the woman in the booth. She was leaning back now, nodding as she focused on the person sitting across from her. For a brief second, I wondered what they were talking about. Normally, local gossip piqued my curiosity. Not today. *Twenty dollars says my story is better than yours.*

The depressing thought soured my mood even further. I drew back from the window and followed Fitz around to the back of the building. He locked his bike near the rear entrance while I pulled mine inside through the heavy steel door. The familiar scents of espresso, chai, and cinnamon fused together, comforting me like a warm hug. *We made it.* I lifted my bike up to the large wall hook Fitz had installed for me a few months earlier. He waited as I secured it, then followed me up the steep, narrow steps to my apartment. Murray's fierce bark could be heard from behind the door.

"You don't have to come with me—I'm fine." I glanced at Fitz, who stood behind me.

"I know," he said. "But downstairs looks under control, so I thought I'd take Murray out for a walk."

A mixture of gratitude and affection flowed through me. I looked back at him. "Have I ever told you what a gem you are?"

"They say diamonds are a girl's best friend. I'm the budget version." He pointed to the door where the barks were now almost frenzied. "You better hurry before the beast breaks through the door, and I have to replace it. Again."

"On it." I turned back and shoved the key in the door.

As the lock turned and the sound jacked up, Fitz raised his voice to compete against the deep-voiced sounds. "This'll give you time to brew some tea before you're pinned down for snuggle time."

Was I that predictable? Yup. "You'll hear no argument from me."

The door opened into my apartment, and a sea of excited black fur approached. Normally, Murray would've come with us for the ride, but in the wee hours of the morning, the massive mutt hadn't budged.

"I've only been gone a few hours, goofball." Murray jumped up, resting his two front paws on my shoulders. Standing on two legs, he was tall enough to lick my face. I cringed, wiping slobber from my cheek as I was engulfed in a sea of kisses. His furiously flapping tail knocked over a plastic vase of fake flowers that sat next to the door. For Murray, two hours was too long.

Fitz ushered past us and grabbed the leash from its nearby hook. Murray's head whipped around at the familiar sound, and he dropped down on all fours, scrambling toward Fitz without an ounce of grace.

Fitz wrestled with the clasp with a groan. "Stop moving, Murball."

Murray stilled long enough to get the leash attached. Fitz opened his mouth to say something but got pulled away too quickly to get the words out, his mussed blond hair flopping over his eyes, reminding me of an agile sheepdog. I waved as the two of them bounded down the stairs together. The spring-loaded door at the bottom of the steps shut behind them, and I was left in silence for the first time in what felt like days. I caught my reflection in the small mirror next to the door and flinched. *Egad.*

How was it that I resembled a creature out of a George R. R. Martin novel, but Fitz looked as fresh as morning dew? *No tête-à-tête with a dead body, for starters.* I dragged myself toward the kitchen. Tea time. The kettle still had water in it, ready to go. Perfect. I pressed the button to start it up and grabbed a large mug out of the cupboard.

The sun was fully up now. Natural light poured into the large open area and reflected on a glass cupboard door across the room. I squinted at the cheery brightness like a grumpy old man. *It's going to be a long day.*

I swiveled around in my chair and faced the window. Down below, a man struggled to load a cluster of bicycles onto the complex roof rack of a parked minivan. He could barely reach the top of the supersized vehicle, and I wondered how he'd manage it. As one of the bikes toppled off of the rack and onto the road, I realized he wouldn't manage it at all. Tires screeched, a horn beeped, and the man waved an apology to the driver of the passing car, who'd stopped just in time to prevent running over the bike in question. On the adjacent sidewalk, two kids exchanged a look of concern while they munched on chocolate-dipped donuts. Their mom stood just behind them, a hand on each of their shoulders, her lips pressed tightly together as she took in the scene. With a big breath, the man gave up his attempts, pulled all the bikes down, then opened up the rear of the van. He somehow managed to shove all four bikes safely inside after patiently rearranging the van's contents.

If only the driver who'd hit Jackie had had the same lightning-quick reflexes the passing driver below did. Jackie would still be alive, and I would've started my day with an excursion that didn't involve finding a dead body.

I drew back and stretched out on the couch, closing my eyes. I thought the silence would comfort me, but it didn't work. After a few minutes, I gave up, unable to shake the feeling of restlessness and dread.

Back in the kitchen, I dropped two slices of bread into the toaster, then ripped open a new packet of lemon ginger tea, breathing in the soothing scent. That didn't help either. With a sigh, I dropped it in the cup, poured the water, and left it to steep.

Another look outside showed more people milling about town. Early risers were out for a brisk walk, coffee lovers filed into the café for their morning brew, and boutique owners arrived at work for another busy day. Lights were switched on, and A-frame chalkboards were put outside, each with daily specials or clever quotes.

The familiar buzz was comforting on one hand, yet cruel on another. Nothing around here had actually changed. Life carried on. The world didn't yet know that Jackie Hunter was dead. Then again, once the news broke, who would lament her passing? There would be no hugging it out, or broken sobs, or quiet weeping. Our town didn't need to prepare extra pews at the church for a grief-stricken community. Jackie was mean and had more enemies than friends.

Is that why she ended up on the side of the road?

Before I had time to ponder the question, my door opened and Murray rushed inside, tongue hanging out and bursting with joy to see me. Fitz was right behind him, an easy grin on his face. "It's really hard to be in a bad mood when Murray is around."

Murray jumped up and planted a slobbery wet kiss across my nose to prove his point.

I grinned at the drooling mass of love. "Settle down, you giant furball."

He sat at attention, and I bent over to rub my head against his. "Go chill out."

Murray grumbled but followed my orders. He hopped over his dog bed and onto the couch.

"I hate to leave you alone after what happened."

"I'm fine," I said, an octave too high. I cleared my throat and lowered my pitch. "All good."

Fitz crossed his arms. "You're lying, but I won't fight you on it. I need to get downstairs and make sure things are running smoothly. However, I can be back within ten minutes if you need me."

"I just need some peace and quiet."

He pulled out his phone from his pocket and looked at the time. "Okay. See you in a few hours then."

"Yes, boss."

Fitz gave me a quick hug, then headed out. There was no need to ask if I'd be by later. Coffee was like air to me, and The Longbourn served the best cappuccinos in town.

My growling stomach reminded me I had toast waiting. I dropped a big glob of peanut butter onto each slice, then stood at the counter and scarfed down the snack. I chased it down with a glass of cold water. Exhaustion kicked in almost instantly once the food hit my stomach. I moved to the couch and curled up next to Murray, allowing my eyes to drift shut. Images of broken doll parts rushed through my mind. I felt around the couch for the nearest throw pillow and pressed it over my face, making it hard to breathe. A shift sideways allowed better airflow while effectively blocking out all nearby sounds. Within a few minutes, my breathing deepened and I could finally feel myself relax.

I awoke to Murray's wet nose nudging my cheek. I reached my hand out and ruffled his fur. "Good boy," I said into my pillow. My eyes opened at the unwelcome sound of my phone ringing. Most people sent texts. Who was calling me?

I dragged myself up and reached for the phone. "Hello?" My voice sounded groggy. How long had I slept?

"Emily?"

The cracking voice was desperate and familiar. It was Becka Hunter, Jackie's younger sister. My fatigue vanished. I cleared my throat. "You okay?"

Her sister was dead. Ridiculous question.

"No."

A fresh wave of anxiety coursed through me. "I'm so sorry about Jackie."

She took a ragged breath. "I guess the whole town knows by now."

There was a moment of awkward silence.

"Is there anything I can do?" I asked.

"That's why I called." Another pause. "Can you meet me downstairs?"

"Of course. When?"

"I'll be there in an hour," Becka said. She hung up the phone without saying goodbye. I pulled the phone away from my ear and frowned at it. Why did Becka want to talk to me?

Becka was a friend. But not *that* kind of friend. She and I hadn't been close in years since our friendship went up in flames, permanently fractured after a betrayal I couldn't forgive. We'd never returned to the status of confidantes.

So her coming here to see me now could only mean one thing. She'd learned I'd been the one to find Jackie and wanted more details. My stomach knotted. Should I give them to her? What if it made her more upset?

Before I could get ready, I had to do a quick post. I dug through my makeup bag and pulled out thick concealer and blush, the kind used mainly by TV makeup artists and morgues. *Was Jackie getting the same treatment right now?*

Heavy makeup was followed by clouds of powder, two rounds of eye drops, and rosy red lipstick. I cleared my throat and looked for my camera. Time to put on a show.

Chapter Five

Half an hour later, I sat downstairs, anxiously awaiting Becka's arrival. The café was buzzing. Clinking cups, grinding beans, and noisy chatter filled the air. Like crashing waves or steady rain, these were my favorite sounds. If only I could turn up the volume to override my darkening thoughts. I was stationed in my regular booth, where I nursed my coffee, trying to forget the grisly early morning. *Caffeine, take me away.* When that didn't work, I tapped on my keyboard and waited for my laptop screen to light up.

My post had gone live. Nothing particularly inspiring, but it was done. There was no mention of Jackie's death. I'd smiled at the camera while horrific images flashed through my mind. *Everything is good. Everything is normal.* I'd repeated these sentences as if they were daily affirmations. I braced myself to review the post, barely able to remember what I'd said, then pressed the replay button.

Saturday, May 4th

Morning people!

I'm back from my early ride, and I made it. Barely. My first tip? Do your make-up and hair after you bike, not before. More importantly? Don't fret. Remember, perfectionism is the enemy of happiness.

Let it go.

That's all for now, peeps. Have an extraordinary day. I'll check in later.

21

Onward,
    Emily

Huh. Could be worse. *When did I get so good at lying?* The beauty of online life was crafted reality. The kicker? I had an unspoken rule to be open and honest with my followers. My posts were messy sometimes. They saw the good, the bad, and the brutal. If my die-hard fans knew I'd willfully kept a major crisis from them, it could be disastrous for my brand.

My *brand.* A deep flush filled my cheeks. Did my brand matter as Jackie lay dead on some metal table, waiting to be poked and prodded like a prized slab of meat? No, it didn't. But I liked my job. I loved my job, in fact.

"Shouldn't she be here by now?" I called over to Fitz, who stood behind the counter.

He looked down at his watch. "Becka said she'd be here at ten o'clock, right?"

"Yup. She's almost late."

He grinned at me. "In other words, she's still early."

I gave him a withering glare and turned my attention to the window. *C'mon, Becka, where are you?* I just wanted to get this over with. Sort of like my first appearance on Jackie's show.

My mind drifted back to that day. The day that changed my life forever.

I still remember the beads of sweat lining my forehead. The bright lights were relentless. I was caught off guard, anxiety crippling me as I met Jackie's eyes from across the room. The only cold thing within reach. Her face was placid except for her top lip, curled back with just a hint of contempt, as if she'd been served a plate of undercooked chicken. Her chin was lifted, and her head was cocked to the side.

"Can you repeat the question?" I asked.

Jackie glowered at me, slowing her speech to enunciate every word. "Rumors are spreading. Are they true?"

"No. I'd never... *we'd* never..."

"Fake your love to maintain your social media status as the perfect couple? How long have you been pretending? Or has it been a sham since the beginning?"

"Of course not." I shifted in my seat and turned to Rob, who'd been uncharacteristically quiet during Jackie's onslaught of accusations. Maybe it was true that we could use a little rekindling. A dash of excitement wouldn't be bad. But we'd been together for almost seven years since we were eighteen-year-old college freshmen. Every relationship ebbed and flowed. So *maybe* we'd been caught up in the frenzy our following had invoked. We had no idea that it would garner so much attention—that we'd become the social media darlings of coupledom. It was easy to get caught up in the image. It felt good to be admired and loved for our relationship. What was wrong with that?

Rob stared at Jackie, his face pale and clammy. Was he coming down with something? "Um..." he stammered. His eyes flashed to me, and he rubbed the back of his neck.

"Rob?" Jackie said, shifting her focus to him. "Do you have something to say?"

Once again, he stared at her. His knee began to bounce.

"Our viewers are very intuitive. We can all see that you have a truth to tell. Go on, let it out. We are not here to judge. We are here to listen."

His Adam's apple bobbed. "It's not that we don't care about each other but..."

The back of my neck prickled. *Wait, what?*

"Go on," Jackie prodded in a softer tone.

He looked from her to me. "I'm sorry, Emily. I don't think we can keep this up."

My eyelids blinked, one at a time, out of sync, in slow motion, like the speed of my comprehension. "Keep what up?" My voice came out hoarse.

With a heaving chest, he confessed. "I don't love you anymore."

Jackie smiled at me. Satisfaction and delight, emanating. The cameras closed in on my face, making sure to capture every microsecond of my fall from grace.

A blaring horn on Main Street brought me back to the present. I shuddered.

"You okay?" Fitz said, sliding into the booth across from me.

"Yeah, totally." A raised eyebrow told me he didn't believe me. "A little on edge," I admitted after a pause.

"Edge of a cliff?"

I barked out a laugh. "Do I look that bad?"

"I'm not sure if I'm reading you right or if I'm projecting my own guilt onto you."

No one had ever known me as well as Fitz. We'd spent countless hours and had been through every major catastrophe and celebration I could remember. But we were nothing alike, not really. Where I was an overthinker, Fitz lived in the moment. If I had a to-do list, Fitz dealt with things as they happened. He had enviable low anxiety and was my rock. Guilt was not in his regular wheelhouse of emotions.

"What's up? Did you run out of whipped cream for the pup cups?"

His eyes widened. "If my regular dog clientele came in and I didn't have their regular treat in stock, you'd have heard the protests of barks, whines, and… smells." He wrinkled his nose with a shudder. " Believe me, I learned the hard way with that one." He leaned closer. "I feel bad I forced you to go biking with me this morning. Had I not, you'd still be sleeping instead of dealing with a tragedy. I'm so sorry."

"Oh no, you don't." I crossed my arms. "I'm the worry wart. There's no space in this friendship for you to start overanalyzing situations and casting blame on yourself for things that are out of your control. That's my thing. Back off."

"But…"

"Did you have anything to do with Jackie's death?"

He balked. "Of course not."

"Did you intend on crossing paths with misfortune this morning?"

He shook his head.

"Then step off, please. If you are upset, we can talk it through. But none of this is your fault, and if you want to feel bad about anything, it's not arming yourself with fresh croissants when joining me at this booth. End of story. Got it?"

"Fair enough." He stood up and did a full body shake. "Wow, I feel so much better, thanks." He looked at me. "Is that how you feel all the time?"

"Nah, it's way better these days."

He left in search of fresh baked goods as I thought about how far I'd come managing what my mom called my worry bug. It's not that I thought Jackie's show made me an anxious person, but it seemed to wake up what had been lying somewhat dormant. Chances were, it would've come out at some time. It just happened to be on a big stage. Literally.

* * *

I tried to remember how the show had ended once I'd been dumped. Did I immediately leave the stage, or was I too stunned? I wasn't really sure. Everything blurred after the initial shock. I wondered if Jackie ever considered what would happen to me after the show aired? The humiliation I'd suffer because of the breakup, along with the accusations of being a liar and a fake. Probably not.

Originally, we'd been scheduled to talk about how to successfully navigate a relationship from college to the real world.

There'd been pre-screened interviews, several in fact. Unbeknownst to us, or at least to me, there'd been a change in the direction of the show. It was kept hush-hush so only her most trusted crew knew the plan. Jackie saw a great opportunity to deliver genuine drama on live TV. Never mind that it had been my real life. My real feelings.

And Rob's, too. How could I be mad at him when it was only under the unrelenting lights and pressure that he'd finally admitted his real feelings? Not that I was able to remain close with him. The moment he dumped me changed everything. Our relationship ended, and our burgeoning play into the world of public coupledom shattered like glass—or my heart, which was also decimated that day.

But Jackie only saw herself as a proponent of truth. It didn't really matter that we were hurt along the way. Her world was black and white. The way she saw it, we'd screwed up by pretending to feel something for each other we no longer felt. And every choice has a consequence. So, to her, there was no one to blame but me. And Rob.

Only maybe a little less Rob's fault. Why else would she start dating him after the fallout? But that was a guess. I never asked her and barely spoke to him after that. I guess I'd never truly know.

The scent of melting butter on puff pastry drew my eyes up. Fitz was back, this time with full hands. He placed the fresh croissant in front of me before setting down his own and digging in. I paused to breathe it in before allowing myself to have a bite.

"Thank you. This is more like it."

"Good timing. The bakery just dropped them off."

"I can tell," I gushed through a mouthful. "Still warm."

Fitz was finished his before I had a second bite. "Now that you're fed, are you feeling better?"

"With this in my hand, how could I say no?"

"Good." He glanced over at the growing line.

"I'm set here. Go help the crew." I waved him off, and he went to assist the baristas with their orders.

What a guy. Best friend ever. After the breakup on Jackie's show, it took him a few days to convince me that I'd be okay. That I'd survive the breakup and the viral mortification. Like always, he was right. In fact, it's what led me to where I am today.

Instead of hiding, or digging a hole and never resurfacing—my first inkling—I did something else. With the support of Fitz and after listening to some good advice from Andrew Huberman's podcasts, I began to journal through my pain. Only I decided to do it publicly through a new blog. My uncurated truth.

As it turned out, the viral breakup worked in my favor. I became the poster girl for dumped women everywhere. My blog became an overnight success, and my social media pages blew up. Tissue brands and cozy blanket companies jostled for my attention, offering lucrative sponsorship deals. Before I knew it, I was making ten times what I'd made as one-half of a couple, only this time, it was *all* my thoughts, nothing left out. Raw and real.

And after an initial apology and an explanation for what really happened between Rob and me, I let it go.

That was three years ago.

Fitz sat down again, the line of customers under control. "I'm baaack."

"I'm fiiiiine."

He studied me, unconvinced. "You've been through a traumatic ordeal. Now you're waiting to talk about it with someone who will be even more traumatized than you."

"And I love that you're here for me. But hovering as if possessed by an overbearing mom is not the help you think it is."

He looked surprised, but not in a bad way. "Kris, right?"

I looked around. "Chris, who?"

"Kris Jenner." He pulled out a pair of sunglasses and struck a pose. "I've always thought we shared a likeness from the right angle."

"I have no words."

"Ah, there it is."

I scanned left then right. "What?"

"Your shoulders slump. Means you've relaxed." When I gestured with my thumb to get lost, he smiled. "Just remember, I've always got your back. I may not be your momager, but I'm always here."

"Lurking?"

"Supporting." He took off the glasses, tucked them back in his pocket, and pivoted back toward the counter.

Couldn't argue that. When the rest of the world had turned its back, my bestie was still there, holding steady.

My first task when I began my blog was to unravel the humiliating breakup in my own words. Once I had it all out, I moved on to navigating the single life. My followers were invested in my story because they'd seen me hit rock bottom. And as much as people loved to watch a juicy fall from grace, there was even more interest in witnessing those same people climb their way back up.

I discussed ways I'd rallied to pick myself up and self-soothe, how to weather humiliation, and elements of my life that were a source of joy. Like

Murray, who became the poster dog for canine companionship.

I became so comfortable airing it all out, I even began to discuss dipping a toe back into dating.

I wouldn't become a millionaire. But I was in a good place and intended to stay there. So, I kept things real.

But...was I ready to share that Jackie Hunter was dead with my audience? I had the final bite of my croissant. No. Not just yet.

Chapter Six

I swallowed as a wave of emotion passed over me. Jackie was gone. No longer in existence. That was going to take time to accept. Time to think about something else. Like Becka. Our history had been another source of pain. But I was fully healed from that wound, wasn't I?

Thinking back, what Becka did was almost worse than what happened with Jackie. Because Jackie never pretended to be my friend. The humiliation I suffered when she tried to destroy my reputation on live TV was not as hurtful as finding out the identity of the person who'd come up with the idea and the ammunition to do so.

That credit belonged solely to Becka.

Bang. Murray's head had hit the underside of the table like a brick, spilling half my coffee in the process. Oblivious, he began to wag his tail and bark.

I braced myself and swiveled around to see her plodding her way to the table. No more time to sort through my feelings. Regardless of what happened in the past, Becka had lost her sister and needed whatever support I could manage to give.

Her uber-cropped bangs shot out in every direction, and her chiseled brunette bob, normally polished and perfect, was pulled off her face with a faded pink scrunchie. I caught her eye and waved. Her black-rimmed glasses framed smudges of dark make-up circling her light brown eyes. She clutched her phone to her chest with both hands.

Becka's jaw tightened as she neared. If she wanted to cry on someone's shoulder, she would've called her bestie, Vera Hansen. But she hadn't. There was purpose in her eyes. My stomach knotted. I should've known she'd come to me for a reason. She wanted details. And she knew I was the only one who could give them to her.

The café grew quiet, wide eyes peeking over mobile phones to get a good look. No one said a word. But everyone knew. Jackie's body had been found only hours earlier. Small town? Big gossip.

Becka trudged into the booth, and her shoulders slumped. I rose up to give her a hug, but she held up a shaky hand before I'd left my seat.

"Please don't."

I reversed my movement and dropped back. I understood. She was barely keeping it together. Any contact might break her wide open.

"Becka," I said. "I'm so sorry."

She removed her glasses and rubbed her face. "Thanks." Her skin was red and blotchy, and the circles around her eyes reminded me of coffee stains. Emotions began to stir inside me, and I felt the sting of tears crop up. Weird. My hard shell had become like armor where Jackie was concerned, and I didn't think anything would crack it—not even this. But looking at Becka made me remember Jackie had been the sum of all her parts, not just the ones that had caused me pain.

"Don't look at me like that," Becka warned. "Sympathy makes me weak."

I knew exactly what she meant. "Sorry." Fitz came by with large steaming teas for both of us. He put the drinks down and looked at Becka.

"I'm so sorry, Becks." He put a hand on her shoulder.

She reached up and patted his arm. "Thanks, Fitz."

"I'll let you two talk. If you need anything, I'm here."

Becka gave him a small smile, then Fitz looked at me with raised eyebrows. It was all he needed to do to ask if I was okay. I nodded. Always good to be reminded he had my back.

Once he was gone, Becka and I both reached for our tea. It was ginger lemon, a Longbourn favorite. Having an object to hold seemed to help Becka relax. She blew on her tea to cool it down. Heavy silence filled the space between us.

A group of teenage girls sitting nearby caught my attention. Their heads were butted together. Excited whispers and eager looks darted between them. I could only imagine the rumors that had begun to circulate.

Becka cleared her throat. The girls faded into the background.

"Noah came to see me earlier and told me that Jackie died in a hit-and-run," Becka said. "He mentioned you were there."

I braced myself, waiting to hear more.

"He wouldn't tell me much," Becka continued. "I hoped you could fill in the blanks. I can't wrap my head around it."

My mouth went dry. "What do you want to know?"

Becka had a sip of her tea and sat back. "Why was Jackie walking along the dark road in the first place?"

Good question. I'd wondered the same thing. "No idea."

She folded her arms across her chest. "What happened at the party, Em? I deserve to know."

The party! I'd forgotten all about it. Last night, Jackie's newish boyfriend, a show consultant, had thrown a party for her. She'd invited her staff and anyone else associated with the show. That included me, since I'd become the designated social media expert six months earlier. My semi-regular visits were mostly to discuss celebrity gossip, specifically who-was-dating-who, although Jackie would sometimes ask me about popular videos or online trends. I'd almost turned down the offer, given that Jackie was still dating Rob at the time, but I was so over it, I didn't care anymore. The opportunity had been too good to decline. It paid well and expanded my audience. Plus, it was fun.

Becka cleared her throat, bringing me back to the present. I shook my head. "Sorry, I wasn't there."

Becka pursed her lips. "What do you mean?"

What I meant was that I'd never attend a party that celebrated Jackie. Yes, I was over the past. It didn't mean I wanted to socialize outside of work. That was a line I wasn't willing to cross. Not that I'd say that out loud. At least not to Becka. "I wasn't at the party. Weren't you?"

She should've been there, after all. She was Jackie's producer, as well as her sister. It's not like it was far. It was at Jackie's new boyfriend's place.

Something clicked. A flash of the invitation went through my mind. That was where Jackie had been found. Mountaintop Road. The address where the party was held was on that street. Why had she been out walking when there was a party inside? It was early May, too. Not warm enough to wander without a coat, especially in the evening.

Becka huffed out a breath. "Something came up, and I couldn't make it."

Pushing aside my inner thoughts, I focused back on Becka. "What about Vera? She usually went to those types of things. Maybe she could fill you in."

Becka's best friend was the stage manager, and from what I remember, the party was mandatory for full-time staff. Only way to guarantee attendance.

"Nope, she didn't go either."

I frowned. "Who did?"

"I assumed you did." Her face grew tight. "Why would Noah say you were there if you weren't?"

I chewed the inside of my cheek. She didn't know I was the one who found Jackie. The idea of explaining what I'd seen and how I was involved was as appealing as a tin of cold sardines. But what choice did I have? Becka deserved to know.

I met her gaze. "When Noah said I was there, he didn't mean I was at the party. He meant I was the one who…"

She frowned at me while I tried to think of how to explain what happened. "Tripped over your sister's dead body" felt a little insensitive.

My sputtering fizzled out when Becka gasped. The truth dawned on her before I could figure out what to say.

"You found her?"

I nodded and let it sink in.

Becka studied my face. "None of this makes sense. Where exactly did you find her?"

"Fitz and I were out riding on Mountaintop Lane. I fell off my bike and…and…"

Becka flinched. "She was just lying there? On the side of the road?"

I pressed my lips together. No more details. She got the picture.

Her eyes narrowed. "Why didn't you call me?"

Huh. Good question. "I'm sorry."

Her expression turned hard. "Yeah, I guess you should be."

I didn't blame her for being angry. "Is there anything I can do?"

"You can make up for it now. Tell me everything you know."

Everything I knew would haunt my dreams for the rest of my life. I'd try to spare her the same. "It was dark and foggy out. By the time I found her, she was gone."

Her eyes continued to probe me. She sat so still I wasn't sure she was breathing. "So, you decided to go home and have a good night's sleep without giving Jackie or me a second thought?"

I shook my head. "You don't understand. It was this morning. Just before sunrise."

"*This morning?*" She blinked. "I thought she was killed last night."

"Right. At least that's what it looks like."

"Why do you say that?" she demanded.

How could I explain it without sharing anything too graphic? For a moment, I was stumped. Then it came to me. "She was wearing a white cocktail dress and heels."

"And?" she said with a hint of frustration.

Touché. For most people, party dresses and heels were evening wear. But Jackie was different. The woman dressed like it was award season on a daily basis.

I thought about Jackie's discolored skin, her ice-cold body. "It's better you don't know."

She drew back, eyeing me warily. "Why?"

"The details won't help you make sense of this."

She seemed to consider my words. "Fine. But there's one thing I have to know."

"Okay, what's that?"

"If you agree with Noah's assessment?"

I frowned. "That she was hit by a car?"

She paused before answering. "That it was an accident."

My breath caught. Becka leaned over the table, closing the gap between us.

"Tell me the truth," she whispered.

"I-I don't know." Anxiety twisted in my gut as her eyes bore into me. "Like I said, it was dark out. Everything happened so fast—I fell, Jackie was there, Fitz came to help… and then the cops showed up."

Becka drew back and picked up her tea. She turned her head toward the window, so I did the same. People carried on back and forth, shopping bags in hand, going about their daily routine.

"Noah said it was probably a hit-and-run," Becka said, finally.

I pictured Jackie's body, left at the side of the road, broken. "I'm so sorry."

"Me too. But I think there's more to it."

My shoulders tensed. "Like what, exactly?"

"I need to show you something."

Becka looked around like a paranoid fugitive, scouring the café to make sure no one was watching. Once satisfied, she pulled out a small crumpled note stuffed in her back pocket.

"Check this out." She slipped the note across the table but kept her hand on it. "This was sitting out on Jackie's coffee table when I went to her condo this morning after the cops came by my place."

The bottom half of the page was ripped off. Becka unfolded the paper enough so I could read the note. There were four words hand-written in block letters.

I WILL DESTROY YOU.

What The Frog.

I stared at her. "Do you know who wrote this?"

She shook her head.

I read the words again. There was no way to mistake the implication. Jackie was threatened, and then she was killed. "Have you shown this note to Noah?"

She gave me a hard look. "No."

"Why not?"

She uncovered the corner of the paper where her hand had been. There was a small hole where a tack might've held the note to a wall. Strange. Even stranger was the familiar logo underneath. It belonged to the Eliot

Hill Sheriff's Department.

Chapter Seven

There were certain facts I knew about Noah Warner. First, he'd been sheriff in Eliot Hill for four years. Second, he'd wanted to be a police officer since we were kids, just like his dad. Lastly, and most importantly, Noah was a good guy.

So when Becka showed me the note she'd found at Jackie's, I knew the sheriff's logo at the top of the page didn't mean what she thought it did. But there was a reason she went there, and it had nothing to do with Noah. More likely, it was because Jackie had targeted local law enforcement. "Lazy and ineffective" had been her usual criticisms. Although she'd gone as far as using terms like "corrupt" and "on the take." Whether or not she believed it, she caused a stir every time she accused Eliot Hill P.D. of being in cahoots with the local motorcycle gang. 'All these yahoos left to roam free on our streets?' she'd say. "Why aren't they locked up behind bars where they belong? Only one thing makes sense. They pad the pockets of our boys in blue." In her defense, she hadn't chosen sides. Both the cops and the bikers had been on her hit list.

Becka watched as I examined the note. "Can you see why I brought the note to you instead of Noah?"

No, not really. I bit my lip. "Noah's a decent cop, Becka. I've known him my whole life."

A dark scowl told me my dismissal didn't sit well with her. "How predictable."

My stomach tightened. "What?"

She scoffed. "Sheriff Hottie could be robbing the bank, and you'd excuse it as redistributing town funds."

Ouch. I opened my mouth to respond, then shut it again. *Don't take the bait. She's just venting.*

She wasn't finished. "Jackie hounded the cops. Maybe Noah or one of his goons got sick of it."

I felt my face flush. Becka was angry. I got that. But wild accusations wouldn't help. "I don't think so, Becka. Why would the police want to kill Jackie? Because she didn't like them? If that were the case, they'd off people on a daily basis."

She didn't look convinced.

As if on cue, Fitz walked over and dropped off a few biscotti. Nothing broke the tension like a sweet, hard crunch.

Becka's hand flew over the note. He took a step back with his hands up. "I'll avert my eyes."

Her cheeks went pink. "Sorry, Fitz. I'm a little jittery right now." She scrunched up the note in her hand and stuffed it back in her pocket.

"Of course you are," he said in a softer tone. "Don't worry. I won't interrupt again. Promise."

He turned and shot me a curious look as he strolled off.

Becka leaned forward. "You can't tell Fitz. You know that, right?"

Briefly, I wondered if those were similar to the words spoken between Jackie and Becka years earlier about the ambush they'd plotted for me on live TV.

Up until then, Becka had been a good friend, second to no one but Fitz. I hadn't known she'd harbored a bitter jealousy—only found out later. But after watching it back, again and again, I knew she'd been the one who'd spilled my sworn secret—my changing feelings towards Rob—as fodder for her sister's salacious show. Because she'd been the only person I'd told after a night of watching rom-coms and drinking too much wine. When I talked it through with Fitz, he felt bad he'd never warned me. He knew, said *everyone* knew, with the exception of me.

Everything changed after that. We stopped being friends. Rob hooked up with Jackie, and Becka was left with no one. I'd learned then never to keep secrets. I guess Becka hadn't. It made me wonder if she'd changed at all.

But for the sake of this moment, instead of questioning her reasons, I simply crossed my fingers under the table as I agreed to her terms. "Okay. I won't tell Fitz."

I began to wonder about the real reason why Becka had called me. She knew I was close to the Warner brothers. Did she really think one random note would shift my allegiance?

She took a bite of biscotti and turned back to the window. My stomach was too unsettled to eat. I settled for another sip of tea and waited.

"Want to know why I really called you?" She kept her focus outside.

"Sure," I said.

Finally, she brought her focus back to me. "There's something I need you to do."

"Absolutely, I'm in." I harbored no ill will towards her, and she'd lost her only sister. The girl could use a break. And a friend. I could do my best to be that for her.

She took her time before speaking. "I want you to share the details of Jackie's death on your blog," she finally said.

My mouth dropped open. *"What?"* I blurted out.

A few heads turned to look at us. I slouched down in the booth, my cheeks heating. "Sorry."

"Listen, Em," she said, her eyes never leaving mine. "You have access to a huge network. Followers from all over the country. You also have an unofficial local fan club. Anytime we've had you on Jackie's show, we've gotten calls from every corner of town demanding more air time for you. People like you. They listen to you."

"So what? I don't get the connection."

"You're a local celebrity. You talk about life in Eliot Hill. Even people who don't like social media follow your blogs."

I wasn't following. "What does my blog have to do with Jackie's death?"

"Maybe everything," Becka said. "If you post the note, maybe someone will come forward."

Crowdsourcing for clues? I hadn't seen this coming.

"Becka, there's no way. We don't even know what happened."

"That's the point. I want you to ask your followers. We could figure out who killed her."

"Slow down, Becka. If the police want to use social media or involve the public, I'm sure they have their own methods to share information."

"Not with the same level of engagement you get."

Something in the urgency of her tone concerned me. The lack of balance between speed and accuracy told me she wasn't thinking straight.

Becka snapped her fingers in front of my face before I could figure out what to say. "Hello? C'mon, Em. You are the only one who can do this. And the more people who see it, the better."

"More people doesn't necessarily mean more answers, at least more right answers," I argued.

She wasn't in the mood for a discussion. The determination in her eyes made me stifle a sigh. I could feel myself waffling. Where was my anti-people-pleasing spine of steel? This was not a good idea.

"Do you want me to beg?" Becka's eyes flashed. "I need to find out who did this as soon as possible. You could post the thread online right now. The first forty-eight hours is crucial. Isn't that what they say?"

"True. It also might muck up the investigation."

"How?" she demanded.

"If we get people sending me wild theories and accusations, it could water down the focus on facts and draw attention away from where it's needed. Your sister was hit on a dark road at night. The most likely scenario is that she was hit by a drunk driver."

"And what if you're wrong?" Becka argued. "What if someone intentionally went after her?"

She pulled the paper from her pocket again and held it up. I reached forward with an open palm. She allowed me to take the paper and flatten it out. I had to admit the note presented doubts about my theory. "Can I take a picture of it?"

With a shrug, she agreed. "Sure."

I snapped a photo with my phone, then handed it back.

She glanced at it, shaking her head before she tucked it back into her pocket.

I drew in a long breath. "The police will sort this out."

Her shoulders sagged. "I'd think out of anyone, you'd know that isn't true, even if it was a case of drunk driving. Or have you forgotten about grad night?"

The implication made me flinch. I hadn't anticipated a reference to a dead friend. Kelsey Minor, who'd succumbed to injuries after a suspected drunk driver hit her, was a tragedy that was never resolved. Rumors and accusations abounded, but no arrests were ever made, no closure ever found. I shoved a biscotti in my mouth and began to crunch. Becka watched as I ate my feelings.

She sighed. "Sorry. I didn't mean to—"

I held up one hand and covered my mouth with the other. "It's okay. You've lost your sister. You're allowed some leeway."

Becka got up abruptly halfway through a crunch.

"Listen, Em, if you don't want to help me, I can't make you. Anyway, I gotta go. I'm meeting Vera. She's probably wondering where I am."

A mixture of guilt and relief washed over me. I didn't try to stop her. Instead, I got up, too. Murray exited the booth behind us. He wagged his tail and stretched his front paws, assuming it was walk time.

"Not yet, Murr. Sit back down."

His tail drooped, his ears dropped, and puppy dog eyes met my gaze. It was so pathetic, I almost laughed. "Soon, okay? I'll take you in fifteen minutes."

Resigned to another nap, he climbed back under the table and curled into a large fur ball. But he kept an eye on me to make sure I wasn't about to stroll around the neighborhood without him.

Becka and I walked through the sun-soaked café as people quieted their conversations and gave her not-so-subtle side-eyes. We paused outside to say goodbye. I gave her a hug, taking in the fresh mango scent of her shampoo. The sweet smell sparked images of hot summer days and visits to the ice cream shop. It was in direct contrast to the dark reality of what she faced. The desire to help weighed on me, and I wracked my brain about how to make her idea work. Then something occurred to me.

"Wait." I pulled away from her. "I have a thought."

Her eyes met mine. "I'm listening."

I held up my hand, "It's a compromise."

"Okay." She crossed her arms and waited.

"What if I ask my followers for help but not share details of her death?"

Becka raised an eyebrow. "What would that do?"

"If someone knows something about what happened to Jackie, whether it was an accident or not, a little encouragement might help. I'll suggest they send me a direct message if they don't want to come forward publicly. Online anonymity might give someone the courage to reach out."

The corners of her mouth turned up. "It's a start. When will you do it?"

"Now?"

She gave me a tight squeeze. "Thank you."

"Don't thank me yet. I don't know if it's going to help."

"It will. I know it."

She said goodbye, then I watched her march down the street and hop into her small blue hatchback. As she drove off, I wondered if I should've talked to Noah first. The words of trailblazer Grace Hopper came to mind: 'It's easier to ask for forgiveness than permission.' Besides, involvement in a police investigation wasn't so bad if it helped out in the end. Was it?

Chapter Eight

Armed with a couple of banana blueberry smoothies, Fitz slid into the booth across from me when I returned from walking Becka out.

I batted my eyelashes at him. "My hero."

Fitz grinned at me and rubbed his hands together. "I'm more of a mercenary. This comes at a price."

I took a sip of my smoothie. "You want details."

"Everything."

I raised my eyebrows. "Sure you've got time?"

"For this? Yes. Longbourn baristas are not only efficient, they're independent. I'm here strictly as eye candy after eight a.m."

He meant it as a joke, but no one in town would disagree. He and Noah resembled a pair of models, cute mugs and chiseled from chin to chest.

I looked around and leaned in. "Becka thinks Jackie was murdered."

He nodded and waited for more.

Irritation flared up inside me. He'd known that she wanted to talk to me earlier but didn't know what about. The claim of murder should've come as a shock to him.

"Why are you not reacting?" I demanded. "You're unreasonably chill, even for you."

He shot me an apologetic smile. It was the look he gave me when I found out he knew something and hadn't told me, a common occurrence. Starting out as everyone's favorite bartender, Fitz not only knew at least half the residents of Eliot Hill on a first name basis, he also held a lot of secrets

42

in trust. Since he'd opened the Longbourn Café, his knowledge had only grown. His cafe was the epicenter of local news or town gossip, depending on your point of view.

"Her urgent need to talk implied she had more than grief to unload," Fitz said. "Plus, you've been on edge since she called. I assumed it must've had something to do with what Becka said on the phone."

Fitz was smart and intuitive. But I got the feeling there was more to it. As a volunteer firefighter, he'd been on hand at several accident sites. Had he seen something this morning that would back up Becka's claim?

"Okay," I said. "So what do you think?"

"I think you're keeping something from me. Why did she want to talk to you specifically? You see her a few hours a month. That's not confidante territory. C'mon, spill." He made grabby hands at me.

Eye roll. "You're like a bloodhound, you know that? Sniffing out secrets from everyone that walks through your door."

He grinned at me. "I knew it."

I wasn't quite ready to share. Tit for tat. "Do you really think Jackie could've been murdered?"

He shrugged. "It's possible. Think of the effect she had on you."

I grimaced. "Yeah, she got me pretty good."

Fitz met my eye. He wasn't smiling anymore. "Jackie set you up to be humiliated on live TV. You reacted by turning the shame inwards on yourself. What if someone else focused their hate back on her instead?"

Huh. He had a point. After Jackie prodded Rob's feelings out of him and he dumped me on her show, mail flooded my blog. I became a favorite target of online critics who didn't like that Rob and I had pretended to be so perfect. Comments like "liar-liar, life on fire" and "fake lives deserve real deaths" were some of the popular quotes. My blog blew up, and I was suddenly in the spotlight. I went to a dark place. And though I had way more supporters than adversaries, the small percentage of negative voices drowned out the rest. I couldn't hear what I didn't believe.

"Remember when I used to call you almost every night at three a.m.?"

He ran his hand through his hair. "How could I not? That's when I was working at Milligan's. I'd finish my shift at the bar and get home just in time. It became like clockwork. It was worse when you didn't call."

Mom had wanted to sue Jackie for exploitation. I'd begged her not to do it. "That wouldn't help," I'd said. "It would just make things worse."

She'd backed off, but it was hard for her to let it go. She'd felt like she'd failed as a parent and began to cry on a daily basis. We could've built our own tissue factory for how much the two of us cried. In the end, it wasn't a bad thing. In fact, a tissue company was my very first big-paying sponsor. It paid enough to cover all my bills, including rent. Even after that, it took a while before I could see the whole experience as anything other than a crushing personal failure.

Luckily, Fitz was there. He shouldered my pain and got me through it, a ride-or-die friend who stood by me. Day after day, he reminded me that I was a good person who was loved. What if someone didn't have a friend to help them through the cruelty of Jackie's wrath? Could the fallout lead to murder?

"You may be onto something," I said. "Someone had threatened Jackie—Becka showed me the note."

Fitz frowned. "Who?"

I shrugged. "Don't know. I took a photo of the note."

"Can I see it?" he said.

I hesitated for a moment. Becka had specifically told me not to share this tidbit with Fitz. But that was like asking a dog not to bark. Even the most well-trained would break eventually, a woof slipping out when a squirrel crosses its path or an ice cream truck rolls by, its dallying pace and sugar-infused aroma breaking their will to follow the command. At some point, I told Fitz everything. And given the note's importance, that point was now.

Ignoring the twinge of guilt, I dug into the deep abyss of my bag in search of my phone.

Fitz tapped his fingers on the table. "There were a few details at the accident that seemed off."

I gave up the hunt to focus on what he was saying. "Like what?"

"Think about the distance between Jackie's body and her shoe."

Jackie had only been wearing one shoe when she was found. The other one had been found in the ditch.

"It was about fifteen feet from where she'd been lying."

"Right," Fitz said. "Think about the impact necessary to knock it that far away. The car must've been going at a good clip to send it that far."

Odd. On a dark mountain road, even if someone were drunk or distracted or fantastically reckless, driving at a high speed didn't make sense. It was a dead end.

I took a sip of coffee. "How fast do you think the car was going?"

"My opinion? The driver had the pedal to the metal."

A sense of unease was growing inside me. "There's something else."

Fitz nodded. "Tell me."

"The supermoon was out last night."

"Okay." He rolled his hand in a circular motion, telling me to get to the point.

"Think about what she was wearing. A white sparkling dress. Under that moon, she would've been practically glowing." It was the brightest night of the season. As always, it lit up our town like a beam of white light descending from a UFO.

He drained his latte. "You're right."

I sat up straighter. "You mean Becka might be right."

"Em," Fitz held his hand up. "Slow down. We're just talking here. It's not time to reboot *America's Most Wanted* quite yet."

My phone pinged from inside my purse. The sound helped me find it. I ignored the incoming text. Instead, I pulled up the photos of the threat. "You might change your mind once you see this."

I swiped through them and found a cropped shot so he could get a good look at the message.

He examined it closely. "Where did Becka find this?"

"It was sitting out on Jackie's coffee table," I said. "She found it this morning."

"That's not good. It's one thing for people to slag her off online or complain to their friends if she talked smack about them. But a direct threat? Someone taking time to write that out? That's a whole new kit and kaboodle."

Were we making assumptions? Leaping ahead? I didn't think so. "It's too much of a coincidence."

Fitz pulled out his phone and sent a text.

I waited. "Noah?"

He nodded. His phone pinged with an immediate reply.

I craned my neck and tried, unsuccessfully, to read the exchange. "What did you tell him? What did he say?"

The corners of his mouth lifted. "I said we wanted to talk to him about what happened. He'll come by, but it might be a while. The fire chief is with him right now."

Fire chief? "Why?"

"Accident reconstruction," Fitz said. "Whenever there's a crash around here that's anything more than a fender bender, the chief helps out."

It made sense. Firefighters were often the first to arrive on scene. And the chief had been on staff as long as I could remember. If anyone could figure out what happened, it would be him.

"Have they learned anything?" I asked.

"Noah didn't tell me. It's tricky in this case because the car wasn't on scene to assess the damage. But there are other clues that will help them get some idea—marks on the road, debris, trajectories of bits and pieces. It's all math and physics."

I had no idea. "That's amazing."

"Yeah, it gives victims a voice. Tells the story they can't tell themselves."

"Jackie would love to know her last story was big and juicy, only this time she was the one who got hurt."

"The reconstruction is normally done to figure out if charges should be laid. In this case I'd guess it's more about sorting out the severity of the charges, carelessness, drunk driving…"

"Or murder," I finished.

"Right." His face was grim. "Has Becka told Noah about the note she found?"

My knee began to bounce. "Um."

Fitz snorted. "So that's a no." He leaned back in his seat and crossed his arms. "Why did she tell you and not him?"

Before I could answer, a friendly barista with blue hair and a sparkly nose ring came over to ask Fitz about a shift change. Escape time.

Murray needed to walk, and I needed to run. Information overload had me itching to go.

I stood up. Fitz put his hand up, asking me to wait, as he finished his conversation with the barista. I adjusted Murray's leash and pretended not to notice. Then Murball and I made a break for the exit before Fitz could stop us.

The breeze had picked up since this morning. Striped awnings flapped as I paused to zip up my hoodie. An A-frame wood sign in front of the gift shop collapsed, barely missing Murray's paws. He jumped out of the way, nearly taking me down in the process.

"Careful, Murr." No way I'd add a sprained ankle to the list of things that went wrong today.

The street was buzzing with people out and about. We passed by the floral shop and felt a tinge of moist air coming from inside. Mary Sheddon had her mister out. She was going over all the bouquets. I watched her do a little dance to an upbeat tune and felt my mood lift.

I checked my watch. Time to move. I'd told Becka I'd post something immediately. Better get to it.

There was only one snag in the plan. I had no idea how to approach the subject of Jackie's death. What should I say? Maybe I should consult with Fitz. No way. He'd tell me it was a bad idea, and he'd probably be right. Never mind that Noah was a capable sheriff and a good investigator. I didn't doubt he'd figure out what really happened to Jackie. But, big but, I'd already told Becka I'd do it, and I didn't want to let her down again.

Gah. How did I get myself into this? Murray glanced up at me. I gave him a quick pat to let him know I was fine. Why had I agreed to get involved? It didn't matter. Too late. There was no way I could back out now.

Plus, like Becka said, I had access to a big online audience, usually hovering around fifty thousand visitors a month. That included a considerable chunk of our local population. Maybe she was right. Maybe I could help. Maybe Noah would thank me.

I raised my chin and squared my shoulders. Time to put the title of *influencer* to the test.

Fitz met my eye when we marched back into the café. He gave me a curious look. It wasn't often I kept things from him. A quick wave and I shot up to my apartment to compose a new type of post—a call for help. Instead of a blog, I decided to do an Instagram story, then share it on my feed. In case Noah didn't like Becka's request for my involvement, I had to get it out before he stopped me.

Chapter Nine

Saturday, May 4th

Hi everyone,

Today, I'm on a mission. I'm calling on all Eliot Hill locals and visitors. I need your help!

Last night, tragedy struck. There was a hit-and-run in our small community. The tragic event has been made worse by a rumor circulating that it may not have been an accident.

Shocking, right?

Let me tell you about the victim. Her name was Jackie Hunter, a local TV host with big opinions and always too much to say. Many of you are familiar with her. For those of you who aren't, I'll tell you this—she wasn't always kind but she was fierce, and never let anyone push her around. My history with her is complicated. But it led me to where I am today.

You may be wondering why I am telling you about this. Let me explain. I'm hoping someone out there might have seen something or knows something about what happened. It only takes one tip to break a case and help justice prevail.

Here's what I can tell you:

Fact number one: I found her. Total coincidence. Now, the cops are going to do their thing and use forensics and science to figure out precisely how she was killed. But I know everything I need to. The car that hit her didn't slow down; she was flung off her feet and left for dead. Either they didn't see her, or they meant to hit her. I'm leaning toward the latter. Outlandish? Maybe not.

Fact two: There is no way someone could've missed seeing her. It was a full moon (a supermoon!), and she was wearing a white dress that would've stood out in the moonlight like a giant glow stick on Halloween.

Fact three: There was no call to the cops, no effort to help her. As I said, they left Jackie for dead.

So there it is. I'm involved, and I don't think I can step aside. I'm going with my gut. This is not about the what and the how that stuff is for the cops. This is about the who and the why. Will you help?

Thoughts, theories, and information are all welcome. Jackie died on Mountaintop Lane in Eliot Hill, along the cycling route, not far from Overlook Point. Anyone from the area knows the place.

Don't be shy and don't stand by.

Onward,
Em

Off it went. New content into the online universe, like a newborn baby into the world. Except this one didn't smell, wasn't cute, and may not be received with open arms. I wondered if Noah was downstairs yet. With a quick splash of water on my face, I took a minute to reapply my lip gloss in the small mirror next to the door.

The landline rang. Only one person had this number. The same person who insisted I have a landline in the first place. Mom.

I toyed with a lock of hair. "Murray, do I have to?"

Two barks said yes. No one ignored his Nanabear.

"Fine." Reaching over, I picked up the phone. "Hi, Mom."

"Emily Jane Dalle, what are you up to?"

Oh, fudge.

"You'll have to be more specific, Mom. I've got my fingers in a lot of pots today."

"Don't be cute with me, young lady. Why didn't you call me sooner to tell me you'd discovered the body of the devil incarnate?"

My mom didn't like people who weren't nice to me. Jackie was easily the worst. My mom never forgave the sin.

"Mom, Jackie was killed last night, and I found her body this morning."

"That is a right shame. But tell me this. Why on God's green earth would you get involved?"

"Trying to help feels like the right thing to do."

"That woman almost ruined your life, hon." She clicked her tongue. "That she died in some unnatural way doesn't surprise me, given the rules of karma. You owe that woman nothing. Not even a second thought."

Ouch. Mama bears are a ruthless breed.

I was about to respond, but Mom wasn't quite done. "Shouldn't you be focused on the show instead? It seems that's where your time and energy would serve you better."

"Someone killed her, maybe intentionally. Even Jackie Hunter didn't deserve that fate."

"If you say so, hon. Either way, let's not dwell on the past."

"It happened yesterday."

"Which means today is one day closer to our big day."

Our new show premiered in less than two weeks. It was a Friday night movie pairing that included Mom and me. It was called Friday Night Nostalgia and featured us as co-hosts. Mom had been the popular singing weather girl at WKRZ when she first moved to Eliot Hill. She was excited to get back to her TV roots. I wasn't as enthusiastic about the idea, but she'd convinced me to give it a go. I didn't like disappointing her.

"I've been working on the first three segments with the production team. It's in good shape. Promise. We have one final meeting. I'll make sure everything is perfect."

"Let's not get cocky, hon. When I was on air, I practiced 'til the cameras rolled."

"Yes, Mom. I know that. But our show is supposed to feel organic, like we're hanging out with the audience, a girls-night-in type of feel."

"Casual and cozy," she said.

"Exactly."

"Well, that takes practice too."

I rolled my eyes. "Maybe for some more than others."

Another click of the tongue. "Emily Jane, wait until you're a mother one day. All that cheek you love to give me will come back in spades."

Time to pull the chute. A few of Mom's friends had become grandmothers in the last year and the hints that I should get busy started coming faster than rain pellets in a May storm.

"Mom, I've got to go. Fitz is calling me." *Or he will be once I message him for help.*

"Listen, hon." Mom cleared her throat. "I'm coming home early. You've been through a terrible ordeal, and I want to be there for you."

Nooooooo. "I'm fine, really."

"Don't bother arguing. It's all arranged. Your father's signed up for a golf tournament, so he's staying. But I'll be there Tuesday morning."

My mouth fell open. That was a full week early. "This Tuesday?"

"Yes. I get in first thing. I've reserved an airport taxi to drive me home."

I slumped against the wall, eyes on the ceiling. Arguing at this point was futile.

"Why don't I come pick you up? I haven't seen you in three months."

"Exactly, Emily. And neither has anyone else in Eliot Hill. If I get into that cube on wheels you call a vehicle, my hair will look like it did the morning after prom." She paused to let out a giggle. "Although I heard no complaints from your father."

A shudder passed through me. Prom was her third date with Dad. "First of all, Mom, ew. And second, why not add an extra layer of hairspray? That way, your hair will double as a helmet yet look exactly the way it did when you set it. And, if that's not enough, I'll put the top back up on the Jeep, and I'll chauffeur you around like the queen you are."

"Save your sass for the cameras. And I'll take the taxi, thank you. I have a meeting, so I need to look my best." She paused. "You should join us."

A request from the LLC, the Ladies Lunch Club, was not an invitation you turned down. They were a powerful bunch, each of the members with her own area of specialty, like the Freemasons or the Illuminati… or the mob. If you needed something done, there was no one better. The LLC met every Tuesday for lunch at the Longbourn.

"Sounds great."

"Thank you," she said. "And hon, please move past the messy business of Jackie's death."

"I'm only trying to help."

"Like I'm doing now, Emily?"

I smiled. With the crackle over the phone, I knew she was smiling, too. My attitude didn't just drop out of the sky.

"Love you, Mom. See you Tuesday."

Chapter Ten

The café was hopping. Fitz was behind the counter, so I sat down with a resounding whump on my favorite stool along the bar. He was faced the other way. I sat impatiently, willing him to notice me.

After a few loud sighs from my seat, his head turned enough so I could see his profile and a subtle smile. He knew I was there but made me wait while he chatted with a tourist about the best place in town for a romantic dinner.

"There's always Sylvie's. It's been here for twenty-plus years and has a warm ambiance. Or you could try the new resto-bar down the block. Excellent apps, and the bartender makes a mean chocolate martini."

When Fitz was younger, he'd dreamed of owning a bar. He became a proficient flair bartender and watched his favorite movie, *Cocktail,* so many times he had the entire script memorized. But the reality wasn't what he'd imagined. He realized after working for years in the industry that he wasn't a fan of excessive drinking and grew tired of dealing with the aftermath. So he pivoted his dream towards opening a café and fulfilled that dream three years ago, after saving all his hard-earned tips and using the proceeds to buy out a run-down coffee shop and renovate it. The trendy renos were on point, and it soon became the town's favorite place to caffeinate, work remotely, socialize, and gossip.

The enthusiastic customer gave Fitz a hearty handshake and left with two classic cappuccinos.

Fitz turned and looked at me with an amused smile. "What's gotten into you? Did you triple your daily caffeine allowance behind my back?"

"I would never betray you like that."

He picked up a few empty cups left on the counter. "Thank the coffee gods. Spill it, then. I can see you're dying to tell me something."

I sat up straight and lifted my chin. "Fitzwilliam Warner, would you be surprised to find out that your best friend is a certifiable genius?"

His smile widened. "Did you finally beat *Are You Smarter than a Fifth Grader?*"

"Think bigger."

He dropped the cups in a bin of dirty dishes and came around the counter. I swiveled on my stool and stood up, beaming with pride. He rubbed his eyes and muttered something under his breath. It might've been something about a bad feeling, but I couldn't be sure. I fanned out my arm, and he led us to our booth so we could talk more privately.

He plunked down into the seat and rubbed his chin. "Tell me what you did, and make sure to leave out anything illegal."

Without taking a breath, I blurted out my idea. "I reached out to my online followers. I asked them to help me figure out what happened to Jackie."

His eyebrows dropped. "You did what?"

I drew back with a frown. Reproach wasn't the reaction I'd hoped for. "Save the lecture, Fitz. Besides, it was actually Becka's idea. I was trying to impress you."

He shook his head. "That isn't a good idea, Em. We don't know what happened. Our conversation earlier was conjecture—not meant for the masses."

"Even if it was a case of a drunk driver and not a pre-meditated killer, somcone knows something. Like Becka said, we can't sit back and watch another hit-and-run go cold."

His expression darkened. Kelsey Minor's death was the only other unsolved hit-and-run in recent history. To make things worse, Fitz's dad had been sheriff. When no arrests were made, the town had come down hard on him.

"Fitz, your dad did everything he could," I said. "I'm just saying..."

"It's okay. No one was harder on my dad than himself when the case went cold. And you're right. He would've done anything to find out what happened." He looked up at me. "Maybe you have a point."

The two incidents were very different. Kelsey was walking along Highway 77, the busiest route into town. People rarely drove under forty miles an hour, including big rigs on long-haul routes. With two lanes and a narrow shoulder, it was a dangerous place to be for a pedestrian at any given time. Mountaintop Lane, where Jackie died, had none of the blatant dangers of Highway 77 other than the lack of street lights.

But there was another big difference. Kelsey was a teenager. She'd thought she was bulletproof, like most of us did back then. She died on grad night after a fight with her boyfriend. She'd been drinking and decided to walk home from a party without considering the dangers of her chosen route.

What was Jackie's excuse? She wasn't spontaneous. And she wasn't a heavy drinker. Where had she planned to go? And why?

Maybe it was a fight with her boyfriend, like Kelsey. All I knew about the guy was that he'd planned a party for her. Chances were he'd have some insight into why she'd been outside alone. Then again, there were no calls made to the police until I alerted them. Why hadn't he reported her missing?

When Kelsey was found, her boyfriend was wracked with guilt. He'd jumped headfirst into a whisky-induced stupor and stayed there for months. Eventually, his parents hauled him off to the West Coast to start a new life. What about Jackie's boyfriend? How was he coping? I hadn't heard much of anything. Was he holed up somewhere, falling apart? If not, why not?

Fitz pulled up my post on his phone. I held my breath as he watched. *Like it, please.* I felt like a kid nervously watching their mom's reaction to a homemade breakfast on Mother's Day. Every promising twitch of a smile was countered by a distinct frown. Gah. If I couldn't get Fitz on my side, I was in trouble.

When he was done, he put the phone aside and sat back. His face was more serious than I was used to. My anxiety spiked.

"Spill it, Fitz," I blurted out. "Tell me I'm not a screw-up. That I didn't risk my fan base, make a fool of myself, and mess up the investigation into Jackie's death all in one short post."

"Okay," he said.

"Okay?"

"Yes, okay."

"What does that mean?" I asked.

A hint of a smile played on his lips. "You've said everything I was going to say. It's good, Em."

I exhaled a long breath. "Sheesh. You had me worried."

He held a finger up. "Let me be clear. I'm still not a fan of your meddling."

My eyes widened. "Even if it helps to find out what happened?"

"Even then."

I slapped my hand down on the table. "Why not?"

He tilted his head to the side. "Because you may have just put a target on your back."

I frowned at him. *Say what?*

"C'mon. Think about it. Whoever did this may see you as a threat. Regardless of whether it was planned, someone left Jackie out there to die. If they're willing to kill one person, why not go for a second?"

I bit my lip. "I hadn't thought that far ahead."

Fitz dropped his chin. "You better start. Especially if Jackie was run down on purpose. What if it was planned? A result of harbored dark rage? Like, what if this was an act of revenge?"

I swallowed. He could be right. And I could relate. "Didn't I make a voodoo doll resembling Jackie and stick pins in it for a while?"

"On a nightly basis," he said.

I'd been so used to being with Rob that I hadn't even recognized we weren't happy anymore. My identity and confidence had become dependent on being part of a twosome. Jackie brought that out. Part of me was actually grateful after my ego healed. Did I feel worse when Rob started dating Jackie within weeks of the episode airing? Of course. I felt worthless and foolish and completely lost. But I got through it and came out stronger.

"Maybe whoever did this decided to skip the voodoo doll and go after the real Jackie instead."

"Em..."

"What's the issue with wanting to find out the truth about what happened to her?"

"Where should I begin? Let's talk basics. Your livelihood. Your platform is based on positivity and fun. How is your audience, and your sponsors, going to react to your decision to go off on a 180 and morph into a true-crime theme?"

He had a point. "I suppose it is a far cry from a pep talk and the occasional makeup tip."

"Exactly, unless you want to temporarily rename your blog. How about *Emily Dalle and the Callous Case of the Weathered Witch?*"

"I get what you're saying, Fitz. But I always include my audience in what's going on in my life. Not mentioning it would feel like a lie."

"True," he conceded.

"And," I continued, "I've already shared that I was the one who found her."

He considered my argument.

"I suppose," he finally said. "But you're gearing up to pair with WKRZ to begin a new show. That should be your focus."

He'd made his point. It was the same one my mother had made an hour earlier.

"Okay, that's fair. But on the off chance my post does reach someone who knows something, maybe it will help."

"Anything is possible," he said. "I just have one more question."

"What?" I asked.

He sat back and drummed his fingers on the table, smiling. "Any chance you cleared your online sleuthing with Noah before going rogue?"

I shook my head.

"He may have a few questions, too."

I shrugged. "I'll tell Noah I was trying to help. It's my life, my decision. There's nothing he can do about it."

He quirked an eyebrow. "And if he doesn't like it?"

I scoffed, "Wouldn't faze me. Not everyone is intimidated by his no-nonsense cop routine. I say bring it on."

With a big grin he circled his finger to indicate I should turn around.

Oh crap. "Behind me?"

He nodded. Pure delight radiated across his face.

I sucked in my breath and turned around.

Standing directly behind the booth was a none-too-happy Noah Warner. His taut jawline pulsed with anger, and his eyes were smoldering. It was so hot, I almost swooned. Too bad he was probably here to arrest me.

Chapter Eleven

When my posting about Jackie had gone live, I felt great satisfaction. Murray and I had exchanged looks of mutual admiration, and a wise quote had even come to mind. *Be the person your dog thinks you are.* In those brief moments, I thought I'd achieved it. Pride surged through me, confident I was working toward the greater good.

Now, as Noah hovered behind the booth, looking down at me, literally and figuratively, I questioned the pat on my back. Should it have been a slap in the face? Doubt blossomed inside me. Had I screwed up?

"Emily," he said.

I tried to cover my anxiety with a brilliant smile. "Hi, Noah."

"We need to talk."

I tilted my head and twisted a curl in my fingertips. "Should we start with the weather?"

Fitz covered his mouth to hide a giggle. Noah frowned.

I felt a growing sense of irritation that my charms were failing. His raging hotness made it worse.

I mustered my courage and raised my chin. "Are you going to haul me in?"

He met my gaze. "Don't tempt me."

An image of him putting me in handcuffs momentarily pushed any other thought out of my mind. *Get a grip.*

Fitz, now back behind the safety of the counter after sliding out from the booth like a silent ninja, called over to Noah to ask if he wanted a coffee.

"Sure, plain black. Thanks."

Surprise, surprise. Mr. Serious knew how to take the fun out of everything. Even coffee.

Fitz brought it over in a takeaway cup. "Any updates?"

"Not that I can share," Noah said, taking the cup with a nod. "This is more of an official visit to our local Jessica Fletcher."

"Gotcha." Fitz threw his hands up and backed off.

My ride-or-die was going to let me hang, the traitor. As he turned to leave us to chat, he mouthed the words 'good luck.' I bared my teeth at him. He repressed a grin.

"You guys can use my office in the back if you want," Fitz called over his shoulder to Noah like the helpful brother he never was. It was novel that it was me, not him, getting into trouble from Noah. Fitz was basking in it.

I exited the booth, ready for my interrogation. Noah turned to me. "Maybe we can chat upstairs at your place instead? Guaranteed privacy."

Of all the times I had imagined Noah coming up to my place, it never went like this.

Were there dishes in the sink? Had I vacuumed within the last day? Week? Year?

"Sure. C'mon up," I said, trying to sound casual. There was no way I was going to put my nerves on display.

I led Noah upstairs and into my cozy little apartment. Murray, not used to a lot of guests other than my parents and Fitz, was all over him. Noah seemed happy enough to give him a few pets on the head, but every time he stopped, Murray would paw at him until he did it again. Eventually, Murray relented and sat on his feet. The distraction gave me a few minutes to straighten up my kitchen and deposit the dirty dishes from the counter into the sink. I offered to make tea. He accepted. He'd already downed the coffee Fitz gave him at an impressive rate.

I called off Murray and Noah made his way over to my island, the divider between my living room and kitchen. My apartment was very small. It suited me fine, but when I had guests, it morphed from cozy to cramped. Noah sat on a stool that was on the far side of the island and looked into the kitchen.

In spite of the circumstances, I was excited Noah was here. The musky scent of his cologne made my heart skip a beat. *Stop it.* I channeled my thoughts back to the reason for his visit. The butterflies in my stomach flew away. There was nothing better to kill a warm and fuzzy feeling than a conversation about a suspicious death. I filled the kettle with water and turned it on. "Have you had a chance to talk to Becka?"

Noah held my gaze for a minute as if trying to decide whether to grant me an answer. With a sigh, he relented. "Barely. She keeps her thoughts close to the vest. At least in front of me. Why do you ask?"

Would Becka mind if I shared what she'd told me? Probably. But I'd do it anyway. In spite of the fact Becka didn't trust the police, I did, especially in Noah's case. And it wasn't up to me to decide what was a legitimate clue or whether something was relevant. That was his call. Besides, the term *withholding evidence* flitted through my mind. Although not sure whether it applied in this scenario, I didn't need more than one reason to get in trouble.

"She came to see me earlier," I said.

He waited a beat. "And?"

"Becka's nervous about trusting you. It's no secret Jackie was pretty hard on law enforcement."

While never stating it publicly, I assumed having a biker dad who was in and out of jail had soured Jackie of both the motorcycle crowd and the police. It was the only explanation as to why she'd badmouthed both on a regular basis. I guessed her dad was the source of disappointment, and the police took him away. Neither role made for warm and fuzzy feelings.

The kettle whistled, and I pulled out my teapot from a nearby cupboard. Hard to look cool when your teapot is in the shape of an oversized dog, with a nose for a spout and a tail as a handle. Sprawled across the white belly of the beast read, "Dogs before Dudes." I drained the kettle into the pot, feeling my cheeks heat up.

He read the slogan, then studied my face again. "What's Becka nervous about? I missed something."

"Jackie was threatened just before she died."

"What sort of threat?"

"I don't know—it was vague. Said Jackie deserved to die for what she did."

He rested his elbows on the island and began to rub his forehead.

I poured tea into the only clean cup I had. It, too, was dog-themed, with a pair of stamped paws on it and a slogan that read, "I Pawsitively Love You."

His eyes drifted to the cup. Nothing.

"Let me make sure I understand," he said. "Becka told you that Jackie had been threatened."

"Yup."

He tapped his chest. "But kept it from me."

"Uh-huh."

He sighed and took a sip of tea. "That's not good."

Either was the fact that it was written on an Eliot Hill Police notepad. Maybe I'd leave that part for now. If I betrayed Becka's trust, she may retreat completely. Wasn't that worse?

"Listen, Noah, I told her you were a good cop."

A stellar report should get me off the hook for my online meddling. I stood across from him and waited to be praised. It didn't come. Instead? Another question. "Is that what prompted you to write about it publicly?"

And here we were. Back to square one.

I kept my tone light. "Becka asked for my help. She was in a bad place, so I agreed. I wanted her to feel better and thought it might help the investigation at the same time. No harm, no foul, right?"

Still, not even a hint of a smile. I shouldn't be surprised. Noah could be prickly. It took him and Fitz years before they were in a good place. There was no wrong or right, just different. In high school, Noah was like a mother hen, constantly checking up on Fitz, worried he'd be an easy target because of his sexual orientation. It drove Fitz nuts. He complained Noah used him as an excuse to fight.

"Emily, what happened to Jackie is a tragedy. In order for me to get justice for her and her family, I need to find out what happened in an orderly manner. Having you hijack my case by luring possible witnesses or leads into online chit-chat about what they know or what they've heard will only lead to misinformation and confusion."

My mouth opened to counter his argument. I closed it again when I couldn't think of what to say.

"It's time for you to back off and let me do my job," he said.

"I'm not trying to make your job more difficult." I snapped. "I did it to help."

"Is that right?" he said.

"If you weren't so focused on the stringent rules of conduct, maybe you'd recognize my unconventional method might actually work."

"Listen," he said in a cool tone. "I appreciate your intention but that's not how things are done. You need to let me handle this."

I leaned toward him. "Noah, think about it. What if my post generates a tip you can use? I'm not saying you'll get a smoking gun or anything, but maybe it'll start a conversation, get people talking about stuff they don't go to the police about, minor details, things that don't seem important."

He took another sip of tea. "And has it?"

"Has it what?"

"Has your post yielded any results?"

My face flushed. He'd called my bluff. He knew it, too. I hadn't expected that. There was a fine line between confidence and arrogance. I was beginning to wonder where Noah Warner fit.

"I haven't had the chance to look yet."

He raised his brows. "Alright, I'm here now. Why don't we look at it together? We can see if your method generated any sort of relevant information. You're so confident about the effectiveness of a public appeal from your platform; show me why. But," he paused and held my gaze, "if you're wrong, I want you to drop it. We will let this go as a well-intentioned mistake and be done with it. Does that work for you?"

He sat back on the stool. A small crack of a smile showed on his face, as if he knew there'd be nothing to find. The crush I'd had on him for so long had suddenly morphed into a desire to plain old crush him instead.

"Sure." I blinked. "Why not?"

My post had only been out an hour. Even in the digital world, that wasn't a lot of time. However, I had to admit, most responses to my posting were fairly immediate.

I marched around the island and hopped up on the stool next to Noah. I placed my laptop on the counter between us and logged in.

I'd posted it as a story, then shared it to my feed. Luckily, the story had generated thousands of views and the post a number of comments. Relief set in. At least I wouldn't have to watch virtual tumbleweeds scroll across my screen. Most were words of sympathy, with a few less-than-kind comments for good measure. Never underestimate cruelty empowered by online anonymity. Then again, if anyone were fair game, it would be Jackie.

I scrolled down to see if there was anything useful losing hope as I came to the end of the comments. I drew back as a direct message popped up. It was from Jenny Park, the local gift shop owner, and my old drama class buddy. Hmm…this could be something. Jenny didn't regularly message me. I leaned into read it.

> *Hey Emily, it's been a while. Hope you're good. I saw your post. I can't believe Jackie's gone. So weird. She and I were in the Eliot Hill Hiking Club together. I may have something that could interest you. I was out last night with a few friends on a hike. Our club uses an app that tracks our movements when turned on. It's private but shared by the group. Anyway, Jackie uses the app, too, and she was active at the same time as me. It was sometime between 8:30 and 9:00, I think. I only remember because I didn't want to run into her. I'd just gotten a really bad haircut (side note—avoid the new stylist at Tresses!). I knew Jackie would say something if I saw her, competitive cow (sorry, my bad). I wasn't going to let a bad hair day ruin the chance to see the Supermoon. Do you think I should call Noah and tell him? I don't really want to get involved. Can I leave this with you? TTYL, Jenny.*

Son of a Goat. This could be a real clue. I looked at Noah. He read, then reread the message, his eyes glued to the screen. When he finally looked back at me, all traces of the cocky smile were gone. His face was like a blank slate, washed clean of any emotion.

65

Now, it was my turn to gloat. "Well, well, well."

He dropped his elbow onto the counter and shut his eyes.

I watched him. "You okay?"

"Yuh. All good. Just give me a sec."

I got off my stool and began to fidget around the room. Murray trailed behind me. I moved onto the couch, pretending to read the latest issue of Us Magazine. Easy breezy. When he turned to face me again, he pointed at the magazine and made a circular gesture with his hand. My cheeks lit up. *Cheese and crackers!* It was upside down. I dropped the magazine and cut the act. "That quiet thing you do makes me nervous."

He groaned. "Listen."

I sat forward, Murray at my feet, ears perked, tail wagging. "Mm-hm?"

He held his hand up. "I think you may have uncovered some valuable information, if it turns out to be accurate."

"Oh yeah?" I tried to sound casual.

He ran his hand through his short, perfect hair. "It would be almost impossible to pinpoint Jackie's time of death within a window of less than eight to ten hours, given the information available to us with the conditions outside. If Jenny's right, her tip could be very helpful."

A small victory. I basked in the moment for a microsecond until his darkening expression told me it wouldn't last.

"Emily," he cautioned. "I'm not saying we wouldn't have found that information out on our own. It might've just taken a little more time. However, since you've been upfront with me, I'm going to extend you the same courtesy. In less than an hour, I'll be publicly announcing the investigation has been officially classified as a homicide. Your instincts were right."

I stared at him. Shock hit me like a rogue wave on a calm shore. Up until now, all this had been conjecture. "How…"

"Forensics. I can't go into detail."

The confirmation that someone purposefully ran down Jackie was terrifying and sickening. Goosebumps crept up my arms.

"Poor Jackie," I said. Two words I could never have imagined put together.

"That's a lot to take in."

"Sure." He pulled out his phone and frowned.

"You know what I don't get?" I said after a minute. "Why was Jackie out for a walk so late? It was the night of her party. And there's no way she was out with the sole purpose of exercise. Not with that dress and those heels. Even for Jackie, it doesn't make sense."

Noah didn't respond. My mind continued to churn. "Why was her hiking app even turned on if she wasn't actually hiking?" Then again, I had a smartwatch. I always turned on the exercise app, even if I was out for a walk around the block with Murray. Every step counted. "Jenny said the group was competitive. Maybe there was a tight rivalry." It was no secret Jackie didn't like to lose. She'd make sure every single step was clocked and counted to stay on top.

Had Jackie given us a clue to her own murder?

"I can't discuss this case with you more than I already have," Noah said.

I held my index finger up. "One question."

"Emily…"

"Where does Jackie's boyfriend live?"

Grant Henshaw. I didn't know much about the guy. I'd seen him around WKRZ over the last few years, but I wasn't sure of his exact role. From what I understood, he was there to streamline costs. And he made everyone nervous. Becka had brought him up a few times but mostly to complain. She didn't like him, but I couldn't remember why.

Noah cleared his throat. "Like I said."

"Yeah, I heard you, Noah. You can't discuss the case. But I just gave you a big clue. I'm not asking for classified information. It's an address, one I could find myself."

"Slow down. I told you about the homicide classification because it will be public knowledge by the end of the day. However, your involvement stops here."

Huh?

"You've made your point and been helpful." He drained the last of his tea. "Thank you for that. But now it's time to go back to your regular blogs with nice photos and life advice so I can go back to investigating."

His words were stern, as if I'd wasted his time instead of providing him with critical information. Anger bubbled inside me.

"You have the traditional police techniques, and I won't get in your way. But I have access to something you don't. People who like me."

He raised his eyebrows.

"That came out wrong." My frustration grew. "I mean, I have a lot of followers who want to help. Jenny is a prime example."

"I won't argue that online tips can be helpful."

"Like they were today?" I said.

"Yes, but we have our own resources to use for that sort of thing."

I marched back to the kitchen and snatched his cup off the island. "Not with the engagement levels I have with my followers. When I post something, people pay attention. A lot of them are from right here in Eliot Hill. What do you have? A hundred followers? I'd guess most people in town aren't even aware the Eliot Hill Sheriff's Department has an online presence."

A ping alerted me that another message had been posted. I ignored it.

Noah's jaw tightened. "That might be true. However, it's generally done through a larger police agency equipped with the technology and staff able to manage and maintain it. Not by ordinary citizens who watch too much *Dateline*. If I haven't made it clear, that means you. I want you to back off."

"No way," I said. Anger took hold of me, and I refused to even pretend I'd listen to his crap any longer. "The great thing about my being so ordinary, as you say, is I am allotted certain freedoms. Freedom of speech, for example. So if I want to use my blog to find out more about how Jackie died, I will."

Noah finally lost the grating neutral expression he'd maintained up until now. His face flushed, and his neck tensed to match his jaw. Finally, I'd gotten to him. *Score one for me.*

His eyes fixed on mine. "Twisting my words and misconstruing my intent won't win you any points. This isn't a game. It's a homicide. That means we're dealing with a very dangerous person."

"I know where you're going. You don't need to worry. I can take care of myself."

"Yeah, I get that. But Jackie was no wallflower either."

"Your concern is noted, officer." I gave him a mock salute, which probably wasn't something cops did, but I didn't care.

"That's not good enough." His voice now raised to a level halfway between a stern voice and a yell. "Don't you get it? I don't want you to get hurt."

It should've been at this point that I recognized Noah was trying to protect me, not control me. But it was too late. Indignation and pride had taken hold.

"You can't tell me what to do. This isn't high school. I'm a grown-up."

"It's time to start acting like one then. If I need to worry about you, it could take my focus away from figuring out this mess."

"Maybe you should start following me on social media. It might give you a little insight into the case."

Noah tapped his hand twice on the island, then stood up.

"Now I can see why you and my brother are so close. Neither one of you listen to reason. In fact, you don't listen to anyone. I'm telling you, as the town sheriff, to back off."

"But I'm not under your command. And, like Fitz, I will choose the path I take. If you want me to back off, get a court order."

He scoffed. "You watch too much TV."

"Maybe you don't watch enough."

He gave me a hard look and left the apartment. He slammed the door and stomped down the stairs. Murray barked.

"You tell him, Murball."

I fumed about our conversation while a seed of fear crept into my thoughts. Fitz had already warned me I could be putting myself in harm's way. Would Jackie's killer look at my blog? If they did, could I actually be in danger? I walked out to my balcony just in time to see Noah about to get into his police cruiser. He paused, looked up, and saw me watching him. Our eyes locked before he got in, put his car in gear, and peeled away.

Chapter Twelve

Saturday, May 4th

Here's the newest shade of #RED by #SUNSMEAR cosmetics #RAGE
    Looks good against a mirror, doesn't it?
    I'm wearing this because this is how I'm feeling. You can't always be happy, right? Sometimes people suck.
    What puts you over the edge?

Signed,
    Single Fuming Female

Fitz texted me ten minutes later, suggesting I meditate. He must've seen my post. After gritting my teeth, I reluctantly conceded meditation was a good idea. First, I'd check the messages that had come in since Noah left. There was only one new message.

It read: *Back off.* Signed *Anonymouse.*

I rolled my eyes. Give me a break. Another hater telling me what to do, just what I needed. I almost wrote back then stopped myself. Engaging in an online feud was not a smart move. Best thing to do was ignore it. Instead, I would do as Fitz suggested.

He had introduced me to meditation years back. Fitz had been an amateur yogi since freshman year. He had integrated meditation into his daily life ever since. I was more of a casual user.

It took five minutes to get the image of a jumbo marshmallow man out of my head, a common occurrence when I tried to clear my mind, brought on no doubt by incessant viewings of the original *Ghostbusters* movie. Grudgingly, the manifestation left, and I was able to focus. I slowed my breathing and let go of my thoughts.

The frustration brought on by Noah slowly seeped out of my system. I was lucky to have a best friend who knew me so well. I'd just posted a photo with the caption that stated I hated being told what to do, but it was easy to justify in the case of Fitz. He was the exception. When I was spun, Fitz was there to help. He knew me better than anyone, and I trusted him completely. It had been that way since I could remember, our moms both Southern transplants who'd bonded over their shared love of cornbread and sweet iced tea. We'd spent so much time together, sometimes it felt like he was more like my conscience than an actual person. I grinned. He'd hate that.

A half-hour later, I felt better. After a quick shower, I made myself some instant noodle soup. With a dollop of hot sauce, I lapped it up, then grabbed a handful of cookies to satisfy my sweet tooth. I popped two in my mouth, then opened my laptop. This was a big week for me. I needed to prepare for my new show with Mom.

WKRZ banked on my popularity to draw in a bigger audience and compete with the online streaming services on Friday nights, one of the time slots they struggled with the most, particularly with younger viewers. I promoted the show and had good feedback, with people excited to see the banter between Mom and me. Mom was a movie buff, like me, and a regular guest on my blog. She knew little-known gossip behind classic films and loved to share it with anyone interested. Her favorite topic was the romantic entanglements of the stars of years and decades gone by. My fans couldn't get enough of her. She loved it, and I had to admit that I did, too.

After stuffing two more cookies in my mouth, I went downstairs. Fitz was chatting to local gossip Queen Bee Marnie Shivers, who reveled in spreading tidbits of useless information all around town. No surprise that today, she was focused on Jackie.

"You know she couldn't have children—infertile." She leaned in closer to emphasize the last word, scrunching her nose as she said it, as if the word itself was dirty or shameful. I stood near the doorway of my apartment and listened. Was it possible she may have insight into why Jackie was killed?

"Apparently," Marnie continued. "That's why she was so mean to all the young, pretty women who worked for her."

Everything Marnie said had to be put in context. Her daughter was hired as a production assistant by Jackie's team. The stint lasted less than a week. Apparently, Jackie fired her when she found the newbie taking selfies on stage her second day on the job. But Marnie may have hit on something. Could a spiteful employee have decided to seek revenge on Jackie? It seemed a little far-fetched from where I stood. But I'd ask Becka about it, just in case. She would have more insight than the hearsay and idle talk of a gossip hound.

While Marnie prattled on, Fitz nodded, making all the appropriate hm's and oh's. He'd argued with her over various issues in the past, but found these days it was easier to let her talk to shorten the time she spent in the café.

When I couldn't take it anymore, I interrupted the tête-à-tête with a clap of my hands. "Sorry folks, can I interrupt?"

Marnie stood up to her full height again—all five-foot-nothing. She jutted out her chin and huffed in frustration, not quite done slinging mud at the recently departed.

Fitz swiveled to face me. "Did you get the order I needed from Connor?"

"Connor" was code for "help me." We'd begun the tradition in high school and it had stuck.

I sighed. "Yeah, but I need to show it to you. There's a discrepancy in the numbers."

He looked at Marnie apologetically. "Chat later?"

She gave him her most demure smile. "Sure, Fitzy. See you real soon." She reached up and copped a feel of his bicep before turning to go.

Once she was gone, he told his crew of baristas he was off-duty, and then I followed him back to our booth.

"Okay, you spill and I'll pour." He dropped the tea bags into the pot to let them steep.

I shrugged. "Noah's mad at me."

His chin dropped, and he gave me his tell-me-something-I-don't-know-face. "That's a given. You're stubborn and he's bossy."

I frowned. "It's more than that. Noah wants me to back off even though I can help. Even though I gave him a big tip."

At the mention of a tip, Fitz perked up. "A clue about the accident?"

"Yeah, a good one, too. Do you think it'll offset that I kept one teeny detail from him?"

"Uh, we better start with the detail."

"I haven't told you either." I began to chew my nub of a nail. "It's eating me alive."

"No, you're eating you alive." He swatted my hand away from my mouth. "Now what is it?"

"The note that Becka had, the threat, is the reason she doesn't trust Noah."

"I don't get it."

I leaned in closer. "It's written on an Eliot Hill Police Department letterhead."

He paused. "What is?"

I looked around to make sure nobody was watching. "The threatening note. The logo at the top of the page is from the EHPD."

"So what?"

I recoiled. "*So what?*"

He stared at me for a minute, then pulled out a notepad from his back pocket. It had the same logo.

My breath caught. "Fitz, where did you get that notepad?"

"From the stack in my office. The baristas mainly use them to write down orders. You must've noticed them before. We've had them lying around the counters for months. I'm pretty sure you actually have a grocery list on your fridge with the very same paper."

I wrinkled my nose and frowned. So much for my powers of observation. "Why do you have them?"

"Noah dropped them off here after Fallfest last year. It seemed they weren't the hot ticket item he'd expected. He tried selling them as a fundraiser with no takers. By the end of the day, he was handing them out for free. There were no takers for that either, so he dropped them off here, thinking it would remind people that the police are part of the community, too."

"I better call Becka and let her know."

"I wouldn't overthink it," Fitz cautioned. "Her reasons are probably more personal."

My head snapped up. "What do you know?"

"Em," he cautioned. "I only have a few minutes."

Fitz, unlike me, was good at keeping secrets. Did Becka and Noah have history?

Fitz crossed his arms across his chest and waited. I let it go. "Fine." I pulled out my phone and showed him the message Jenny sent about the hiking app.

"Jenny's quick." He scrolled through a few screens on his phone. "I hadn't thought about it, but she's right. It's an app called *Hike to It*."

He held up his phone and pointed to an orange icon with the outline of a boot on it.

"You're a member?" I asked.

He nodded. "I cycle more than hike, so I don't use it all that much. But it's popular. The Eliot Hill group has at least a hundred members."

"Why didn't you ever mention it to me?" I huffed. "I hike."

He suppressed a grin. "I'm not sure that morning outings every two weeks in flip flops qualify. The app is used by hardcore hikers. It's pretty competitive, too. Every step is recorded, and there's a real-time tracker of the distance hiked. There's a ranking updated daily."

"That would explain why Jackie was tracking her movement, even if she wasn't technically on a hike."

"Maybe," Fitz said. "Let me check her standing."

He went into the app and played around for a minute. "Yeah, that makes sense. People don't use their real names, but if I were a betting man, I'd guess, based on the user I.D., that Jackie's number two."

He held up his phone again to show me. In the number two position was a user named *FierceBitch1*. No question, that was Jackie. She was a close second, meaning she'd use every opportunity to take the lead. Jackie didn't like to lose.

I wondered who was in the first place. "How can you find out who is in the Eliot Hill group?"

"Only the administrator knows. Even that's supposed to remain anonymous. Privacy laws, or something."

Inconvenient but not insurmountable.

"How does someone join? What's the process?"

"It's not hard. You submit an application and wait for approval. After that, you choose your username, and you're all set."

"Right. So, are you going to tell me who it is?"

He blinked. "Who?"

"You said the administrator is supposed to remain anonymous. The addition of 'supposed to' tells me you know who it is. Go on. It's your turn to spill the tea."

"Em…"

I shook my head. "The vault has been compromised, Fitz. You can't close it again without sharing everything you know."

"Why not?" he said, with slightly less determination. "If I tell you and Noah finds out you were interfering again, making use of information *I* provided, he'll be angry. At me."

"When did that ever stop you from doing anything? Besides, the app has already helped narrow down Jackie's time of death. Maybe the administrator could look at the data and see if there's anything else it can tell us."

"Like what?" Fitz said.

"I don't know, heart rate, maybe? It could tell us if she'd been running away before she was killed. Or maybe they could check for other hikers nearby at the time she was killed?"

Fitz picked up a cookie and took a big bite. He was stalling. I waited until he was done chewing and looked at him expectantly.

"You better prepare yourself," he said.

"For what?"

"Not for what, for who. Let's just say you won't be jumping for joy when you find out who runs the app."

I wrinkled my nose. "Go on, tell me."

"Rhymes with knob."

Rob. I groaned. Of all the people I'd rather it not be, he'd be the top pick. Rob Chaser was my high school sweetheart and Jackie's most recent ex-boyfriend.

I slumped back in my seat. Why did it have to be him?

Every time I thought back to my relationship with Rob, it was hard to refrain from going down a rabbit hole of anger and regret. He was the boyfriend who dumped me on Jackie's show and who then moved on with her. How very cozy.

When was the last time I'd even spoken to Rob? Eliot Hill was a small place. I'd seen him around. We both lived here, so it was inevitable for us to run into each other. But we didn't communicate beyond a quick flash of a fake smile. I didn't blame him for what happened any more than he blamed me. Jackie hadn't ruined our relationship; she'd simply picked up on what we'd yet to recognize. Had she done us a favor? In a way, yes. But doing it on live TV and mortifying me in the process, then adding salt to the wound by hooking up with Rob soon after? That hurt.

"You going to talk to him?" Fitz asked, his lip curling up. No need to ask if he thought I should. Fitz hated the guy, and I was pretty certain that would never change.

"Probably," I said. "But not now. I've been through enough hardship today."

Visible relief set in, and he relaxed, which was exactly what I intended to do for the rest of the evening. Suddenly bagged, just the thought of climbing the stairs up to my apartment made me dizzy with exhaustion.

I'd planned to get much more done, but I knew when to call it a day. After saying goodnight to Fitz, I booked it upstairs.

The rest of the evening was just me and Murray. I ordered a pizza and sunk onto the couch with my snuggle buddy. It was Netflix time. The pizza arrived in minutes, and soon, I was knee-deep into extra cheese and reality TV. The perfect pairing worked well as a good escape until I couldn't keep my eyes open. A final jaunt outside, then I crawled into bed.

My thoughts soon drifted back to Rob. His relationship with Jackie never made sense to me. I found out after the fact that they'd hooked up while prepping for our show. But it was almost as much of a surprise when the two became more than a passing fling. Rob seemed so different from her. Jackie was five years older and had a successful television career whereas Rob was still starting out, finding his path, his identity tangled up with mine. But, against the odds, they became a hot and heavy couple. Inseparable, I'd heard. I'd always wondered what had brought them together and, more recently, split them apart. First thing tomorrow, I would find out.

Chapter Thirteen

Jackie thought in black and white. There was never a gray zone. Everything could be categorized as right or wrong, good or evil. The way she saw it, when Rob and I went on her show, we'd been actively deceiving the public by creating a fantasy and selling it as reality. Afterwards, she explained to her viewers that she wouldn't stand for duplicity. Choose the behavior; choose the consequence. She took no accountability for any pain caused as a result. And weeks later, when she and Rob began dating? She put out a statement saying that their unforeseen romance was only further proof that our relationship was curated and that I deserved no sympathy. Not that I wanted any. Far from it. But her lack of empathy was something I never forgot.

After waking up late and taking Murray for a nice long walk, I wrote a blog but left it saved in drafts. After a slice of buttered toast and a big cup of coffee I skipped out the back entrance of the building, avoiding the café. I soon found myself across the street, at the door of Chaser's Bicycle Shop. How many afternoons had I spent here after school, doing homework and hanging out with Rob? A rush of memories hit me. I paused to take a big breath before pulling the door open and entering a space I hadn't been in for a very long time.

Rob still worked at the bike shop, having taken it over from his dad. But he didn't only run Chaser's Bike Shop; he'd also begun to design and support mobile phone apps as a hobby.

According to rumor, he'd done well for himself and only kept the bike shop because he enjoyed spending time there. Bigger responsibilities were transferred to hired employees, so he came and went as he pleased. Of course, everything I'd been told was hearsay, not fact. Sort of like when I first heard rumblings that he and Jackie had hooked up. Of course, that juicy nugget turned out to be true.

As I looked around the shop, marveling at how little it had changed, Rob walked out from the back. He stopped in his tracks and blinked. A smile slowly spread across his face.

"Wow. Emily Dalle. You are not who I expected to see."

I took a minute to look him over. He was a classic jock who hadn't changed much since high school. His chestnut hair was still in a crew cut, and his brown eyes were still warm and friendly, fringed with long lashes that garnered a lot of attention. He even had a little dimple that told moms he was a decent guy with a sensitive side. He liked to display it whenever charm played to his advantage.

I gave him an awkward wave. "Hi."

"Hells yeah, hi," Rob said. "It's good to see you, Emmy. Although, I have to admit, I'm a little surprised."

"Yeah, me too."

Rob walked around the counter to lessen the distance between us. His spandex outfit, with neon orange and black shorts and a sleeveless t-shirt, drew my eyes downward. He followed my gaze.

He put his hands on his hips proudly, as if he welcomed more than a quick peek.

A snort escaped from me, and I fought back a smile. "Same old Robbie. Strutting around like a rooster."

"You betcha," he said with a grin. "See something you like?"

"No." My hand covered my face. "Can you please change?"

He crossed his arms and puffed out his chest. "Why would I? It would be a disservice to the general public, in particular those of the female persuasion."

How was I ever into this guy?

"Your clothing, Rob. I meant, can you change your clothing? I need to talk to you, and that outfit bars any chance of adult conversation."

He chuckled and gestured to a couple of nearby stools. "You take the fun out of everything, Emmy. Have a seat. I'm supposed to be going for a bike ride in about twenty minutes, if you must know. I was waiting for a staffer to arrive so I could leave."

"Fair enough," I said. My mom always said Robbie would never grow up. Guess she'd been right.

He grabbed a pair of baggy camouflage shorts from under the counter and threw them over his spandex.

"Better?"

With the goods under wraps, I sat down. "Much."

He sat down next to me. It had been years since we'd been this close to each other. Axe body spray filled my nostrils. A string of memories ignited in my brain and flashed before my eyes like a spliced-up old movie reel.

Our relationship had been passionate and powerful, and I'd never experienced anything like it before. Neither had he. We were so into it, the emotional highs of love that we wanted to share that overwhelming joy with the world. So we did.

Setting up an Instagram account dedicated to our love was a passion project. We never set out to profit from it. We'd gushed and laughed and doled out sage advice, thinking we'd done something right to find each other. We believed we had insight to pass along to others so they could be like us and find their person.

Then, it got a major boost from a celebrity. A well-known actor who was filming a romantic comedy in town. Rob hooked him up with a loaner bicycle, and in lieu of payment, he shared our handle on his page, recommending it to his followers. Overnight, our account grew a hundredfold, and we were thrust into the social media limelight. It became so popular we started a blog, too, answering questions and counseling singles on how to find their own true love, as well as spewing out guidance to other couples on how to keep the fire burning.

Not long after, companies began to reach out to us, offering paid sponsorships for all sorts of items. We decided to accept a few, including both date-night idea kits and his-and-hers terry cloth robes. We were on a roll and enjoying it.

Unfortunately, we were so busy telling others how to nurture their relationships, we forgot to take time for our own.

Over time, our passion became passive, and our coupling felt stale.

I hadn't wanted to tell Rob because I thought I still loved him. I was ashamed of my dwindling affection and felt I just needed to try harder. I hadn't wanted to hurt him or cause any ripples in our 'perfect' relationship.

It had nothing to do with our brand—that had been placed on us by others, including Becka. Yes, I'd been flattered and completely bought into it. But not because I was trying to manufacture a lie or chase fame. I was naïve and foolish to believe that Rob and I were soulmates.

Looking at him now, I was surprised at how good it felt to be here. Did I still have a soft spot for him? Maybe. Despite the torpedoed ending, we'd shared some amazing times. Whispers of old promises brought a faint smile to my face. Part of me wanted to sit in the nostalgic comfort and remember all the laughs we'd shared.

Whoa.

Fast forward to the end. There were no red roses and sweet memories there.

He leaned forward and patted my knee. "What's up, Emmy? Why are you here?"

I pushed the past away. "It's Jackie. Can I ask you about her?"

His face darkened, and a scowl replaced the grin. "Didn't see that coming."

"Are you talking about my question or her fate?"

"Both." He shuffled awkwardly in his seat.

When we were together, Rob hated to talk about anything deeper than how to deal with mud in the tires of his road bike.

"I can't imagine what you're going through," I said.

"We weren't exactly getting along." He stretched out his muscular legs and shoved his hands in his pockets. "What can you do? Life goes on, I guess."

His callous words didn't surprise me. He'd always played it cool. To anyone else, he would come across as uncaring. But I'd known him well enough to recognize the signs that told me otherwise. When his father used to reprimand him for a missed opportunity during hockey games, his hands would begin to tremble, and he'd experience a tingling sensation brought on by anxiety. Hands in pocket told me it hadn't changed.

"When was the last time you saw her?" I asked.

"C'mon, Emmy, you sound like Noah. Cut it out."

Rob and Noah were good friends. Although quite different, they'd been close since they were on the local hockey team. Now, they watched pro games together as armchair athletes at the local bar.

"Did you avoid the question when Noah asked you?"

"No, he's the sheriff. It's his job to ask," he said with a tinge of irritation. "What does it matter to you?"

"I'm curious."

He scoffed and shook his head. "Same old Emily."

I frowned. "What does that mean?"

"How many times did those words come out of your mouth over the years?"

My blank look told him I didn't know.

"Why do you think your nickname was monkey?"

I shrugged. "Because I could climb to the top of the evergreen near the back door of the gym."

He shook his head. "Nope. Half the school could do that. It was because curiosity always got you in trouble. You know, like *Curious George*."

Huh. How had I never made that connection?

"And before you ask," he said. "Friday night, I was out riding. I left work and went straight home afterwards. Alone."

"I wasn't going to ask." At least until I'd tried my hand at small talk.

His eyes narrowed. "Then what is it? I can tell you're not done asking questions."

"It's that app you created. I want you to explain how it works."

He rubbed his hands together and sat up taller. "You'll have to be a little more specific. I'm quite prolific in the app department, among other things."

There were so many insults on the tip of my tongue. But I wanted his help, so I bit down on them instead.

"The hiking app," I specified.

"*Hike To It*. Yeah, one of my best." He grinned at me. "What do you want to know?"

"Jackie was using it when she was killed," I told him. "It would've shown her location, right?"

He blinked. Then blinked again. "Okay. Why does that matter? Everyone knows she was killed on Mountaintop Lane."

"If someone was after her, I want to know if that app could be used to find her, to track her down."

He flinched. "Jesus, that's dark."

I flushed. "It's just a theory. Will you help me find out?"

"I guess so. What do you need to know?"

"I want you to give me the names of all the members who were using it when she was killed and tell me where they were."

His body stiffened at the request. "What time are you looking at?"

"Between eight-thirty and nine Friday night," I told him.

He looked uneasy but tried to cover with a smile. "I guess I could look at the data and send you a list. As long as you're discreet. Confidentiality is important to people."

"I'll keep that in mind."

He slapped his hands on his shorts. "Are we done?"

"One more question."

"Shoot."

"Any idea why Jackie might've left her own party?"

The smile faded. "Ask Grant Henshaw, the idiot boyfriend."

"Guess you weren't a fan?"

"Em, this might sound ironic coming from me, but that guy treated her like crap." He stabbed himself in the chest with his thumb. "I may not be perfect, but at least when we were on a break, I made sure not to get anyone else pregnant, and when I proposed, I meant it for life. Unlike him."

Pregnant? Propose?

I held my hands up. "Whoa. Slow down, Rob. You're dropping bombs here."

"Tell me about it." His gaze shifted to the floor. "Last time I saw her, she was a mess."

"What do you mean?" Jackie was never a mess. Vulnerability was a weakness to her.

"She'd had a fight with Grant." His voice cracked. He cleared his throat. "Jackie was legit hysterical. I don't even know if half of what she was telling me was true or whether she was just paranoid."

"Back up. Why would she come to you after a fight with him?"

He scoffed. "Because I was still her best friend, and she knew I loved her. Ironic, isn't it?"

I frowned. "What is?"

"When I finally became a decent guy, it burned me. She was upset, so I pushed my feelings aside and listened. Maybe I should've pressured her more. She might've come back to me." Sadness clouded his features. "Maybe she'd still be here."

My voice softened. "Why didn't you tell her how you really felt?"

He leaned back, lifting the front two legs of his chair. He stared at the ceiling. "Because Grant gave her what she wanted most. A reason to leave town."

Leave town? "Why would she want to take off? Her whole life was here."

He dropped the chair back on all fours and shrugged. "Ask Becka. She might know more. All I can tell you is that there was some major shake-up being threatened at work, and Jackie didn't know if she was going to make the cut."

Becka hadn't mentioned that before. Then again, maybe she didn't know. If Jackie had pissed off WKRZ president, Mitch Myers, it was possible Jackie's position was the only one at stake. Lord knows it wouldn't have been the first time he'd threatened to fire her. But I knew a better source to ask than Becka. Someone who had the ear and the trust of Mitch Myers.

The sound of a bouncing ball interrupted my train of thought.

"Wanna play?" Rob asked. Leave it to him to have a toy within reach at all times. It was his way of telling me he was done with the conversation.

"No thanks." I stood up. "I should get going."

He stopped the ball bouncing for long enough to give me a fresh smile. It was almost enough to make him look cute again. Almost.

"Now that you're a fancy pants influencer, you think you're too good for me?" he teased.

"Of course not." I shot him a grin. "I've always known I'm too good for you."

He snapped his fingers. "Dang, Emmy, that's cold."

Another snort. I reached over and grabbed the ball from his grip.

He managed to take it back and threw it toward the hoop, not far from where we stood. I reached out and intercepted it before he scored a point. No matter what was going on behind the scenes, Rob always exuded carefree ease, as if nothing at all was wrong in the world. It hit me for the first time that this was not necessarily a good thing. What went on behind that grin?

When I reached the door, I tossed the ball over to the net. If I'd gotten it in, it would've made for a fierce exit. Instead, the ball hit the rim and took a sharp turn. Maybe that was what I needed to start looking for.

Chapter Fourteen

Sunday, May 5th

Hey guys,

You have been my rock during the last few days, and I wanted to say thanks. Jackie's death shook me. It was so unexpected and shocking. Death seems so final, and it's been tough to wrap my head around.

My complicated relationship with Jackie left me with a bunch of feelings, and none of them were the good kind. We still don't know what happened. There are so many questions. Luckily, we have a smart, dedicated sheriff who has been working around the clock.

The truth will be found. Justice will be served. Someone knows something, and secrets never stay hidden. A lot of you have reached out to me. It's been helpful and reassuring. I'm not sure whether I should've dumped all this on you. Life's path is not always clear. For a recovering people pleaser like me, uncertainty creeps in as my inner saboteur whispers doubts in my ear. For now, that voice has been silenced. You've helped me recognize that my thoughts and opinions count. Getting over the need to please matters.

Anyway, let's switch lanes. You ready? I sure am. Let's focus back on positive vibes. My new weekly show, Friday Night Nostalgia on WKRZ, will be starting in less than two weeks. Mom and I will whip up a perfect, easy snack, and we'll show you how to make it so we can all eat and enjoy the movie together. Movie pick? Stay tuned for details.

I'll give you a hint. Early nineties and lots of angst...

Thank you for your unwavering support.

On another note, I will be sharing my favorite new products of the season by Sunsmear Cosmetics next Thursday morning. There are some fabulous new nudes!

Onward,

Em

I settled into my booth at the café after catching up with Rob, and I ordered a green tea, a BLT bagel, and a double chocolate chip cookie to balance it out. On a full stomach, I reread the blog I shared this morning, then began work on next week's talking points, brainstorming ideas for both the content of the blog and social media posts to support it. The casual tone and upbeat message of my narrative took time to curate. Bloggers and influencers often worked more than most people realized.

With so much competition out there, I had to stay relevant without becoming repetitive. My platform was based on my own experience. People pleasing almost ruined my life, and I believed it was a soul crusher. Not a new message, but one that seemed to garner a decent audience. I also had to make sure to keep it light and fun. That wasn't too hard. I had Murray, a hundred pounds of happiness, to help me out.

My phone rang. I picked it up, not recognizing the number.

"Hello?"

"Hi, Em. Glad you picked up."

"Becka? That you?"

"No, it's Vera."

"Sorry, Vera. What's up?"

"I'm calling from the studio. Can you come by? Becka wants you here for a meeting."

"Really? Why?"

"Not sure. Sorry, I gotta run. Please come, it would mean a lot. The meeting starts at 3:00. Talk soon, bye!"

She hung up before I could answer. I held out my phone and looked at it. Odd request. Then again, maybe Jackie's show was the reason for the meeting. It made sense to address her death as soon as possible. Things were probably a hot mess right now at the studio, and as a producer, Becka would be under a lot of strain. I could see why she might request a little extra support. Besides, maybe I could pick up a few clues into what happened.

Murray shifted under my feet. "No, you're not coming. I need to go to the studio. No dogs allowed." A low rumble of protest made me roll my eyes. I bent down to address him. "Don't start with me."

Fitz caught my eye as I sat up. I waved him over. "Favor?"

"Depends."

"Can you keep an eye on my oversized baby for an hour or two? I have to head over to the studio for a meeting."

"Will you be long?"

I shrugged. "Not sure, it's last minute, so I don't know what to expect. If you're busy, I can drop him off upstairs."

"Nah, leave him with me. The Mahjong Maidens are on their way. It's better if I'm not around. A walk with Murray is the perfect excuse."

I grinned. "Dare I ask why?"

He shook his head. "Last time they played, the game got super intense. Their language turned so blue I had to ask them to tone it down three times. If you need my support to cut out your cursing, I can't be under the influence of that unruly bunch."

"Aren't they all in their eighties?"

"Uh-huh. Your point?"

"My point is I have to go." I stood up and elbowed Fitz out of the way. "Watch out, I see a cotton top heading this way."

Fitz's eyes widened. "Save yourself. I'll get Murball ready and see you back here later."

I thanked him, then zipped upstairs to get ready.

* * *

The studio wasn't far. Although not actually situated in Eliot Hill, it was only a thirty-minute drive beyond the town limits. It felt shorter today. My head buzzed with information and was so overloaded, I barely remembered the ride over.

If the execs held an emergency meeting at the TV station, they must want to discuss how to handle Jackie's show. Although unsure why Becka wanted me there, I was grateful to be included. It could give me some insight into what had been going on recently with Jackie.

The Morning Dish was normally taped the day it aired, shot beforehand to edit out errors and make sure it ran smoothly. An audience was brought in for the hour-taping at six a.m., and the show aired four hours later.

From what I remembered, they had a few shows shelved and ready to go in case of an emergency, like a snowstorm, or an illness. Would murder classify, too?

It felt odd, inappropriate, to air one of the previously taped episodes as if everything was status quo. Jackie's death was actually trending on X. Although the show wasn't aired across the country, Jackie had made her mark in the entertainment business and created a name for herself. *Queen of Mean* wasn't just a local term. Since her death, the most common tweets associated with her were #thequeenofmeanisdead and #karmakilledher.

What would Jackie think of the attention her death attracted? Most likely, she'd relish it, whether or not she was cast in a good light. For her, fame was the goal, period. She was like a misbehaving child. Negative attention was better than none.

I paused at the entrance and took a deep breath as I approached the studio's back door. In stark contrast to the stylish public lobby, the private entranceway, where on-air personalities and guests accessed the studio, was basic and industrial and not in a trendy modern way. The first thing people encountered was an old steel door with dents from who-knows-what over the years. Far from welcoming, it was intimidating and cold. It made me wonder if that had been chosen with intent, as if to remind VIPs to check their egos at the door.

I knocked. It didn't take long before I heard heavy footsteps make their way toward me. A sturdy-looking woman in a security guard uniform opened the door.

"Hi there." My tone was friendly.

Her demeanor was not. "You're not on the schedule for today."

Although a semi-regular guest on Jackie's show, I wasn't here enough to warrant a pass. But it was enough to irk the guard, although her greeting today was particularly frosty. "Emergency meeting re. The Morning Show. You can check with Vera or Becka if you like. It's Emily, Emily Dalle."

She looked me up and down. "Come in." She held open the door as I entered. The industrial design carried on inside. It resembled the interior of a garage more than a TV studio.

Not much had changed over the years. Except for the addition of a Keurig Coffee machine. A small but vast improvement over the old drip coffee maker. Now, instead of the incessant scent of burnt coffee, it always smelled like a freshly brewed cup.

"Meeting's on the second floor," the woman instructed.

"Thanks." It was a familiar path.

My second appearance on the show was not something I'd anticipated doing after the first time. The invite had come as a shock, and I'd almost turned it down. Both Fitz and Mom hated the idea of a return visit. But I hated leaving things unfinished and hated it even more when I avoided things that scared me for no good reason. Not that Jackie wasn't a good reason. Still, I was curious and had accepted the offer. Plus, it was a great opportunity to expand my audience and have a do-over.

It had turned out better than I'd thought. We'd discussed how dating had changed over the last few years and both refrained from bringing up the fact that she was currently dating my ex.

Instead, we ranked and classified apps—everything from best for relationship goals to short-term companionship to a quick night out. She even helped me nail down my brand, which, up until then, I hadn't considered much. Up until then, I posted anything that felt genuine. It was very organic. But Jackie suggested I pair it down to what she called 'my specialty.'

"And what is that?" I asked.

"How to stop being a people pleaser."

I felt my guard go up. "What do you mean?"

"The first time you were here, the need to please outweighed standing up for yourself. But today I can see you've changed. You are less focused on what you think is expected and are more direct about how you really feel. Sharing opinions without wondering if they are the right ones. It's refreshing."

I stared at her. "Is this some sort of backhanded compliment? Because I'm not here for that. You want to see honest? I'm prepared." No way I'd be the deer in the headlights again. I could—and would—take her down.

She looked amused. "No need to get your back up. I'm a hundred percent here for you. My goal has always been to know thyself. You have come full circle, and I applaud it. Some of my staff didn't think you could handle coming back here, but you did. That takes courage. You should lean into that and share your tips on it with that world."

"As an anti-people pleaser?" I said, ensuring I understood her suggestion.

"Sounds about right. I just finished reading Mark Manson's book, The Subtle Art of Not Giving a..."

"I know the book," I said.

"Yes, well, it reminded me a little of you."

"I've made a concerted effort to no longer curse in my blogs."

"Not just that. It's your tone. You're not perfect, and have embraced that. I found it refreshing."

Something happened in that moment. I felt seen. I felt understood. It was as if she'd edited my work and helped me find the underlying theme. And I loved it.

From that day forward, I'd run with it.

I'd ceased being the lonely girl and moved on to being an individual in charge of her own voice, her own career, and her own destiny. No longer trying to be someone people thought I should be, or even could be, I accepted who I was proudly and encouraged others to do the same. Perfection was the enemy, and I gave up trying to reach its peak. It was fun to embrace the lighter, brighter me, and I'd learned that rejecting the need to please was the key to a happy life.

It's not that I hadn't shifted my blog up until that day—I really had, giving advice on the rejection of anyone who doesn't make you feel good. But that was only one aspect. There was so much more to anti-people pleasing than breakups and boyfriends. And since then, I'd been sharing my experience about it with my followers.

Some of my sponsors left, but with a fairly sizable audience, I had the flexibility to pick and choose others that fit my new mission statement.

Plus, Murray was a natural star, so leaning into his best doggy life brought unexpected sponsors I gladly embraced.

The only moment during the show that drew my ire was when Jackie attempted to take credit for my success. "Some of our viewers may not know I had a hand in thrusting you into the spotlight," she told the audience.

But I'd learned a few things since the first time I'd visited. Like not being caught off guard. "Jackie," I'd said in response. "That was one of the worst days of my life. You had a hand in that, too." She'd looked surprised by my comeback.

"Well, well, well." She'd raised an eyebrow. "Okay, I'll accept that. You turned a personal crisis into a personal success. All on your own." She pivoted toward the audience. "Let's give this woman a hand."

The studio erupted, and the episode garnered the best ratings of the season.

The experience left me feeling better and stronger. And the disdain I'd felt for Jackie was thrown for a loop. It made me realize that maybe her intention had always been to keep it real and call out BS, even if it came across as cruel.

After that visit, I became a regular. I gave her audience tips on how to navigate the social media world without feeling inadequate. We also discussed the newest self-help blogs and books, and local haunts for fresh air and fun. We always ended by engaging with the audience, and the latest and greatest light-hearted gossip usually centered on who-was-dating-who.

The sensational nature of her show didn't bother me. When I was on the show, it was never mean-spirited and always brought a few new followers. My former resentment dissipated over time. And I felt stronger and more confident for seeing it through. It was a full-circle moment.

I never trusted Jackie again, but I understood where she'd been coming from, and we'd formed a jocular type of banter, on and off the air, almost as if we were friends.

Chapter Fifteen

I wandered out of the elevator and into the open studio, then paused to look around. There were still photos up all over of Jackie in extravagant outfits with various celebrities. Each one managed to capture her larger-than-life spirit. Her presence was so big here it almost felt tangible. Even her distinctive sweet honeysuckle perfume hung in the air and wafted into every crevice of the kitschy pink and orange décor. It was enough to make me question if the last few days had really happened.

I automatically made my way to the staff lounge. It had been a refuge for Jackie's employees. The Hideaway, as it was usually referred to, was the only place fun was allowed. The walls were covered with pictures of current staff members enjoying themselves on set but off the record. I recognized most of the faces. Becka stood on stage holding a microphone, emulating Jackie's hand-on-hip pose, an exaggerated smile on her face. Another photo showed bearded cameraman, Merle Fisher, giving the thumbs-up gesture as he pretended to pour a beer into a coffee mug under a clock that read six a.m. Becka's best friend and stage manager, Vera Hansen, was holding out the t-shirt she wore, a black and white skull surrounded by red and blue roses, and sticking out her tongue.

"In my defense," a voice said from behind me. "It was my birthday. The guys gave me the t-shirt, then took a picture to remember."

I spun around on my heel. Vera stood behind me, smiling.

"I don't get it," I said.

"One of the admin assistants decided to spill the tea about my real name. She was mad because her boyfriend asked me out. The photo is from a band.

The Deftones. The song's called 'Minerva.'"

I scrunched my nose. "You're a Minerva? As in McGonagall?" The hot blonde was a far cry from the stern professor in *Harry Potter*.

She grinned. "As in Minerva Lois Hansen, after my grandmother. My grandpa calls me Minnie. What's worse?"

"I can see why Vera is your go-to. What's with all the goofy photos?"

"Things can get tense around here. Becka started the tradition by daring each staff member to do something silly on camera without getting caught by—" Her smile faltered. "Sorry," She brought both hands to her lips in a sudden wave of emotion. "It's been a tough few days."

My heart went out to her. "Jackie was a big presence. It must be hard to imagine being here without her." We were quiet for a minute. "You okay?"

"I'll manage. It's just hard to believe."

I rubbed her arm. "I know. How's Becka handling everything?"

Her head bobbed from one side to the other. "She's up and down." Vera took a deep breath and swallowed hard. I'd gotten to know her during our hikes with Becka. The two had become attached at the hip. They had a lot in common, including having targets on their backs from Jackie. Becka, for sisterly reasons, and Vera because she was the prettiest employee on set. Vera wasn't fazed. She'd come from a background of beauty pageantry and competitive dance, where the rivalry from jealous contenders could be fierce and cruel. Vera, like most of the staff, was grateful for her position, since WKRZ was the only gig around.

She gave me a practiced smile. "Anyway, I'm glad you're here."

"Do you know why Becka wanted me to come?" I asked.

"A little extra support. She's going through a lot."

"Okay."

She held up her phone and checked the time. "We better go."

We left the staff room and continued down the hallway. Vera's posture was polished and perfect. It made me feel a bit troll-like. She wore a silky red and white polka-dot blouse over a fitted black pencil skirt, somehow making it look chic and sophisticated. The pattern reminded me of a sweater I'd had in high school. I loved that sweater. Fitz said it made me look like I had chickenpox. Is this how Becka felt under the star of Jackie?

We slowed just outside a meeting room. Vera turned to me. "Ready?"

I nodded. "Sure."

Vera pushed open the heavy wooden door and sailed through. She veered ahead and grabbed a front-row seat. I paused, unsure if there was enough space, but she waved me over.

I approached and was about to sit beside her when a gruff man sidestepped in front of me and took my spot. I was so close to sitting down, I barely managed to stop myself from landing on his lap. I stumbled forward, furious. When I turned to object, my glare was met with a patronizing smirk from the bearded middleager. It was Merle Fisher, the camera operator, whose photo I'd been looking at in the Hideaway. He was also Jackie's rumored henchman.

"Sorry, Doll. I need a front seat for the show." He extended a hand to steady me. His forearm was tattooed with what looked like the scales of justice, weighed down on one side by a mouse.

I met his eyes. He winked at me and did a double click with the side of his mouth, the sound you might make if trying to speak to a chipmunk. His beard was so long it could've actually housed a family of chipmunks, if he'd wanted. As far as I could tell, its only occupant at the moment was a dollop of ketchup.

Too flustered to respond, I looked around. Almost every other seat was taken, all twenty or so. The crew of familiar faces looked strained and unsettled, with the exception of Becka, who'd slipped in at the last minute. She looked a lot calmer than I expected, polished too.

Her brunette hair was back to its blissful bob, and her bangs were runway-ready. She must've felt my eyes on her because she met my gaze with a small nod.

Her greeting was a little chilly. But what could I expect? The poor girl had just lost her sister.

Before I could make small talk with any of the familiar faces around me, the door of the room closed. A wispy-haired man with deep smile lines and a small paunch covered by an expensive suit stood up and waited for the hum of conversation to quiet down. In mere seconds, the room fell completely silent. It was the executive we were waiting to hear from. He looked at me and gave me a quick wink. Although likely surprised to see me there, Uncle Mitch didn't give it away.

"Thanks for coming today, everyone." His voice boomed. "Obviously, this is a hard day to be here, so I won't keep you long. For anyone new, my name is Mitch Myers. I'm the founder and President of WKRZ. I'd like to begin by telling you all that I'm so sorry for everyone's loss. Jackie was larger than life, and her presence will remain with us each passing day. However, I'll save the sentiment for a later time, as I'm sure Jackie would appreciate it. I'd like to get down to business now and establish the plan going forward. We've made some decisions I'm eager to share with you."

Head nods and murmurs went around the room as people looked at each other, with concern and apprehension.

"Let's get right to it. Jackie's show is popular and does well. It would be a shame to shut it down prematurely, even without its star. We all have a stake in the success of this show continuing, so I am going to propose the best option we've come up with for the foreseeable future. Is everyone up for the challenge of working through our loss to keep the camera rolling and our jobs secure?"

There was a light round of consensual applause to show that everyone was on board, without exception. As cringe-worthy as this whole process seemed, what other choice did they have? The studio produced more shows than Jackie's, but hers was one of the biggest.

"We'll be passing the reins to the closest figure to Jackie, both on and off the stage. Becka, you're up."

All eyes shot to Becka, including mine. *Ex-squeeze me?*

I stared at Becka, trying to wrap my head around the announcement. She flashed a stellar grin as if her name had been called at the Emmys for Best New Talk Show Host. Son of a monkey. I didn't see that coming.

Chapter Sixteen

Becka hopped off her chair with a little shimmy shake. She let out a giggle and clasped Uncle Mitch's hand with both of hers. He gave her the Oscar. I mean the floor. The Emmy would have to wait for award season. I'd be putting her name in the running for best actress. She deserved to win.

I shoved my balled-up fists into the miniature pockets of my stretchy jeans, grateful for the give. Either Becka faked joy now, or she'd faked heartbreak yesterday. There was no way someone could go from the depths of despair to the top of the world in twenty-four hours. No. Freaking. Way.

When I'd reconnected with Becka, a little voice inside me said, "Don't trust her." I ignored that voice. Years earlier, she'd been one of my closest friends. But when she decided not to warn me that Jackie planned to ambush me on TV, our friendship fizzled out.

So when Becka reached out and asked to join me on my bi-weekly hikes, I'd been slow to agree. I couldn't help but wonder now if it had been a mistake. *Who was the real Becka—grieving sister or TV star wannabe?*

The chair next to me squeaked. I jumped. A hum of voices began as the news settled into the room. Upbeat and energized, the tone lacked the sour milk feeling I was experiencing. Why was I the only one who needed time to process this announcement?

I looked at Vera. She beamed at her bestie, then joined the growing round of applause. She held her hands up as she clapped, encouraging everyone to join in. When her eyes met mine, she gave me a quick thumbs up. I forced a smile. Then she swiveled back around and let out a holler. Like everyone else, she seemed eager to join the excitement that filled the room.

Then it hit me. Vera showed no sign of surprise. I cast my eyes around the room. No one else did either. What was going on?

Becka was smart, hard-working, and devoted. She garnered the support of the crew. Passing the reins to Becka was a good call. Worth a shot, at least. But how could this have been planned in mere hours? Talk shows required a lot of prep behind the scenes. More than could be organized in less than a day.

Becka avoided eye contact with me. At least, that's what it felt like. Maybe that wasn't fair. The whole room wanted her attention. She was in demand. I wasn't her priority. She's been propelled into a new role, and everyone wanted her light on them.

It would've been an awkward moment, anyway. I wouldn't have been able to hide that none of this sat right with me.

Uncle Mitch cleared his throat, indicating he had more to say.

"We're going to start out with a bang. Big-name guests and fan favorites. We've already spoken to a few, and we have the first two weeks planned. We'll be increasing the segment time with guests, recipes, and giveaways while Becka has a chance to get her feet wet."

The staff applauded, and Becka gave a wave. Then she put her finger to her lips. Becka pulled a neatly folded paper from the sleeve of her shirt. I flinched. She'd planned a speech?

Becka cleared her throat. "First of all," she began. *Uhhhh.* I had the urge to run. Becka continued. "I want to thank you for coming out today, for your years of dedication, hard work, and loyalty. Jackie relied on you, and you delivered. My sister wasn't always easy to work for. You all know that I'm speaking from experience." She paused while titters filled the air. "Going forward, this show will be more collaborative, more positive, and more enjoyable."

Another round of applause. Uncle Mitch joined in, beaming at her. She waved again and let him take the floor. He nodded at the enthusiastic crowd, shushing the crowd to settle them down. "Okay, okay. Thanks, everyone. I hope you're this excited next week." He paused as the audience laughed.

"Seriously though, we're going to need everyone to pitch in. *The Morning Dish* has a fresh face. I want everyone to take a few days off and come in Wednesday ready to hit the ground running."

Chatter filled the room, and chairs scraped the floor as people got up and left the room. No more mention of Jackie.

I watched Becka talk enthusiastically with the small crowd who'd gathered around her. After a few minutes, the crowd dispersed, and she met my gaze. I tried to smile. What else could I do? She pointed down toward the exit. It was her way of telling me to meet her outside so we could talk.

We shared an elevator downstairs with a few smokers, who each took a turn letting Becka know they supported the decision and were glad to hear it was official. We all then went outside, squinting in the sun's bright light. The smokers veered left to the designated area, where they began to talk amongst themselves.

Becka and I looped around a nearby corner. Once there, we fell into an awkward silence until I broke the silence with the only thing I could think to say. "Congratulations."

Becka beamed at me. "Thanks. I would've told you myself, but I never got the chance. The call came an hour ago. I had to come in and get ready. Fastest makeover in TV history."

"They made the right choice," I heard myself say. As she thanked me, I realized I actually meant it. Maybe I'd overreacted earlier. Maybe I hadn't. But either way, it was only fair. After all, Becka had filled in whenever Jackie was unavailable. To hand her the reins was the only decision that made sense.

I thought back to the first time Becka filled in for Jackie as host of *The Morning Dish*. It had been after a botched Botox session. Jackie's left eye was droopy, and she'd refused to film until it went back to normal. She'd offered up her sister as backup.

Left in a lurch, they hadn't had a lot of options. Becka lit up on stage and was better received by audiences than anyone had expected.

"Thanks, Em," she said, bringing me back to the present. "I appreciate your support." She dropped her voice. "I wanted to talk to you about that other thing I asked you to do."

"Yes," I said, relieved she brought it up. "I was hesitant at first, but it was a good idea. You were thinking outside the box."

"I appreciate that. But," she paused and let out an awkward laugh. "Noah came to see me, and we had a good talk."

My eyes widened. "I didn't tell him, I swear."

"No, *you* didn't, but Fitz did."

My cheeks flushed. *The rat!*

"I'm not mad," she said.

"I'm sorry, I—"

She held up her hand. "It's okay, really. Noah was good about it, and we've straightened everything out. So, you're off the hook."

I frowned. "Okay, but like I said, I think you were on to something. My post snagged some important information. I was thinking I could—"

She shook her head. "Thanks. But I'd like Noah to handle it now." When I opened my mouth to argue, she cut me off. "Please, Em. I shouldn't have put you in that position in the first place."

I stammered. "Right." I forced a smile. "Anyway, why don't you tell me more about the show."

Her face lit up. "Unbelievable, isn't it? In darkness, find the light, isn't that what they say? Besides, in show biz, you take any opportunity given. Am I right?"

Opportunity. Is that how she saw the murder of her sister?

Before I could say anything, Becka began to describe the set changes she had in mind. "Softer lighting, artificial plants. It's all about branding."

As she spoke, a sinking feeling set in. Not only did she dismiss me, she seemed to have moved on from Jackie's death. As she prattled on about mood boards and chill vibes, I couldn't help but wonder if Jackie was even in her peripheral. Had she lost interest in who'd run Jackie down?

"Em?"

I felt my cheeks warm. "Sorry?"

Becka looked at me impatiently. "I asked if you prefer millennial pink or a lavender purple? I need to make some decisions, and I'm waffling."

"Um…" I cleared my throat. "Both are nice."

She pursed her lips. We were on different planes, and we both knew it. "I should probably…" She gestured with her thumb toward the door.

"Yeah, of course," I said, nodding.

We headed back inside. With a quick goodbye, she headed toward the elevators. I watched her disappear, then turned to go.

Vera came in as I was on my way out. She had a small shopping bag in one hand. "Thought I might need a few supplies if we're going to be here for a while."

"Anything good?" I asked.

"Promise not to tell, and I'll make it worth your while."

I raised my eyebrow. "Whatcha got?"

With a small grin, she let me peek inside the bag.

I pointed down to the only item inside. "What's that?"

She waved her finger at me. "Don't play coy with me, Em."

Busted. The hot pink box had to be from *Bitten,* Eliot Hill's premier bakery. Right now, cupcake therapy sounded just about right. She pulled it out and opened the lid. "Go on, take one."

No need to ask me twice. Of the dozen to choose from, I grabbed a vanilla cupcake with sprinkles. A classic. "Thanks, Vera."

"You're welcome." She closed the lid carefully to make sure the cupcakes were safe and secure. "I better get back in there."

"Free for a hike in the morning?"

"Sounds like a great idea." She gave me a little wave and headed inside. I hopped into my Jeep and took a bite. Were cupcakes an official form of therapy? They had a calming effect like no other. I texted Fitz as I chowed down.

Me: You told Noah about the notepad?

Fitz: Yes, of course. I assumed you knew.

Me: Nope.

Fitz: Sorry. But in the end, it's good, right? You're off the case.

Me: True. Guess I'm not mad then.

Fitz: You're welcome.

Me: Talk later.

Fitz: OK.

I dropped the phone on the passenger seat and let my head fall back, cramming the rest of my cupcake in my mouth. *Off the case?* I wasn't really *on* the case. A little digging here and there was all, and now I wasn't so sure I was ready to give it up. I was actually beginning to get somewhere. *Am I really going to quit now?* My shoulders slumped. *Who do I think I am? Jessica Fletcher? Veronica Mars?* Maybe in another life, I would've made a good detective, but I wasn't ready to make that leap.

Time to shift my focus. But how? I should try a little meditation. Fitz would be so proud. Up until recently I'd relied on power naps and reality TV to get my mind off things, although I'd recently added nature walks, which was proving to work wonders.

I was surprised at how much I'd come to enjoy hiking. My outings with Becka and Vera had proven to be one of my favorite hobbies. I enjoyed their company and Vera had begun taking photos I used on my social media feeds, an added bonus. I'd even been invited to their next big trip, a week in California. Hollywood, Disneyland, and Malibu. Although I wasn't quite ready for round-the-clock togetherness.

I picked my phone up and canceled the silent mode I'd switched on for the meeting. A ding alerted me to one new voicemail. A motorcycle pulled up next to me, making it impossible to hear the message. Sparking irritation, I shot the helmeted rider a withering side-eye before tossing my phone back onto the seat.

It was probably Fitz, anyway. How would he react to the news of Becka replacing Jackie on the show? Hopefully, his incessant optimism would pull me back from the feeling of dread I couldn't shake. I looked at the time. A walk would have to wait. I had a blog to post and an audience to call off. I'd ask them to leave the investigation to the professionals. But could I do the same? I wasn't so sure.

Chapter Seventeen

Sunday, May 5th

Hi everyone,

I've got the inside scoop about the direction of Jackie Hunter's show, The Morning Dish. Does it seem odd to be discussing it so soon? Of course. But Jackie would be the first one to tell you the show must go on.

I'm excited about the direction of the show. Things move fast in show biz, kids. Let's get ready to support its new format. What is it, you ask? Tsk tsk, you know it's not up to me to say. Stay tuned, and I'll let you know as soon as I've been given the green light.

In the meantime, I hope you've set your reminders for Friday May 17th. Watching a classic nineties movie with my mom is going to be a treat. A guaranteed pick-me-up for anyone feeling down. Lord knows we could all use that right about now.

On another note, I'm be posting photos of Murray with his new doggy goggles in the next few days. Perfect eye protection for an open-air ride. Poochies Eyewear is my newest sponsor, and I couldn't be more excited. Hilarious? You betcha. Unique? I'd say. Awesome? Definitely.

Until then, stay on the path of kindness.

Em

When I first got back to the café, Fitz wasn't there. Neither was Murray. They were likely out for a stroll. It gave me the chance to grab a bite and post a quick update on my blog. Armed with a black bean wrap, I plunked myself down on a stool along the counter and pulled my laptop out of my bag. I took a big bite and logged onto my account. Instead of asking my followers to let the case drop, I switched lanes instead. If anyone had information to share, I wasn't ready to discourage them. If nothing came of it, I'd move on.

I always posted a new entry before I went through the replies from my last one. It was a habit I'd gotten into not long after my blog first blew up. I learned that if I went through reactions to my previous post beforehand, it sometimes changed the direction I'd planned out, often as a reaction to something negative. As much as I pretended not to give a hoot, words still hurt. To maintain the upbeat tone of my blog, regardless of content, I needed to write first, read after.

Once my new posting was up, I circled back to sift through comments as I chowed down on my wrap. A dollop of avocado plopped onto my keyboard. I wiped it away and finished off the food. It was a relief to see most of the remarks were positive. I went into the message board, visible only to me. Desperate men often thought of the function as an invitation to sleaze. Today's included a message with a different vibe, although no less nasty.

Play with fire, you'll get burned. Better stop now before the flames get too high. Anonymouse.

There was always someone who wanted to dump their bad mood on me. *No thanks. I'll pass.*

Another message piqued my interest. It had a photo included. Huh. Shot from Overlook Point, it was taken at an angle almost directly above the place where Jackie was hit. This could be something. I leaned in to get a better look.

It was easy to identify by the recently erected statue of Rita Walsh, a world-renowned skier from Eliot Hill, placed in the forefront of the shot. It was sent by a follower who'd come across the photo online not long after reading my request for information about the night Jackie died. They'd marked up the photo with a virtual pen. The date was circled at the bottom to draw my attention to it. May third at seven thirty-two pm.

If the photo had a wider scope, it would show Mountaintop Lane. This may not solve the case, but it was a start. A good one.

Immediately, I thanked the sender and replicated their search. I scanned through a popular photo-sharing app with the hashtags full moon, super-moon, EliotHill, and mountaintop.

Within minutes, I spotted the original photo. The photographer was a tourist who'd visited Eliot Hill on a weekend getaway, according to their post. I sent them a note. It said I loved the photo and asked if they had taken any other photos with a wider scope from the same night.

I sat back and stretched my arms over my head while I waited. I glanced around and caught the eye of a familiar face. It was Merle Fisher, the cameraman from WKRZ.

He looked from my screen to me with a tight-lipped smile. I turned and closed the laptop, wondering if he'd been able to see what I'd been looking at. *Note to self: watch out for creeping creeps while amateur sleuthing.* When I turned back around, he was still watching me. Was this his attempt to be cordial? I couldn't tell but decided to give him the benefit of the doubt, responding with a friendly wave.

"An interesting choice today, wasn't it?" His booming voice cut through the buzz of the café.

I leaned forward and raised my voice. "What do you mean?"

"Swapping out the dead sister for the live one?"

His crass words caught me off-guard and made me recoil. I gripped the underside of the stool to steady myself, hoping he hadn't noticed.

Red-hot anger flared up at his insensitive remark. "Becka will do a good job," I snapped back. I wasn't sure how I felt about Becka's reaction to the decision, but I wouldn't stand for this jerk trashing her just the same.

"Will she?" his pudgy hand lifted toward his face, and he rubbed his beard. His small, dark eyes studied me.

In an effort to avoid them, I focused on a faded tattoo on his forearm.

A proud grin spread across his face, exposing stained yellow teeth as he followed my line of sight. "You like that, huh?" He flexed his forearm and dragged his stubby fingers over the tattoo, making a mouse dance on the scales of justice. He chuckled at his own cleverness. It morphed into a hacking cough. He wiped the back of his hand on his mouth. He pointed at me, top to bottom, then bottom to top. "Got any ink yourself?"

I glared at him and shook my head in an emphatic no.

"At least not where you're willing to show the likes of me, right?" He chuckled louder. It made his protruding belly bounce.

The creep factor on this guy was intense. I had the urge to smack his eyeballs clear out of his skull. My computer binged, and I turned, grateful for the distraction.

I opened the screen back up. It was the reply I'd been waiting for. I hesitated. Was I paranoid, or could I still feel Merle's beady eyes on my back? I half-turned and glanced in his direction. *Yuck.* He was next in line at the counter now but still watching me.

I pointed to my computer. "Gotta get back to work."

He ran his hand through light brown thinning hair in an effort to smooth it out as if suddenly aware of his sloppy appearance. He made a clicking sound with the side of his mouth, then heaved his belted jeans up over his middle. "Okay, Emily, I'll see you soon."

Trying not to show my discomfort at Merle's use of my name, I simply nodded and moved my focus back onto my screen. It was impossible not to hear him order a small drip coffee with triple cream and triple sugar, with a shot of vanilla syrup for good measure. The barista passed him the coffee, and he clumped through the café, untied boots leaving dirt tracks as he went. I shifted my gaze to watch and he turned to look at me one more time, with a slight upturn on his lips, then yanked open the door and stomped away.

I reached for my laptop when a familiar tinkle told me my furry friend had returned. The side door opened, and Murray burst through with bright eyes and a wagging tail. He stood near our regular booth until I carried my stuff over and sat down. He ducked underneath and dropped his big head onto my lap with a sigh. His eyes met mine, and I gave his chin a good scratch. "I missed you, too, bud."

Not far behind came Fitz, who'd made a pitstop behind the counter to make sure things were running smoothly. As per usual, all good. With premium wages, paid vacation, and health insurance, he had a loyal, hard-working staff. He joined me a minute later, two large lemon waters in his hand. He slid one toward me.

I eyed him suspiciously before taking a sip. "What's this novel luscious lemon libation?"

He glugged down half the glass. "We need to up our H2O. Healthy body, healthy mind."

The drink was cool and tart. Not bad. I crunched down a cube. "First exercise, now this? Are you trying to change me, Fitzwilliam Warner?"

He drained the drink and wiped his mouth. "I'd have more luck teaching a mule to dance. Now, drink your water, then fill me in."

"Fine." I downed a few more sips. "I could use a little refresher. I came back from the studio feeling a little sour myself."

"What's going on?"

"Becka is replacing Jackie on *The Morning Dish*."

He nodded. "She's a logical replacement. You're not happy about it?"

I scoffed. "I am, but you should've seen her, Fitz. She was practically glowing. How could she go from a mess this morning to a shiny new star? Her sister has been gone two days. I've been trying to convince myself she's a superior compartmentalizer, but even still, it makes me uneasy."

"Yeah, there's an element of cringe. But what do you expect? That's showbiz."

"But her sister's dead. It's bizarre."

He shook his head. "Don't be like that. Judgey doesn't suit you. Jackie wasn't a doting sister. You come from a world of family and friends who support you. Becka never had that. Let her have a moment."

I folded my arms over my chest and slumped back. "I guess."

He leaned forward. "Listen, Becka's a complicated person. There's a reason you pulled back from her years ago. But the woman lost her sister, and she's trying to survive. Life hasn't been easy for her. Maybe give her a break, huh?"

I twisted a curl around my finger. "She doesn't need me tearing her down, does she?"

"You're not." He pointed between us. "This is a circle of trust. What's said here doesn't go further. You learned the hard way that circle doesn't extend to Becka. But right now, you should cut her some slack. She needs people in her corner."

He was right. "Sometimes you remind me of Yoda. Have I ever told you that before?"

He sat up a little straighter. "Am I that wise?"

"Oh no, it's the sharp point in your ears."

He laughed. I did, too. "Thanks. I needed that."

"Anytime," he said. "But now these ears are hearing my name. I've got to go sign for a delivery. Back in a flash."

He took the empty glasses and slid out of the booth. He was right. I felt so much better. I returned to my laptop with a clear mind.

Good timing. There was a note back from the photographer who'd sent me a message earlier.

"Hi, Emily. Vince Castro here. Thanks for your note. Eliot Hill has the best views this side of New York City. I took a gander through the shots. Didn't see any showing the street below. Sorry to disappoint you. There were a few other amateur photographers up there, so maybe you'll have more luck with them. One of the gals mentioned she was local. Her name was Carol or Cheryl, I think. Anyway, I enjoy your posts. Keep it real. Vince."

I sent a quick note of thanks and sank back in my seat. *Rats.*

Fitz slipped into the other side of the booth. He leaned over to see what was on my screen. "What's got you so deflated?"

"I thought I was onto something." I shrugged. "Guess not, unless you happen to know any amateur photographers named Cheryl or Carol?"

He eyed me with suspicion. "Nope. Are you still snooping around Jackie's death after Noah told you not to get involved?"

I leaned down to scratch Murray's chin. "Absolutely not. Just tying up loose ends."

"Loose ends?"

I huffed. "I can't exactly ignore people who are responding to my earlier post. But that's all I'm going to say."

He folded his arms and raised an eyebrow. "Because?"

"*Because* you'll feel compelled to tell Noah that I'm not listening to his orders. Then Officer Tight Pants will undoubtedly come down here with those smoldering eyes and that pulsing jawline. Then both of you will be mad at me, and I'll feel like crap."

His elbows dropped onto the table, and his head sunk into the palms of his hands. "Oh no," he said through his fingers. "Not that again."

"What?" I said defensively. "Someone sent me something, and I had to look at it. I'm like a mouse going for cheese, Fitz. There's no stopping me."

"Not that." He pulled his head up and gave me a pained expression. "That's bad enough. But the brother lust is worse. Much worse."

Double crap. "What did I say?" The word *jawline* echoed in my mind.

Fitz pointed at me. "You need to stop it. You know what I'm talking about, you dirty bird."

My cheeks flushed. "Fine, you caught me. But I didn't mean it as a compliment. Noah looks like some sort of Hollywood stereotype when he glares at me with that chiseled face of his." I scoffed. "It's almost embarrassing."

Fitz groaned and slapped his forehead. "Please stop talking. You're making it worse. Can we switch back to talking about your investigative interference? It's become less distressing for me at this point."

"Deal." I stuck out my hand, and we shook on it.

Focusing back on my screen, I made sure to scroll past the threat so Fitz wouldn't see it. I didn't need him worrying about some Grumpy Gus who took his bad mood out on me. I pulled up the photo and turned my computer around.

He leaned in. "Not bad."

"Getting close," I said. "Don't you think?"

He pushed the laptop back to me. "I don't know if that's something to gloat about."

I shut the computer and stretched my arms above my head. "I'm not gloating. I'm sharing. Big difference."

He groaned. "Fine. Ready to head out?"

"Go fo' it," I said in my best/worst Stallone impression.

"Strictly taking out the 'r' doesn't make you sound like Rocky. You know that, right?"

"Then I'll let my fists do the talking." I gave him a one-two jab as I exited the booth. Fitz feigned injury as he went out the back of the café to grab his bike.

I checked my watch to make sure I had downloaded the hiking app that Jackie used the night she was killed. *Got it.* I set it to start. To get a better sense of how it worked, I needed to try it in action. Although biking instead of hiking, I assumed the relevant information would be the same, including the tracking and the heart rate.

So far, the app was the only clue that had panned out. By going through the motions, maybe something else would click. The hours were ticking by, and there was a killer on the loose. It was time to rein him in.

Chapter Eighteen

Sunset was expected at 7:30, according to my watch. Not much time before darkness hit. Murray drooled on my shoe as I tied up the laces, inches from the tip of my nose. "Can I help you?"

A loud bark told me to move quicker. "Alright, alright, alright." On my last ride, Murray stayed home. This time, I wanted him nearby. Just in case. "One of these days, we need to talk about personal space."

I opened the door, and he shot out like a furry cannonball, making a beeline for my bike. "The monster is free. Let's go!"

Fitz did a wheelie and headed out. I scrambled onto my bike and pedaled to keep up. Fitz led the way through the back alleyway to his favorite bike route, a forest trail just off Main Street. Murray stayed close while we made our way through town to the base of the hill. The crisp air felt good.

Tall trees bordered the path, hovering at the edges, like an over-protective mother. Cruising through the path, I hit a good rhythm. Murray took off after a chattering chipmunk, and Fitz dialed into his karaoke sing-a-long streaming app on his wireless earphones. He began to sing an off-key version of a Shania Twain song and took off ahead. I had my phone mounted on my bike and was synched into the *Hike To It* app. I focused solely on that. I wanted to watch it in real time to see how it worked.

The sun began to fall below the tree line. It was darker in the woods than at street level, although with the trail lights, visibility was still decent. Fitz waited at a narrow opening up ahead that would lead us back to town. I gave him a thumbs-up, then called for Murray. Fitz disappeared through the trees.

A screech of tires nearby sent a wave of panic up my spine. I yelled for Murray, then peddled like a pro down the path. *Fitz!*

I exited the path and dropped my bike. Fitz was nowhere in sight. There was a car pulled over, and just next to it lay his bike, wheels still turning. I ran to it. *Where is he?* My heart slammed against my chest. I couldn't breathe.

"Fitz!" I screamed.

I heard him before I saw him.

"Whoa—Em! *Emily*!!"

The sound of his voice stopped me mid-panic. I whirled around to see where it came from.

Fitz was standing under the canopy of a tree. With a sharp exhale, I keeled over in relief, my hands dropping to my knees.

After a brief pause to let my heart rate settle, I stood back up and hustled toward him, taking a closer look at the beat-up car as I went. It was parked at an angle, just off the shoulder; tire marks and the smell of burnt rubber wafted through the air.

As I approached, I noticed someone else was with him. I squinted to get a better look, but it didn't help. Whoever it was remained in the shadows.

"What happened?" I demanded. "Are you hurt?" My voice was loud and shaky as I began to examine him.

He reached out and put a firm hand on my shoulder in an effort to settle me down.

"Em, it's okay. I'm okay," he said. "It was a close call, but I'm uninjured. Lightning reflexes."

He mimicked a one-two punch to demonstrate his supposed skill. I ignored the joke. Instead, I poked and prodded his lean frame to ensure there were no undetectable breaks or bruises. Once satisfied, I drew back and took in the scene. Outrage replaced concern.

"Who was the careless jackass who almost killed you?" I pointed toward the obscure figure. "Is that him? Is he trying to hide from me?"

Fitz shushed me. "Em, take it down a notch. Like I told you, nothing happened. Just a few squeaky brakes."

I huffed. "Smells more like incompetent driver to me."

The tree branches rustled, and the figure came forward. I let out an involuntary peep. Unfortunately for me, it was motorcycle club affiliate and all-around bad boy William Vaughn, AKA Billy Bones. *Seriously?* This was not my week.

"Sorry, Sweetie," Billy said in his deep, grisly voice.

To counter my feeble squeal, I crossed my arms, jutted out my chin, and glared at him. No way would I let Mr. Tough Guy intimidate me. Easier said than done. He was dressed from head-to-toe in black leather and moved towards me like a shadow, quiet and dark. His shoulder-length hair was pulled back in a messy ponytail, stringy bangs half-covering his intense brown eyes.

His ominous figure was large enough to block out any light. "I wanted to let you cool off for a minute." He loomed over me when he spoke to ensure he had the upper hand.

I cranked my neck to meet his gaze. "Is that so?"

He smiled down at me. "I would never hide from such a pretty face." Handsome in that bad-boy way, I might've been flattered if he wasn't quite so intimidating. I could appreciate a rebellious nature, but only if it wasn't based on criminal activity.

At G&R Auto, Billy kept a low-key profile. Most of the time, he remained inside the shop and had his part-time employees deal with the public.

Fitz was one of the few people I knew who wasn't put off by Billy, having served him beer and whiskey for years. But I was no fan and had always kept my distance.

Subtly, Fitz drew me away from Billy, allowing me a little breathing room. "Our unscheduled rendezvous was my fault," he explained. "My headphone volume was cranked, so I didn't hear the roar of Billy's motor. I barreled out of the trees and right onto the road."

"Didn't you notice his headlights?" I demanded. "It should've given you a heads up."

Billy cleared his throat. "I'll take credit for that part. I had a little run-in the other day with a raccoon. It cracked one of my headlights, I'm afraid, so

I'm riding one light shy of a pair."

I looked over at his car. It was also missing a license plate. Odd. Even more troubling? The front end was damaged on the left side. I turned back to gauge his expression. "Big raccoon."

He shifted the lower part of his jaw, making it crack. "Uh-huh."

I bit my tongue to stop myself from flinching. I hated bullies. Anger edged out fear. "When did you say that happened?"

"I didn't."

Fitz rested his forearm on my shoulder casually. "Billy was on the way over to his shop to get it repaired." His tone was chipper, but he shot me a look that said what-the-heck-are-you-doing?

Just then, Murray popped out from between two trees and rushed to my side, tail wagging. My irritation temporarily shifted. I leaned over and shook my finger at him. "Where were you?"

Murray barked as Fitz picked up his bike and brushed it off. "Let's go, Em. We all have someplace to be."

"We do?" I asked.

"Yes," he said curtly. I opened my mouth to argue until I saw his stony expression. Thinking better of it, I hopped on my bike without another word.

"I'll be seeing you," I heard Billy say. I turned back to see he was laser-focused on me.

I lifted my hand to wave before I could think it through, the gesture almost causing me to lose my balance again. *Gah!* I turned back and steadied myself, feeling the burn of humiliation. Billy might be intimidating, but he had nothing compared to the beast that was etiquette.

I pedaled hard to make some distance between us and the metal mouth. With Murray by my side, we followed the winding road back into town. Fitz stayed right behind us. He didn't let me out of his sight until I said goodnight and locked my door.

Chapter Nineteen

Monday, May 6th

Good morning!

Murray and I will be posting some action shots after our outing today. We are going hiking, so the photos will show the big guy on top of the world (or at least on top of the town). Check-in later to see the results.

On another front, thank you for continuing to support me from near and far. While I can't give you any official updates on the death of Jackie Hunter, I met with the sheriff and he is working around the clock. He and I are both grateful for the tips and encouragement. The only thing I can say at this point is our hunch was right—the sheriff has officially classified the case as a homicide. Wow, right?

Let's all take care of each other and keep our focus on the future. For now, I will leave you with a recipe for Doggie Delights—an easy recipe that will keep your puppy love alive. I'm posting it now. All you'll need is flour, eggs, pureed pumpkin, and a pinch of cinnamon.

See ya!
Em

I'd dragged myself up extra early for the busy day ahead. I fed the dog, scarfed down two eggs on toast, and did a quick Instagram post. I was about to head out when a ping alerted me to a direct message. Murray's head whipped toward me.

"Sorry, Murr. With everything going on, I better check that, just in case."

My laptop sat open on the island. I pulled it toward me. It read: *Stop coming for me, or you're next. Anonymouse.*

My irritation spiked. "You were right, Murray. Just another troll."

I didn't have time to deal with that type of garbage. Cyberbullying was an unfortunate reality for anyone with an online presence. The worst part? The inability to escape. They could reach you anywhere, anytime. Combined with the ease of anonymity, it was a constant problem. *Not today, creep.* I shut my laptop and got moving.

Murray waited at the door, ready to move. "Okay, Murr, time to go."

I could hear Fitz moving around in the café already, prepping for the day ahead. It felt like we hadn't had time to process everything going on. I was glad for the opportunity now.

Murray zoomed out the back for a quick nature call before racing back. He bombed through the side entrance of the café and lunged at Fitz with all his weight. If I didn't know better, I'd almost think Fitz was his favorite.

"There he is." Fitz gave Murray a good rub. "Good morning to you, too, furball."

Satisfied with his greeting, Murray padded over to the window and pressed his nose against it. After a glance into the darkness, he trotted back to our booth and curled up underneath for his first nap of the day.

Fitz puttered behind the counter. He'd made me a quad-shot latte with a sprinkle of cocoa. It was still steaming when I perched myself on the nearest stool.

Like every other java devotee, I breathed it in before I had my first taste. The warmth hit all the way down to my toes. "You're a mind reader."

He rolled his eyes. "Just a lucky guess."

I grinned at him. "Today is going to be a better day. I can feel it."

"Good. We could all use one."

"Even Billy Bones?"

Fitz dropped his head back and groaned. "Why can't you start with the weather like any decent human being? I don't want to side with your mom

117

on the subject of etiquette classes, but..."

I threw my napkin at him. "Billy is a convicted felon, and he has a dent on the front bumper of a car with no plates. All that together spells suspicion in my book."

Fitz gave me a pained expression. "It's really none of your business. Noah told you to back off, and Billy has gone through enough the last six years. Trust me, you don't want to go there."

I drummed my fingers on the granite countertop, twisting on my stool.

From what I knew, Billy was nothing but bad news. He'd been released less than a year ago from federal prison after a five-year stint for involuntary manslaughter. I didn't know any of the details except what had been printed in the local news. The victim was an out-of-town biker. He was found dead at a local farmhouse the day after a tense verbal exchange with Billy. I wasn't sure why Fitz felt the need to protect him. "C'mon. You know something. Spill it."

"Billy was railroaded into pleading guilty for something he didn't do. I'm not saying he's a standup dude, but I also know he didn't kill the biker he went to prison over."

Fitz had told me this before but I hadn't been willing to get into it. I'd never pressed him on it, but this time, I couldn't let it go. "How are you so sure? I've never understood why you're so protective of him."

At the time of the trial, Fitz had been called to testify as a defense witness. He hadn't been allowed to talk about the case while it was ongoing. In the end, Billy was convicted and went to prison.

"Look," Fitz said, running a hand through his hair. "I know Billy didn't kill that biker because he was here at the time of the murder, okay?"

I stared at him. The biggest secret I'd ever kept from him was that I thought his lemon squares were too dry. Was this for real?

He continued. "I didn't tell you because there was nothing we could do, according to the prosecutor. Besides, you were dealing with your own stuff, and I didn't want to burden you with more stress."

I had a million follow-up comments and questions. *How could that happen? Who was the real killer? Is there any recourse to right the wrong? I'm sorry you felt you couldn't come to me. I should've been there for you.* My mind spun, and for a minute, I almost went off track. But now was not the time. That conversation would have to wait. I reined it in and stayed on point.

"Are you sure about the timing? You rarely know what day of the week it is, let alone hour of the day. What if you're wrong, and he did it again?"

Fitz retrieved a tray of double-walled espresso cups from under the counter. He began to polish them and stack them up next to the espresso maker behind him. "Billy was at the bar when Lady Gaga performed my favorite song at the Grammy's. He didn't know who she was, and I asked if he'd been living under a rock."

My mouth dropped open. "That sounds like a solid alibi. Why didn't Noah believe you?"

"My dad had just retired, and it was before Noah took over. A reserve deputy was in charge temporarily. Not a good time. Plus, there was no one else at the bar to corroborate my story. The guy thought I'd fudged the timeline to help Billy out."

I felt offended on Fitz's behalf. Everyone knew that he was a stand-up guy. Everyone but that guy, apparently. I knew Fitz hadn't liked him but I assumed it was because he'd replaced Fitz's dad. How could I have been so clueless? Shame mixed with alarm. "That's a complete injustice. Was there no way to appeal or call another police force? The FBI or something?"

Fitz poured himself a cup of coffee and added a splash of almond milk. "I was ready to summon the media, call the attorney general, the governor. But..."

"But what?"

He took a sip of coffee and looked at me. "Billy pled guilty before I had the chance."

I drew back. That made no sense. "Why would he do that?"

"Bikers don't like attention. I assume he was asked—or told—to take one for the team, or the club in this case."

Icy prickles went up my arm. "Club or gang?"

"Yeah, good question. Anyway, his lawyer managed to get a shorter sentence in exchange for Billy's cooperation. That's why he's out."

119

"I guess Billy doesn't have a lot of faith in law enforcement?"

"Loyalty trumps everything in that world. Pretty sure that bought him a lifetime of goodwill from the brotherhood or whatever they call themselves."

"If they wanted Billy to take the blame, does that mean someone else in the so-called brotherhood was actually guilty?"

"Draw your own conclusions."

"Seriously, Fitz, how have you never told me this?"

Fitz raised an eyebrow. "He asked me to keep quiet about it. Billy may not have killed anyone, but he has a past. The impression I get is that he wants to keep that past buried. So don't go digging into it."

"Billy is not someone I want as an enemy," I admitted. "I'll try to stay clear of him, okay?"

He looked up, his hands clasped together in prayer. "Thank you."

Fitz wanted the subject dropped. Message received. I let it go. We had enough to deal with, and I trusted his judgment. Besides, it was a relief. Billy gave me the creeps.

Fitz opened the industrial fridge and began to take out the various types of milk. "Soy, almond, coconut, and cashew. What have I forgotten?"

"Moo."

He slapped his forehead. "Right."

I reached over the counter and grabbed the full fresh coffee pot, adding a splash to my mug. There was just enough time for a few more sips before going to get Becka and Vera. Once the cup was drained, I stood up and stretched my arms over my head. "I better head out."

"A favor?"

"Sure."

He picked up my empty cup. "Can you avoid mentioning what happened last night?"

"Your near-death experience?"

He sighed. "If you must call it that."

"My lips are sealed." I turned to go. "Uh-oh."

"What now?"

I pointed toward the door. "Look outside."

Coffee zombies, also known as patrons, took turns pressing their faces against the window, trying to see inside the still-dark café. Five or six of them stumbled about outside, clearly unhappy about their inability to get their morning fix.

Fitz glanced at the clock and swore under his breath. "It's seven-oh-two."

"Do two minutes really make a difference?"

He nodded adamantly. "I usually have the doors open five minutes early. That means customers have been waiting an additional seven minutes for their caffeine."

I shuddered. "Then what are you stalling for? There's been enough suffering in this town over the last few days. Unlock that door!"

Fitz flew across the room and opened for business. The onslaught of customers rushed inside as he slid behind the counter, ready to serve.

I scanned the room as I left. The zombies transformed back into Eliot Hill's citizens. Things were feeling back to normal. It balanced the unease I felt about seeing Becka. I was ashamed I'd reacted so poorly to the news she was chosen as Jackie's replacement. Instead of giving Becka the benefit of the doubt, I'd allowed mistrust to get the best of me. She'd just lost her sister. She needed friends, not detractors. No more basing opinions on old fears and assumptions. New day, new attitude.

"Murray." I patted my leg, "Let's go." A long stretch, and he sauntered over to me. We headed out the back exit and hopped into the Jeep.

It was a sunny morning with milder temperatures than we'd had in the last week. It took a few minutes to get the top down on the Jeep and put Murray's dog goggles on. Then, we were off to our first stop. A quick refill for the thirsty tank.

We pulled into the gas station, G&R Auto. There were a few other fill-up stations around town, but this was the most convenient. It doubled as a repair shop and had a stellar reputation. Owned by Billy Bones, the business had been originally opened decades earlier by Billy's grandfather, who'd also been a biker.

A young attendant approached me.

"Can you fill it up?" I asked.

"Sure, no problem," the kid replied with a friendly smile. He pulled out a wireless payment terminal, and I pre-paid fifty dollars with my credit card. Once it cleared, he gave me my receipt and tucked the machine into his oversized jacket pocket. Then, he set the amount on the fuel dispenser and inserted the gas pump into the Jeep. With a click, the gas started to flow, and he moved towards another customer.

While I waited, I decided to stretch my legs and take Murray for a quick walk. I took the goggles off Murray, and we hopped out.

G&R had a big lot. Located along the fence line was a stretch of grass. Right next to that was a number of parked cars in various stages of repair. Since we were here, maybe we'd hit the grass. Murray could relieve himself while I checked to see if the car that nearly took out Fitz was here, too.

A twinge of guilt hit me. I'd promised Fitz I'd stay away from Billy. I scanned the property. No sign of Billy Bones. *Phew.* No promises broken. We carried on.

The lot was full, making it hard to spot a single car, especially since most of the vehicles were SUVs, a favorite in our town.

At first, I didn't see Billy's car. There was no sign of it when I glanced around. We weaved in and out between cars, moving to the next row. That's when I spotted Billy's, tucked in between a Cadillac Escalade and a Ford Expedition.

We moved closer. The front bumper was still wrecked. Billy said he'd hit a raccoon. I needed to get a better look. We shuffled over, and I crouched down to examine the damage. With no experience in car repair or road kill, my opinion was an uneducated guess. But it was smashed up pretty good. Could a twenty-pound creature cause this much damage? I rubbed my finger along the crunched-up metal to check for signs of blood. Nothing. Like, not even dust. There was a scratch along the bumper, straight lined abrasions from where a license plate may have been mounted. Had one recently been removed?

I grabbed my phone out of my pocket and snapped a few photos. There wasn't enough space between the car and the back fence to fit, so we squeezed along the side. I craned my neck to see if there was a rear plate. Nope. This car had had all of its identifiable markers removed.

My phone dinged as we hustled back. I dug around inside my jacket pocket to retrieve it and pulled it out. I was so distracted checking who'd texted me, I walked straight into some sort of obstacle. I stepped back and looked up. Small world. A very angry-looking Billy Bones was looking right back at me.

Fudgenuckles.

"I'm beginning to think we're either destined to marry or you've chosen to spy on me," he said.

"Is that a proposal?"

His mouth twitched. A micro snarl came and went. Maybe he wasn't the marrying type.

Murray came forward and sat at my feet. He snarled back.

Billy knew to take a step back. "What do you want, Ms. Dalle?"

I swallowed. "If we're talking in the immediate sense, I'd like to walk around you and leave."

"We're not."

Murray took another step further, making it clear he didn't like Billy's tone. I followed up with a sweet smile. "Your car is damaged, and I'm curious about it." True statement, lacking an accusatory tone. A pat on the back was deserved.

Billy craned his face closer. "What are you suggesting?"

Another growl. I rubbed Murray's ear but kept my eyes on Billy. "I'd like to answer that question, but I really have to go. Maybe we can pick this conversation up another time?"

I decided not to wait for a response and began to inch away. Murray took some convincing. He didn't like it when people were mean to me. On top of that, Billy blocked the only open path. I pulled Murray away reluctantly in the other direction. Cars parked so closely to each other that moving a few feet away felt like I'd entered an elite yoga competition. Billy watched in silence as I willed my limbs to bend around side mirrors and running boards. Luckily, Murray was much more athletic and had no problem maneuvering around the tight obstacles.

Once in the clear, I turned to see if Billy was still watching us. A big yup on that front. I wondered if he'd ever entered a staring contest. Sure-fire winner right there. I gave him a half-hearted wave before I turned back around.

"Have you heard about the dangers of curiosity, Miss Dalle?" he called out. "I'll give you a clue. It didn't end well for the cat. Likely wouldn't end well for a dog, either. Or a person."

"Yup, got it, Mr. Bones," I called over my shoulder as I quickly hoofed it back to the Jeep. "Lovely to see you again, as always."

Murray leapt into the passenger seat. I climbed into the driver's side, pressing my hands firmly on my legs to stop them from shaking. The big lug leaned over and gave me a big lick on the ear.

"Thanks Murrbear."

I turned over the engine and revved loudly before peeling out. If Billy started to threaten me again, I didn't want to hear it.

Chapter Twenty

I pulled over once the gas station was out of sight. My hands shook, making it difficult to shift gears. Just breathe. I looked in the rearview mirror, just in case. Billy Bones was one scary dude. No wonder Fitz didn't want me to get on his bad side. Was that what happened to Jackie? Was I in danger? My phone pinged, and I pushed the thought out of my mind. It was way too early to contemplate a murderer may be after me. I hadn't even had a second cup of coffee. I dug my phone out again. I'd been so distracted by Billy's dagger eyes, I'd forgotten to check who'd pinged me. Noah. That was more like it.

Give me a call.

I rubbed my hands together, then hit the call-back button. Noah picked up on the first ring.

"Hey, thanks for calling back. I hope my message didn't wake you."

"No, I'm awake." I hoped the surrounding wind masked my still-shaky voice.

A pause. "Where are you?"

"En route to a hike. What's up?"

"I wanted to talk to you about your run-in with Billy Bones."

I turned around and scanned the area. "Are you following me?"

"What? No. Why? Are you being followed?" His voice was more alert now with a sharper tone.

I shook my head. "Sorry, no. How did you know about my run-in with Billy?"

"Fitz called me."

Wait. What?

When I didn't respond, he continued. "Fitz said you two saw him near the bike path, and there was front-end damage to his car."

I slapped my forehead. "Oh! Last night. Yes, that's what happened. Among other things." Like Fitz almost becoming one with the pavement.

"What do you mean?"

"Nothing, sorry, rough morning. Can we start again?"

There was a pause. "Did you have another run-in with Billy this morning?"

"Uh-uh."

"You know I'm a detective, right? That's my job, and I can tell, very clearly, that you're lying to me."

I really needed to work on my deception skills. "Can I try again?"

"Emily…"

"Just saying, it was more like a walk-in."

"What the heck does that mean?"

"I literally walked right into the man. Then he got mad at me. Maybe the guy's more delicate than he looks."

"How mad?" Noah demanded. "Did he threaten you?"

I shook my head. "No, he was too busy talking about a cat."

"Billy doesn't have a cat and you have a dog."

I let out a short laugh. "I know, right?"

"Should I ask what you were doing when you collided with Billy?"

"Technically, I was trying to find my phone in my pocket because you'd texted me." I cleared my throat. "However, it was in the vicinity of a damaged car Fitz and I saw him driving, now parked at the back of his lot."

"This just happened?"

"My shaking hands don't lie, Noah. Does that mean you're going to check it out? If so, head straight to the back row, near the shop's car entrance doors."

"What a mess," Noah said under his breath. "I had a feeling it might be, but without a warrant or permission from Billy, I can't just waltz in there. Want to tell me how you spotted it way in the back?"

"Not really," I said. "Did Fitz tell you the license plate had been removed?"

"He did. I'm on my way over there now. Hopefully, he'll let me take a look."

"Don't count on it. He seems to be in a pretty bad mood."

"Billy is not on the community welcoming committee. You know that, right?"

Here comes another lecture. I didn't have the time or patience for it. Before he could continue, I cut him off.

"Sorry, Noah, the wind is picking up out here. I've got to go. Talk to you later?"

"Wait," he said in a warning tone.

"Bye Noah. Talk soon."

I hung up before he could say any more. I felt a little guilty I'd hung up on him but pushed the feeling aside. Noah would get to the car in time. Before the damage was repaired. That's all that really mattered. I turned the phone to silent, shoved it in my pocket, and focused back on the morning ahead.

* * *

Vera and Becka were standing on Vera's porch when I arrived. Becka had likely stayed at Vera's overnight. Given the events of the last few days, it wasn't a surprise that Becka didn't want to be alone. They both waved as I approached. I was a few minutes late, unusual for me.

I attempted a normal greeting. "Good morning, guys. Sorry about the delay."

"No worries," Becka said. "I crashed here last night so it almost makes up the time difference of having to stop in two places. The view will be as stellar as always."

She looked more relaxed than I thought she would. A good night's sleep and the company of a best friend can work wonders.

I pulled the front seat forward, and Vera hopped in the back with Murray. He had his goggles in his mouth and dropped them in her lap. She put them back on him, and he looked very pleased with himself.

"Morning," said Vera once Murray allowed her a chance to say hello. He sat next to her and drooled on her lap.

Becka put the seat back in place and jumped in. Her smile told me she was in a good place. "I'm so glad we're going today," I said. I'd decided I was ready to be her cheerleader and let go of the past. "Are you ready to dish out more details about your new gig?"

She shrugged, but the smile remained. "Not much to tell as of yet. There's a lot to work out still. This may be one of the last days off I get for a while."

"Let's head out then," I said. I glanced back at Vera to make sure she was ready to go. There was a large bandage on her calf.

"What happened?" I asked.

She rubbed her palm over the injury. "My curling iron dropped out of my hand yesterday and caught my leg."

"Ouch," I said. "You okay?"

"Way better today. And don't worry, it won't stop me from taking some great shots of the big guy or beating you two up to the top."

Becka elbowed me. "Her legs are longer than both of ours combined."

"We may not stand a chance." I revved the engine and put the Jeep in gear. "But I'll try anyway. Let's go!"

It didn't take long to get to our destination, Pebble Lake Trail. It was a favorite of mine because it was so close and so pretty. The easy path led to a natural outcrop of conglomerate rock on an unglaciated plateau. I never got tired of looking at it and the natural beauty in the surrounding area. We parked near the path entrance. It was still early, so we had the place to ourselves. I took Murray's goggles off and tucked them into my backpack. Vera brought her professional-grade camera. She knelt down next to the Jeep to grab it out of the case. It was attached to a heavy-duty neck strap for easy access.

Becka did a few leg stretches while she waited for us. I set my watch to start on the *Hike To It!* app. She leaned over to see what I was doing. "Getting serious, huh?"

"Apparently, Jackie always tracked her steps. I wanted to see how it worked."

The grin slid off her face. "Why?"

128

I wanted to kick myself. "No reason, really. I just thought it was a neat idea."

The color drained from her face. "Was she using it when she was killed?"

Vera shot to Becka's side. "You okay?"

My face flushed. "I'm sorry. I didn't mean to upset you."

Vera shot me a warning look. "Isn't our goal to ease tension, not add to it?"

Becka frowned. She stepped away from Vera. "Em, is that why you're trying it? Are you still playing detective?"

"It may have helped pinpoint the time she was killed," I admitted. "I thought maybe if I tried it, I'd get more insight into what happened." I swiveled the watch back and forth on my wrist and shrugged. "Chances are, it won't. It might be a stupid idea."

Becka shook her head. "I'm grateful you're trying to help, but like I said yesterday, I was wrong not to trust Noah. Besides, he's confident he'll find the truth. You can bow out."

Vera nodded. "Now that we have that sorted, can we get moving? It's almost the golden hour." She held up her camera. "Best time of day for photos."

"Gotcha." I snatched my water from the back, grateful for the distraction.

Murray hopped out of the back and bounded up the familiar path. The three of us followed.

It was an easy haul to the top of the mountain since we chose to drive up most of the elevation. We were still newbies, so we opted for the easiest route most of the time.

The trail soon opened up to a large plateau overlooking the town. It gave us a bird's eye view of the surrounding landscape.

My followers loved the action shots I'd started to share of Murray. Vera's camera captured him in motion, running free on the mountain, bounding from one place to another, in all his doggy glory.

We took a break at a grouping of large rocks arranged in a semicircle not far from the pathway. It was the perfect view with ample room to sit.

I paused the hiking app. Vera turned toward me at the sound of the beep.

"Learn anything?"

I shook my head. "I don't know what I expected to find."

Becka sighed. "I'm still having a hard time accepting that she's gone."

"It's incomprehensible," Vera agreed.

"Have you even had time to grieve?" I asked.

"Not really. Within a few hours of finding out what happened, I got a call from the studio. Everything seems to be moving at warp speed. I'm ashamed to admit that part of me is excited. Isn't that awful?"

I shook my head to indicate no. I hoped she couldn't see the look in my eyes. Because if she had? She'd know what I really thought. That, in spite of my best efforts to be supportive, I still didn't understand how she could prioritize the show when her sister had just been murdered.

Chapter Twenty-One

Becka talked about some of the changes being discussed, a set makeover, a new format, and a few celebrity guests that might boost the show.

"I have another favor to ask you," Becka said.

"Okay," I said.

Vera smiled. "Don't worry, this one doesn't involve any murderers."

"Don't be so sure," Becka said.

I frowned. "I don't get it."

"To lighten the overall mood, we want to start the show with something fun. One of the ideas being tossed around is dating do's and don'ts."

"Okay." I nodded. "Jackie and I have had fun with that in the past. Why not?"

"Excellent. We want you to come on the show and talk about your worst dates ever."

I'd done a few posts talking about bad dates but I tried to keep most of my content on the positive side. Even when a date was a miss, I didn't like to target people. My blogs centered around my life in town. It wouldn't take much digging to figure out who I was talking about. I'd leave that sort of fun to the master, Taylor Swift.

"Most of us using dating apps are mere mortals. But you're a step up—an influencer. It would be fun to hear it from your perspective."

My eyebrows shot up. "I talk about shunning the need to please. I'm no expert on dudes and dating."

"I volunteered to be on it, too," she said. "If I share my worst dates, would you reconsider?"

"They'd have to be pretty bad."

"Want to hear about my latest disastrous date? You might be surprised." Before I could argue, she barreled ahead. "His name is Chris. Age thirty-two, divorced, financial analyst..."

Chris turned out to have a habit of eating french fries with his mouth open and never outgrowing the urge to make out in a movie theater. On top of that, he'd yet to remember his wallet and often picked his nose. Gross, for sure, but it didn't trigger any desire in me to share my own experiences.

When Vera was done, Becka turned to me. "So? What do you think?"

"We all have stories like that," I said.

Becka sighed. "Please? I need something fun to kick off the show, and we don't have a lot of time. Viewers love you, and you're great on camera."

"The very idea fills me with dread. It's a literal nightmare," I said.

Vera cleared her throat. "Okay, look, I have a real doozy."

I shook my head. "I want to help, but I don't think I can. I'm sorry."

"What if I had a story so bad, no one would even remember you were on the show?" Vera said.

Becka's eyes widened. "You don't mean..."

Vera nodded. "I do. Mortify me, my friend. Give the audience what they want."

"Guys," I said, trying to keep my voice level. "Seriously, I hate to disappoint you, but I've been humiliated on TV before. I'm not doing it again."

Vera put her hands together in prayer. "We could beg? C'mon, Em, we'll make sure your stories are fun and cute, minimal embarrassment. I'd be the only one cast in a bad light."

"You don't want the kind of attention I got, Vera, trust me. I can't stress enough what a bad idea it is to allow yourself to be publicly disgraced."

"You don't get it. This is my big break, too. Finally, I'm going to be a producer. I promised to deliver a great show. I'm not ashamed of who I am or the mistakes I've made. Sensationalism sells, and I want to succeed."

Then why humiliate yourself on live TV? I wanted to ask, but I didn't. I had my own battle to fight. One I hadn't been expecting.

"Wait until you hear Vera's story, please?" Becka asked.

"It may involve a certain TV consultant and a love triangle," Vera said. "Although I will stress, in my defense, that I dated him first."

"Absolutely," Becka admitted.

Obviously, I was short on the details. But I had a guess. One that made my stomach churn. "Are you talking about Jackie's boyfriend, Grant...?"

"Henshaw. Grant Henshaw," Vera said. "And yeah, I'm afraid so. We kept it on the down-low. He wanted to keep things casual. But we had a spark. And when he turns his charm on, it's hard to resist."

"Let me get the full picture here," I said. "You went behind Jackie's back, while working on her show, and dated her boyfriend?"

"Who was *my* boyfriend first," she said. "But the good times didn't last as long the second time around."

Becka giggled. "Sloppy seconds is never a good idea."

"Shush you," Vera said, slapping her leg playfully. "It took me about three dates to recognize he was too much of a schmuck, even with all his money."

Was this really something Becka planned to discuss on TV? I'd fantasized about evening the score with Jackie, but those days had passed. Actively hating someone felt like injecting poison into my veins. I'd forgiven her and moved on. Becka obviously had her own issues with Jackie that she hadn't resolved. But I wasn't about to get into all that. One crisis at a time. Still, someone had to point out the issues at hand. "Guys, Grant would never agree to his personal life being discussed on air. He'd look like a two-timing creep." This was sensationalism at its worst. I'd assumed Becka would be lifting the show to a higher standard. Apparently not.

"Grant's contract ended last week. And we won't mention him by name," Becka said.

"Did Jackie know about you two?" I heard myself ask.

"She must've suspected," Vera said. "Jackie was the only person he dated publicly, but I left a few things around his place, a crop top and a spare earring."

All of this was making me feel very uncomfortable. But I had to admit I was curious. "Why did you go back out with him, knowing he'd moved on with Jackie?"

"The guy's loaded," she admitted. "I figured it was worth a shot. But I learned my lesson. She went nuclear on me, and I paid the price."

Holy crap. "What'd she do?"

"Made me feel like I was two feet tall. She couldn't fire me, but she made it clear she would make my life suck. *And* she ended up with the guy. You'd think that would be enough of a win for her."

This conversation was making me feel more uncomfortable by the second. Had I just stumbled upon a motive for murder? What if Vera was hiding deeper feelings? Could she be a woman scorned? Jackie flaunted her engagement. Maybe Vera didn't like losing her golden ticket. Maybe she didn't like having her career threatened, either.

Becka leaned forward and tapped my knee. "So, what do you think? Can we add you to the roster?"

"The idea makes me uncomfortable. I'm sorry."

They looked at each other and shrugged. Guess they hadn't counted on my participation. My obvious concern did nothing to dissuade them, however. Good thing there was a whole production team that worked behind the scenes, including executives that gave the final yes or no to segment ideas. This would never get past the pitch phase.

This morning had gone from bad to worse. I couldn't stop thinking that if Becka was willing to gossip on air about her dead sister's love life, what else was she capable of doing? Beyond cringey, that was downright cruel. Was she showing her true colors? If so, what did that mean? The thought filled me with unease.

"Becka, how about you then?" Vera said, pulling me from my thoughts. "We knew Emily was a long shot. How about Plan B?"

I was almost afraid to ask. *Almost.* "What's that?"

Vera clapped her hands and smiled at Becka. "Are you ready to share?"

Becka flushed and let a small grin slip out. "No reason to keep quiet anymore, I guess." She cleared her throat. "We thought it might be fun to talk about bad dates with good men and good dates with bad ones."

"What? Who?" I was way past urging caution at this point. I was also surprised. Becka's dance card was normally as empty as mine, as far as I knew.

She looked between Vera and me. "I've been seeing someone for a while, but Jackie didn't like him, so we kept things quiet."

"Do I know him?" I asked.

She tilted her head to the side. "Maybe."

"Spill girl," I demanded.

She bit her lip. "Okay, do you know Billy Vaughn?"

"*Billy Bones?*" I almost shouted.

Her smile faltered. "So you know him?"

This has to be a joke. But neither Becka nor Vera was laughing. Was Becka really dating the guy I thought might've killed her sister?

"I see your face, Em. And I'll admit, Billy's a little rough around the edges."

"To put it mildly," I blurted out.

She laughed. "Yeah, and that's a good thing. He's not trying to be anything he's not."

"Extra good since we can spin it into our human interest episode on dating," Vera added. "Although he doesn't want to be named, maybe we can work on that."

"Wonderful." I swallowed and forced out a toothy grin. "I'm happy for you."

"Thanks, Em," Becka said. "We'll have to go out some time so you can get to know him better."

Oh, I knew him alright. Did she?

Vera dug into her backpack and pulled out three mini bottles of champagne.

"I wasn't sure whether I'd pull these out, but why not? Even though you've spurned our idea to include you in our first show, Em, I'll let you toast with us anyway. These are to help us celebrate a dream come true."

I put my hands up. "Driving, remember?"

"Relax, they're alcohol-free. The only place open when inspiration struck was the 24-hour grocery store, and they were out of the real deal."

Becka reached over and gave her a hug. "Thank you for giving me permission to celebrate a personal achievement amid the chaos of the last few days."

"You're my best friend, Becks. You deserve it."

I cemented the smile on my face, hoping it would trigger a feeling of joy the other two shared.

Once the drinks were poured, Vera raised her glass. "To the bravest, hardest working friend I've ever had," Vera said. "Congratulations."

We all clinked and had a drink. *Not bad.* Twenty years ago, nonalcoholic drinks had a dire reputation. But the rising sober-curious trend had demanded a better product, and this was a prime example. Did it do anything for frayed nerves? Unlikely.

By the time we were back at the Jeep, however, the sun wasn't the only thing that had risen. My mood had, too. After all, if Jackie was here, she'd be the first one to encourage airing a story if it drew an audience. When asked about her antics, she'd repeatedly said that she didn't care what people said, as long as they were talking about her. At least in that sense, she got her lifelong wish. The circumstances of her death certainly had tongues wagging. Of course, someone knew something. Would we ever find out what really happened, or would the truth be buried along with her?

Chapter Twenty-Two

Champagne. Delicious as it was, sometimes it gave people liquid courage and fostered bad ideas. Given that ours had no alcohol, we should've been given a pass. Nope. Somehow, the effects remained. Which is probably why Becka decided it was the perfect time to pay a visit to Jackie's ex-boyfriend. I resisted mentioning that she'd just told me to back off and let Noah handle it.

The truth was I wanted to see Grant Henshaw and get a sense of what kind of person he was outside of work. I'd never actually spoken to him. But I was torn. This felt more like an ambush. Not only that, we were going to confront a man who was a plausible suspect in Jackie's death on a fairly secluded road—the very road where Jackie was killed.

"Do we have a plan?" I heard myself ask.

"I'll ask him about participating in the show," Becka said. "Give him an opportunity to tell his side of the story."

"If we're going to go there anyway, maybe we should ask about that." What was I doing? Were we sure that champagne was nonalcoholic?

"Guys, I'm having some major reservations about this," Vera said.

Becka shrugged. "If you guys don't want to come, I'll come back later on my own."

"No way," I said, shaking my head. "I'm in. Vera, we can drop you off beforehand if you like."

"Nah, forget it. I'll come. Besides," she said with a rueful grin, "he's suggested threesomes in the past. He'll finally get his wish."

"Watch what you wish for, am I right?" Becka said. The pair high-fived.

What was I getting myself into?

I pushed the thought aside. It would be better for all of us to go together than for Becka to visit him alone. If this man was responsible for Jackie's death, what would stop him from going after Becka, too?

Vera seemed to lose some of her nerve as we got closer. "Is it okay if I stay in the Jeep with Murray?" Vera said. "I'd be much happier sitting here with this dog than that one."

"If you want," Becka said. "But I'll play nice—promise." The steely look in her eyes told a different story, though. We drove on in silence.

As soon as we reached the street, I looked ahead to the spot where Jackie had died. The police tape was gone. Any evidence that a horrible crime ever happened there had vanished. It was no different than any other regular stretch along the unassuming mountain road. A feeling of dread made it feel like a rock suddenly formed in the pit of my stomach.

"Here we are," Becka said. With only the briefest of glances to where Jackie had been killed, she pulled into a private entrance with a long, winding driveway. Lined with shrubbery and pine trees, it was even steep enough that I had to gear down the Jeep to proceed safely.

There was a large area at the top, cleared and leveled. I pulled around to the side of the house, where it looked like space had been reserved for visiting cars. Before turning off the engine, I took a minute to study the well-kept home. It was a traditional A-frame dark wooden house with forest green trim. It wasn't huge, but certainly more than enough room for one or two people. Most of the homes in Eliot Hill with that design had two bedrooms and the kitchen on the main floor, with the primary bedroom and the living area up top to maximize the view. At the other end of the property, there was a separate garage. Could there be any motorized toys inside, such as a heavy-duty four-wheeler? They were as popular around here as bicycles. If so, was it big enough to run Jackie over?

Becka hopped out of the Jeep, and I followed her lead.

"You don't have to come," she said.

"There's no way I'm going to let you go alone," I said. "Are you sure you want to see him?"

Becka nodded with no sign of hesitation. Vera and I exchanged a look of concern. She and Murray stayed put.

There was a flashy red Porsche parked sideways in front of the house, as if in a hurry. The license plate snagged my attention. Playboi. Who did this guy think he was? Harry Styles? Leonardo DiCaprio?

Becka marched toward the small front porch, with me lagging behind. Each step forward made me realize with more certainty this would not end well. Why had I agreed—no—encouraged this plan? If this man was involved with Jackie's death, dropping in on his home turf didn't seem like the wisest move. *Is it too late to abort the mission?* Maybe not. I stopped. "Becka? We need to think this through a little more."

Becka glanced back at me, then charged ahead. My shoulders slumped with a groan. *Cheese and crackers.* My wariness turned to dread. Becka approached with tight fists and stomping feet.

I sprinted forward and reached out to grab Becka's arm. I had to try to stop her. As if reading my mind, she sidestepped me with ease, lunged onto the porch, and raised her fist to knock on the door.

I held my breath, but she stopped just shy of hitting her mark. I slowly straightened. Had reason finally kicked in? A little slow, but I'd take it. I huffed out a loud breath and relaxed. "C'mon, we'll sneak out of here before he even sees us."

Once again, she ignored my words. I hustled onto the porch. Becka brushed past where I stood. Something behind me had caught her attention.

It was a standard cardboard moving box. A piece of beige masking tape hung off it with the word 'junk' scrawled across it with a black marker. The flaps were still open, and stuff was carelessly piled inside.

Becka grabbed something shiny from the top of the pile.

I scanned the area to make sure no one was watching. "What are you doing?"

She held it up to take a closer look, her face draining of color. "Do you know what this is?"

There was a gold cross in her hand. It was about three inches tall and had a mount at the back. I shook my head.

She held it to her chest. "This is Jackie's bedside cross."

A splash of fear hit me. "Are you sure?"

She gripped it tighter. "It was the only thing that she was superstitious about. She wouldn't go to sleep without it. Our mom gave us matching ones when our dad left. She said it would protect us better than he ever did."

The sentimentality Becka described seemed uncharacteristic of Jackie. But then again, I never really knew her well. I only saw the side she wanted to show the world. Becka knelt down and rummaged through the box. She began to pull things out.

The sound of footsteps from inside the house drew my attention back to the door. Becka must not have heard it, now crouched next to the box, digging through its contents. Before I could warn her, the lock unlatched.

The scent of cinnamon wafted out as the door swung open, and Grant Henshaw stood before me. He wore a long black robe and had such an intense fake tan, he'd have to be classified as orange. I'd seen him around the TV studio but had never noticed before. Then again, there had never been a reason. He was a suit in charge of cutting costs. Not exactly the type that made me weak at the knees.

Between the sweet scent and the pairing of colors, I couldn't help but conjure up images of Halloween. Fitting, if he'd just tossed out his dead girlfriend's personal items. He was a monster.

He gave me a once-over before meeting my gaze. "Good morning. Can I help you?" He had a British accent. A very posh one.

I scratched my neck and forced a smile as I took in the textual Versace logo print and the baroque-style gold trim and wrap belt of his robe. This was a man who loved luxury. He had a perfectly trimmed salt-and-pepper beard and slicked-thin hair.

I crossed my arms and stood tall. "Good morning, Mr. Henshaw."

"Hello," he said with a certain reserved charm. He was squinting, obviously trying to place where he knew me from. "Can I—"

Before he could finish his question, he heard the scuffle next to me and craned his neck to see behind me. He stiffened once he recognized my companion. "Becka," he mumbled, saying her name as if reminding himself who it was out loud. She didn't seem to notice his voice, or at least give him the satisfaction of acknowledgment.

"Becka?" he repeated in a louder voice.

She whipped her head around and glanced at him coldly before she turned back around and continued to sort through the box.

I stepped forward. "My name is Emily Dalle. Becka and I wanted to—"

"Ah, yes. The social media *expert*." He enunciated the last word with disdain before turning his attention back to Becka, glowering at her suspiciously. "What are you doing?"

She held up a handful of photos. The one in front had a photo of Jackie and Becka as kids, arm-in-arm, smiling. Becka was barely recognizable as the same person, her face red and blotchy with anger. "Getting rid of Jackie's things already?"

He flinched. "I beg your pardon, but if you'd like to be standing here on my front porch, you'll have to use better manners than that. Or should I simply ask you to leave?"

The direction of this conversation told me we weren't going to get very far unless something changed. Fast.

"Mr. Henshaw, Grant." I summoned my confidence and continued. "Becka just lost her sister. Perhaps you could extend a little empathy."

He let his shoulders drop and heaved a sigh, then turned toward me and away from the grumblings of Becka. "Yes, of course, I'm very sorry for what happened to… to Jackie. A tragic loss." He said it in a way that made me wonder if he might have temporarily forgotten Jackie's name, too. *Seriously?*

He must've sensed my disdain because he tilted his head toward me and said in a low voice, "I tended to call her by her given name, Jacklyn. It was more sophisticated than her TV persona, like the real her." Another rattle from the side brought his attention back to Becka. He folded his arms across his chest and heaved a sigh. "Is there something in particular you're looking for in there?"

"No, I'm good." The sarcastic tone in her voice was thick. "This all her stuff?"

"Anything that might be of interest to you, I suppose. And, although I owe you no explanation, there is a valid reason her things are thrown so hastily in that ill-suited box."

Becka stood up. She edged past me as if preparing to literally bite his head off. "Let's hear it." She leaned toward him. "Was it a guilty conscience?"

He drew back. "I'm not sure I like what you're implying, but it was Jackie who put those things in the box herself. She was in a mood. Since her death, things have been so chaotic I haven't had the chance to bring the box back inside yet."

She glared at his loungewear. "I can see you've been run off your feet."

The scrutiny in her tone flustered him. "Becka, this is an awful time for all of us who cared for your sister. I've been meaning to reach out to you but I've been overwhelmed myself."

Becka continued to look at him with unrelenting scorn. "No doubt. So busy, I'm sure. I have questions about that, too."

This was beyond awkward. And the way it was headed was only going to make it worse. Mentioning that Becka planned on dragging his reputation through the mud on TV could turn it positively nasty. Time to steer the conversation back to common ground. "Could you tell us what made Jackie so upset?" If we could focus on the person they both cared for, maybe we could avoid an ugly confrontation, at least for the duration of our visit.

His eyes went back and forth between us. He straightened up. "There's no reason for me to keep Jackie's things. Take them if you want, Becka."

Becka didn't move. "Guess I should. Don't want them to end up in the trash."

Grant stood his ground. "As I said, Jackie packed that box, not me."

"Why?" I asked again. "Did you have a fight?"

He raised an eyebrow and looked pointedly at Becka. "It wasn't me she was fighting with."

The words made my stomach drop. What was he implying?

Chapter Twenty-Three

I cleared my throat. "Becka?"

I was here to learn what happened. I didn't get to pick and choose the answers. I needed to find out what I was missing.

Becka turned to me. "My sister was fighting with two writers because of a joke that fell flat, Vera for wearing a dress that outshined her, the makeup department for choosing a blush that made her cheeks look ruddy, and one of the camera crew members for filming a close-up at an angle he knew was not her best. Oh, and me for dating Billy."

"I'd say there was more to it than that," Grant said with an acid tone.

"When did she pack up her stuff?" I asked.

He rubbed his beard. "Friday, I believe."

"The night of the party?" *And the same night she died?* Odd timing.

"As it turned out, she wasn't in a party sort of mood, after all. However, by the time she had a change of heart, it was too late to cancel."

I looked from him to the box. "So she tossed out a few personal items then went for a stroll?"

"Very specific items," he said. "All the things that reminded Jacklyn of her dear sister."

Becka's chest heaved with exaggerated breaths, but she remained silent. What was I missing? Had Becka and Jackie had a blow-up fight the day she died? She'd mentioned Jackie disapproved of Billy. Was there more to it?

"Not so high and mighty now, are we?" Grant said, keeping his eyes on Becka.

I cleared my throat. "Grant, was Jackie in her white dress and high heels when she left the party?"

He hesitated before answering. "Yes, a few minutes before people began showing up. Not that many did. Still, it was quite awkward, if you must know, and I expected her to come back in some dramatic fashion and bless us all with her presence."

"But she didn't," I said. "Any reason she chose to walk away instead of drive?"

He nodded. "Her car was in the shop. A detail she likely forgot in her dramatic exit."

"What time was that?" I pressed.

He pulled his hands out of his pockets and waved us back. "Enough of your questions. I've gone over this with the police. I don't owe you, Becka, or anyone else an explanation. Please leave now."

I hopped off the porch, then turned back. "Just one more. Why not call the cops when she didn't come back?"

He huffed out a breath as his face went a deep shade of crimson. "I might not have then, but I won't make the same mistake now. Leave immediately, or I will call the police and have you escorted off the premises."

Becka folded her arms against her chest. "Not without my sister's things."

"Good. Let me help." He swept past Becka. "I'll bring them to your car."

Becka scowled at him but allowed him to pick up the box without complaint. He heaved the box up with both hands and carefully trudged down the steps. Becka hustled after him. "You won't get away with what you did."

He turned, eyeing her over the large box. "I had nothing to do with Jackie's death, if that's what you're implying. As I've already told the sheriff, I have an alibi, remember? I was throwing a party."

"She was gone by the time the first people showed up. You said that yourself. Or maybe you slipped out."

He hooked a thumb toward his flashy ride. "Not in that baby."

He had a point. The sporty engine had a large exhaust. People would've heard the revving engine. Plus, there would've been damage that likely couldn't have been fixed in so short a time. His car looked in perfect condition, not even a scratch on the front. I looked back at the double garage. It could easily be storing another vehicle that was out of sight.

He paused. "Where's your car?"

I pointed to the area we'd parked, just hidden from view. He charged ahead, box in hands. Becka kept up as if it was some sort of race. I lagged a few steps behind, but close enough to listen.

"It may be hard for you to understand," I heard him say. "But us Brits tend to keep a stiff upper lip. I am grieving in my own way but, unlike you or your sister, I don't do emotional outbursts."

"Can I quote you on that?" Becka said as we rounded the corner toward the Jeep.

Grant stopped, so suddenly, my chin hit his shoulder blade. I recoiled from the heat emanating through the silky fibers of his robe.

I scrubbed my chin with the back of my hand and peered around his tall frame to see what made him freeze. It was an unexpected sight. Vera, evidently bored of waiting, had uncorked the last bottle of champagne. She was leaning against the Jeep, taking a swig straight out of the bottle. Murray sat at her feet like a furry sidekick, happy to be of service.

"Good morning, Grant," she chirped.

Grant heaved with anger. He glared at each one of us in turn. All three of us grinned back. I wasn't even sure why.

He stomped his foot. "What the Hell is going on here?"

Vera had tied her yoga top into a knot, exposing an impressive six-pack. Between windswept hair and her bare midriff, she reminded me of a 1950s pin-up girl.

I patted his shoulder. "Don't worry, she's not driving."

He flinched at my touch but kept his eyes on her.

"Vera, put that bottle down," he said authoritatively. "Stop being so reckless. What's wrong with the lot of you? Is life a joke to you all?" He shoved the box into Becka's hands roughly. "I don't know what sort of game this is, but all of you must leave at once."

Becka looked ready for a fight. Before she could take aim and fire, I grabbed the box from her hands with a warning. "Let's go."

She paused as if deciding whether to stay and add fuel to the fire. It wouldn't take much. The aging slimeball was shaking with anger. If Becka mentioned she'd planned to humiliate him on TV, I'd be legitimately scared it would send him over the edge. What would that mean? A heart attack? An attack on us? I wasn't prepared to find out.

I stood in front of her, blocking her view of anything else. "Becka, listen. This man is not worth your time," I said. "You've made your point."

She finally relented. "Fine. Let's get out of this dump."

We walked toward Vera and hopped in the Jeep. I placed the box behind me while Vera strolled closer to Grant. She smiled at him and poured the rest of the champagne out on nearby flowers. He stood aghast, rage in his eyes.

I turned the Jeep on. I gave the stony-faced man a big wave. "Nice to meet you."

"Enjoy the rest of your morning," Becka called out.

Vera blew him a kiss.

Then, all of us burst into laughter.

Grant turned on his heel and stomped back toward his house. I turned to take one last look. Something about his chin jutting in the air as his robe flapped in the gentle breeze, knobby knees exposed, made him look perfectly ridiculous. He stood at his doorway and waited for us to go.

"Guess he's not a morning person," I said. "Want to get the heck out of this place?"

"Desperately," Becka said.

"Just don't drive too fast," Vera said. "There's a lot of bubbly in my system right now. And I'm not normally a champagne-in-the-morning type. I may have overdone it."

"Gotcha," I said.

I backed up the Jeep into his garden, slowly and deliberately.

Vera leaned over and got sick in the garden, covering the only flowers not yet crushed by my tires.

"Nice touch," Becka said with a grin.

"I think I'm starting to feel a little better," Vera said.

CHAPTER TWENTY-THREE

I put the Jeep in gear and spun the wheels in the dirt, leaving a trail of dust behind us as we went.

Chapter Twenty-Four

While Becka and I jockeyed with Grant, Vera had gone through the photos of our morning outing and sent me the best ones. Back at the apartment, Murray curled up on the couch, and I climbed onto a stool in front of my MacBook. It sat open, the photos already on my iCloud account. Good. Seeing the photos on a bigger screen would help me choose the ones to post. I was about to pull them up when inspiration struck.

I scrolled to the Google homepage. Maybe more photos had been added from the night Jackie was killed. I repeated the searches I'd done before, using the same keywords and hashtags. My heart sank. Nothing new. *Come on.*

I stared at the screen. There was a camera icon in the corner of the search menu. It wasn't new, but I'd never thought much about it. Until now. What exactly did it do? When I scrolled over top, it read *search by image*. I clicked on it. Huh. Apparently, I could paste or upload a photo into the search engine, and similar images would be found. I considered entering the picture taken by Vince Castro. His photo missed the mark, but he'd said in his note there'd been other people taking photos from the same vantage point. If one of them had a slighter wider scope, it may include Mountaintop Lane around the time Jackie was killed.

My plan would only work if the exact spot could be identified. There had to be something other than trees and sky that could distinguish the location and make it stand apart from thousands of similar vantage points and millions of online photos. I went into my messages and clicked on the attachment of the initial photo I'd been sent. I expanded it to full size.

My stomach clenched. *I've got it.*

There, hovering at the edge of the photo, stood the statue of Rita Walsh, competitive skier and Eliot Hill legend. This was my best shot. I uploaded it into the search engine and waited for the results. Initially, several came up of what I'd expected, unspecified groupings of trees and forests. But when I scrolled further down, the photos became more specific. Photos of the statue started to appear. Since it had only been erected six months ago, it didn't take long to narrow down the date. Then I saw it. A photo of the statue with the moon. The supermoon. Of course, there'd be photos of that night. It was an amazing photo op. And from one of the best vantage points in town. I narrowed it down to three photos. The last one encompassed the largest area, including where Jackie was hit.

The Supermoon was up. There was no sign of Jackie, but there was something significant—two cars were parked at the end of the road.

My stomach flipped as I recognized a yellow BMW coupe. The only one I knew of with a bike rack attached to the back. It belonged to Rob Chaser.

I tried to think back to our last conversation. Had he told me he'd been out riding when Jackie was struck? Maybe, but he certainly hadn't mentioned where he'd parked that night. Why not? Probably because when things went sideways for Rob, he had a tendency to panic. Like I was doing right now. *Think. Why would his car be there that night?*

Easy. Supermoon. Like everyone else, he wanted to check it out. Why not from the bike path? He loved to bike. Simple. That spot was an easy access point for the cycling route. Under any other circumstance, this would be a normal sight. Then again, a lot of the path was covered over with a tree canopy. It wouldn't be a good choice.

What about the other car? I zoomed in for a better look. A basic black hatchback. I recognized this one, too.

My mouth went dry. "Murray, I'll be back."

Too hurried to tie my shoes up, I threw them aside and grabbed my slides. Laptop in my hand, I raced downstairs and thrust open the door.

"Fitz!" I searched the café. "Fitz!" *Where is he?*

His head popped up from behind the counter. "Em, you okay?"

"Get over here," I hissed. "I have to show you something."

He stood up and breezed around the counter. "What's going on?"

"I found something." I latched onto his arm and yanked him toward the nearest booth, dropping into a seat. "C'mon!"

Stumbling, he caught the edge of the booth before his entire weight crash-landed on top of me. "Whoa!" He looked at me warily as he regained control and took a seat alongside me. "What is it? What did you find?"

I held my hand over my laptop and whipped it open in a dramatic display. "Look. It's from the night Jackie was killed."

He leaned in and studied the picture. I'd zoomed in on just the black car. He craned his neck closer to the screen to get a better look. His brows drew together. "A black car?"

Clearly not picking up the significance, I huffed out a breath of frustration. I tapped on the screen. "I zoomed in to show you the important part. In the background, the Supermoon is out, and it's taken from Overlook Point."

Understanding dawned on him. He slumped against the backrest. "So you have a black car parked near where Jackie died. Don't jump to any conclu—"

"That's Billy's car!"

Fitz bolted upright and clapped his hand over my mouth. "Shh. You don't know that. There's a million plain black hatchbacks around."

I brushed his hand away. "Oh, please. What are the chances it belongs to someone else?"

"I don't know. Guess who might? Noah, my brother. Sexy sheriff dude you obsess over. Remember him?"

"Haha. I wanted to show you first."

"Okay, can I look at the rest of the photo while you give him a call?"

"Fill your boots." I slid the laptop over to him, then pulled up my phone. A call felt too personal. Best to send a text.

Me: Hey, you busy?

No response.

"Em?" Fitz's voice was quieter than normal.

I glanced over. "What's up?"

CHAPTER TWENTY-FOUR

He kept his eyes on the screen. He pointed to the BMW. "Is that..."

"Rob's car?" I finished. "Yup. Wrong place, wrong time."

"Or, maybe the creep went too far."

"*Creep?*" I tsked. "C'mon, that's a little harsh."

He pulled his focus away to give me a disapproving frown. "You're joking, right?"

My back went up. "I'm not saying he was ever a stellar boyfriend. But I think doofus would suffice."

"Oh c'mon, Em. You've got to be kidding. He's a class-A sleazeball. Always has been."

I opened my mouth to argue.

Fitz shook his head. "Let's not go there. For now, all that matters is that the photo is turned in."

"You're right. Maybe Noah will be able to pull up the second license plate to see if it belongs to Billy. It's hard to see, but that car doesn't look damaged, and it still has a license plate."

Fitz shook his head. "Maybe, but the numbers are obscured in the shadows."

"Don't they have crime-scene photo enhancement technology?"

He blinked twice. "You're kidding, right?"

"No, they must have some sort of lab there. My guess is Rob was out on his bike. Not so sure about Billy. At the very least, he might be a material witness."

He patted my hand. "Do you even know what a material witness is?"

Like, duh. "A witness who has material to share."

He grinned at me. "Not quite. A material witness is someone with information that could affect the outcome of a trial. We're not there yet."

"What about the lab?"

He gave me a shrewd look. "You've been to the police station. Where do you think they'd have a lab hidden? In a bat cave under the earth's surface?"

I frowned. "Not when you say it like that."

"The only lab at the Eliot Hill Police Station is Jim Holler's overweight yellow one. You know, the one who pees on the floor whenever someone pets him behind his left ear?"

I threw my hands up. "Well, crap then, Fitz. How are we going to positively identify the car?"

He closed the laptop. "Call me a do-gooder, but maybe we'll have to leave it to the authorities to sort out."

I groaned. "That could take forever. What if they have to send it away to a state lab for photo enhancement?"

"Then that's what they'll do. The whole town has been hit with budget cuts. Noah hasn't been given a new computer in years. Photoshop could probably do it, but I don't even know if he has that."

"You do, though."

He shook his head. "Nuh-uh. Not a good idea."

"Why not?"

"Because we aren't cops. I serve coffee. You serve attitude. Speaking of which, aren't you supposed to be on right now?" He tapped on his watch.

Argh. He was right. If I didn't hurry, my post would be late. I opened my laptop again and sent the photo to him. I paused only long enough to give him my best sad puppy face before scooping up the computer and running upstairs.

Chapter Twenty-Five

Ibrewed a fresh pot of green tea, helped myself to a few chocolate chip cookies, and put together some fun posts for the day. Typically, I liked to send out positive vibes throughout the week, with loads of fun photos, my favorite being those of Murray on our sunrise hikes to help set the tone.

Spotify, do your thing. A few taps on my phone and Dua Lipa began to sing. Better. Mood music was key. Within a few minutes I polished off my video and sent it into the world. Did other bloggers or social media professionals see each posting like a bright new baby, or was it just me? Mom would probably tell me it was the first sign of my biological ticking clock. Better keep that nugget to myself.

My phone pinged with a text from Noah.

Noah: Hi. Saw your message. You okay?

Me: All good. You busy?

Noah: Yes, but I can make time for you. I'm at the station. Do you want me to stop by?

And repeat last time? No thanks.

Me: Can I come by there instead?

Noah: Anytime.

A smile spread across my lips. *Easy tiger. He's a cop, and he's working.*

Me: See you soon.

I changed out of my slides and into real shoes with laces. I chose my pristine new white sneakers. *Good start.* Murray raised his head as I grabbed my keys.

"Next time. Promise." I threw him a treat. All was forgiven. Maybe it would be that easy with Noah. Unlikely. "That's why you'll always be my number one, Murr." He wagged his tail, and I headed out.

The sheriff's department was only about a mile away, but I drove anyway. I'd done my ten thousand steps for the day. Why push it?

Noah sat at his classic wood-paneled desk, one of three identical work areas when I strode into the station. He caught my eye as soon as I walked in and smiled. *Friendly. Professional.* Oh, please, who was I kidding? The man was hot.

His easy demeanor gave me hope that all was forgiven after our last meeting. Since then, I was in a better place. I felt a little guilty for my lifted spirits since Jackie was still dead and there was a murderer on the loose, I couldn't help but separate it from myself.

"Hey." Noah stood up. "Thanks for coming in. I'm not used to people volunteering to come and see me."

"Anytime."

He held out his hand. "Have a seat."

"Okay." I sat down. He watched me. I felt my cheeks go hot.

"Should I brace myself?"

"Uh…"

He leaned forward, ushering in the fresh scent of his woodsy cologne. "I'm kidding. I always know to brace myself when I see you."

"Haha," I said, returning the smile. Was Noah flirting with me?

The moment passed as he stood up. "Coffee?"

Eyes wide, I nodded. "Should I be scared? Police station coffee doesn't have a good reputation."

"C'mon with me. Nothing to fear." I followed him across the room to a corner that served as a makeshift snack area. "See?" He pointed to the only thing in the room that didn't look like an old prop from *Columbo*. "Fitz is my brother, remember? He donated this fancy coffee maker after suffering through a cup from our old machine last year. It even has a cappuccino setting that I've yet to figure out."

"Let me take a look." He stepped aside. While I didn't have the skills of Fitz,

I was able to sort out how to program the machine to make a cappuccino.

"You've just earned yourself a free pass on your next speeding ticket."

"Really?"

"No."

I laughed as he tried to repeat what I'd shown him.

After a few missteps, he managed to make two cappuccinos. "Glad that's done." He then pointed down a narrow hallway. "Can we go talk now? I feel like I've earned a break."

I bit back a grin and made my way down the dim hallway until I reached the small room. I peeked inside before entering. Ah, right. An interrogation room. Just like on *Law & Order*, minus the windows and fancy lighting. There was an empty table with a chair on either side. It smelled like industrial cleaner. We sat across from each other, but his chair was much nicer than mine, with padding and armrests. It sat a little higher, too. A subtle reminder as to who was in charge.

"Sorry, I'd offer you this seat, but it's against protocol."

I could've sat there all day, happy to have his full attention. "No problem." I caught his eye. "I don't mind."

"Thanks." He held my gaze for another minute before looking away. "So, I hear you've found another photo."

"Did Fitz send them to you?"

He nodded. "Want to tell me about them?"

"The first one was sent to me by one of my followers. The second was easy to find once I figured out what to look for."

"But now you're done, right?"

"A hundred percent. The idea popped into my head involuntarily."

"Right. I appreciate your wanting to help. But next time an idea pops up, call me."

"Okay." I paused before continuing. "I also wanted to check in and see if you found Billy's car at the shop."

"I did, thanks."

"Did Billy let you examine the car?"

He closed his notebook and tucked it back in his pocket. "Do you want to go for a walk instead? It's a little stuffy in here."

"Sure."

Noah rose and opened the door. I got up and exited the room. A sense of relief washed over me as I left the claustrophobic space. As much as I enjoyed Noah's attention, sitting in the perp chair made me realize I never wanted to break the law, not even if he was the arresting officer.

Noah grabbed his jacket from the back of his chair, and we walked outside. A deep breath of the cool air felt good. He took sunglasses out of his uniform pocket and put them on. Cop glasses. Go figure. I had to bite my lip to refrain from smiling. Or gawking. I had to remind myself this was business, no matter how much pleasure it gave me.

"Can we stick to the café for our chats from now on?" I asked. "It's a little intimidating in there."

He smiled but kept his focus straight ahead. "Good. That's the point."

We walked in silence for a few minutes before he spoke again. "We need to talk about the other day. It got a little intense."

"Yeah."

He stopped and took his sunglasses off. "I want to apologize for my behavior. I was out of line."

It was nice to see he was willing to admit when he messed up. Most of the guys I'd dated rarely admitted their mistakes. Not that this was a date. Definitely *not* a date.

"I'm sorry too," I said.

"Truce?"

"Yes," I agreed. We started walking again. "Does that mean you can't get mad at me again?"

He grinned. "I can't make any promises."

"Commitment issues?" I teased.

"Nope. I just know you too well."

I couldn't tell if he was kidding or not. "Since I've already got a bad reputation, I may as well ask about where the case is at."

"Good. Let's talk."

"Really?" Maybe sharing the photos made him feel like he could open up about the case.

"Yeah. Why don't you tell me about what Rob was like as a boyfriend."

I gave him the side eye. "Rob Chaser?"

There was only one Rob he could be referring to, only one I'd ever dated. But they were friends, and it hadn't occurred to me that Rob would be on the official suspect list.

"He was in the vicinity when Jackie was killed, as you now know from the photos."

"Don't you want to know about Billy Bones?"

He looked surprised. "I already know you were snooping around his private property uninvited. Was there something else?"

I sputtered. "Billy's car was in the vicinity of the murder, too. And it's got front-end damage."

"Didn't we agree to let me handle the case?"

I was confused. "Yes, but I thought we were going to talk about it."

The smile faded from his lips. "Yes, I'll ask questions, and you'll answer them."

My cheeks felt hot. "Right."

"Can we go back to Rob now?"

I shouldn't have been surprised. With no alibi and a recent breakup with the victim, Rob had to be a strong contender in the suspect list. Was it possible I'd dated a murderer?

Chapter Twenty-Six

"Rob didn't kill Jackie," I said. The question of his guilt came and went quickly, like my fleeting obsession with Bratz dolls or my carb-free diet. After our conversation the other day, I just couldn't see it. "Aren't you two buddies?"

"Yeah," Noah said. "Unfortunately, friendship doesn't give people immunity in murder investigations."

"I get that. And Rob's a goof, for sure. But a killer? Are you looking at him because his car was parked nearby?"

"Doesn't help."

The wind picked up, and I shuddered. "Care to elaborate?"

"Maybe we should head back. You look cold."

I shook my head. "I'm fine." The only chill I was feeling was in my bones. Did Noah really think Rob could be a killer?

"Look, past behavior is often a good indicator of someone's character. He hasn't had a lot of girlfriends other than you and Jackie. So I'm trying to get a better picture of his character as a romantic partner."

Just questions. Due diligence. "What do you want to know?"

"Did you ever fear for your personal safety when you were together or after you broke up? Was he possessive? Jealous?"

My dating history wasn't a topic I'd expected to be discussing when I'd dropped by today. Going back to my first love and the crushing heartache that followed was never something I enjoyed delving into. Noah was right to ask, though. It made sense. I hadn't thought about it like that.

"There are a lot of unflattering things I could tell you about Rob. But he never laid a hand on me, and it never occurred to me that he might."

As I said it, a flashback of a bad night came to mind. He'd been jealous over a college study buddy who'd confessed to have a crush on me. I'd told the guy I wasn't interested, but Rob wanted me to stop speaking to him altogether, and I thought that was unreasonable. It ended in a shouting match. He punched a hole in my wall, and I'd been freaked out. Rob had lost control.

The next day, he came by and repaired the damage before my parents saw it. He apologized about it for months, got over his jealousy, and never did anything like that again. Was that worth telling Noah?

As if reading my mind, he reframed the question. "Did he ever do anything that scared you?"

His eyes were fixed on mine. I glanced away, then down at my shoes. I'd made up my mind not to tell him of one bad night. The fallout could ruin Rob's life. "Can't think of anything off the top of my head."

"Okay." Noah paused and studied my face. "But if you remember something—"

I cut him off. "I won't."

He rubbed the back of his neck and let out a sigh.

Now, it was my turn. "Can you tell me again why you aren't looking at Billy Bones?"

"There's a lot to be considered, Emily. I can't go around accusing people of crimes because they have a dent in their car."

"But Billy's car was at the scene. You can see it in the photo I sent you."

He shook his head. "There's what appears to be a black vehicle in the photo. Do you know how many black cars are in New York state?"

"Yes, but Billy is being evasive about how the damage was done to his car."

He glanced at his watch. "I had a chat with Billy, like I said I would. He had a reasonable explanation for the damage to his car. It's not consistent with a hit-and-run, and I see no reason to press the issue. Didn't he tell you he hit a raccoon?"

I huffed. "Only after I prodded him."

"Motive is important, too."

I shrugged. "Jackie hated bikers."

"So do a lot of people."

"Did you know he was Becka's boyfriend? Jackie disapproved of the relationship." Even as the words came out, I knew my argument was weak. We arrived at the steps of the station and paused. He turned and faced me. "Finding Jackie's body must've been extremely upsetting. I understand your wanting to help. But it's time to let it go."

I wasn't ready to give up. I'd been tossing an idea around in my head. I bit my lip.

He dropped his chin. "Spit it out. I can see you want to say something."

Now or never. "What if Billy is playing on the guilt you feel about him going to prison for a crime he may not have committed?"

He blanched. "I had nothing to do with that."

"Are you keeping him off the suspect list because of what happened in the past? Is it possible he's using that to try and manipulate—"

Noah touched my arm. "I appreciate you coming in, Emily."

"Seriously, Noah. I think he's hiding something. Can't you get a court order or a subpoena or whatever it's called and test the front end of his car?"

"Not without a reason. And at this point, I have no reason. TV shows love to play into the idea of police having intuition and feelings about people. But in the real world, there's protocol. Preconceived ideas about people lead to nothing but trouble. I follow facts."

His logic shut me up. Maybe he was right. Why was *I* so convinced Billy was involved in Jackie's murder?

"Okay," I finally said. "I'll trust your opinion."

The strain on his face eased. "Thank you. Does that mean you'll back off my case?"

"I can't stop people from contacting me. That's my job. But I'll call if anything else comes up."

"Thank you."

I smiled at him. "It was kind of cool sitting in the perp chair. You know, in a life experience sort-of-way. Gave me a different perspective."

He shook his head. "Just watch out for yourself, okay? The fact is someone killed Jackie, and they did it with intent. The whole town knows you've cast a net searching for clues. You need to keep your guard up."

"Will do, Officer."

He held my gaze. "Don't be a stranger."

I bit my lip. "Okay. Now that I know you've got decent coffee, you may find me here more often."

"I'll make sure to thank my brother for that."

"Let's keep that between us."

The corner of his mouth lifted. "Okay. I will."

With a final glance, I turned to go. "Bye."

"Bye, Emily."

I left the station and almost glided toward where my Jeep was parked. My whole body buzzed. What was happening? I turned over the engine and sat for a minute.

My smile faded as I went over our conversation. Had I been wrong about Billy? And Rob? Both Noah and Fitz thought so. I needed to know why. It was time for a heart-to-heart with my BFF.

Chapter Twenty-Seven

Eliot Hill was a happening place these days. Film crews were descending more and more upon us to shoot small-town scenes for big-time movies. It was a boost for the local economy, expanding the appeal of our town. It was also a reason Jackie had been able to get so many big names on her show. Movie stars were milling about, making it easy and convenient for them to pop into the studio and do a five-minute segment. It was a great way for them to ingratiate themselves with locals and start a buzz for their newest project.

Today, there was a gaggle of girls in the café quizzing Fitz on a movie that had just come out. It featured one of the hottest new actors, and it was rumored he'd frequented the café. They peppered Fitz for every detail he could remember about the actor's visit.

"He ordered an almond biscotti every morning to dip in his quad shot oat milk cappuccino."

One of the girls held up the biscotti in her hand. "Like this one?"

"Like, exactly the same as that one."

She swooned, and her friends giggled with delight.

"But how could he have those abs eating that much sugar?" one girl asked. "So many carbs," her friend added.

Fitz swiveled his head right then left, making it look like he was sharing very private information. "You know what he did right after?"

"What?" demanded the same girl.

"He dropped down and did fifty pushups." Fitz pointed to the floor under his feet.

A collective gasp. "Here?"

"In the middle of the café. Busy or not. That guy was hardcore."

I was so busy watching the exchange I bumped into an unexpected obstacle en route to our booth. My ear connected to a soft cotton fabric covering something that felt firm, warm, and muscular. Startled, I glanced up to see I'd walked right into Rob's chest. A smile played on his lips. He smelled like Dove Soap and wore a fitted t-shirt and skinny jeans over his lean physique. No doubt this man was trouble. But the only real pain I could see him causing was as a heartbreaker. I was immune to his charms but had no doubt many others wouldn't be so lucky.

He was holding a muffin in one hand. He gently pulled on one of my curls with the other. "Do you normally greet customers with a cranial chest rub, or are you just happy to see me?"

I swatted his hand away. "You're the first one." I took a few steps back. "I wasn't expecting you, or anyone else, to be standing here."

"I've been waiting for you," he said. "Fitz said this was your usual seat, so I thought I'd hang out and see if you'd show up."

He seemed more relaxed than the last time we'd talked. Fully clothed, too, without any prompting. Two points in his favor.

"Guess it's your lucky day." I smiled at him. "Maybe you should pick up a lottery ticket."

"There's a few things I've been thinking about picking up lately." His eyes lingered on mine.

Rob had always been the king of cheesy pick-up lines. It was hard not to laugh in spite of the fact I wasn't interested.

I gestured my hand out, signaling an invitation to join me in the booth. He was pleased by my encouragement and sat across from me with a goofy grin. It was the same look Murray gave me when I told him he'd been a good boy.

"What's up?" I asked. In all the years that Longbourn had been open, Rob had never graced it with his presence. He was here with an agenda. I needed to remember that.

He split the muffin in two and passed me the bigger half before taking out a neatly folded piece of paper from his pocket. I gladly accepted the muffin, taking a bite as he held up the paper. "I printed out the list you requested. The name of the members from my hiking app."

I rubbed my hands together to brush off the crumbs, then took it from his hand. He held on for a minute, so our hands almost touched. Our eyes locked, and I pulled away, taking the page from him.

"Thanks." Was he trying to fluster me? If so, it wasn't working. But why was he doing it in the first place?

"My pleasure, Emmy," he said. "I also wanted to come by and personally invite you to join the local hiking group. I saw you signed up for the app, too. I'm glad. It's competitive but fun. If you like, I can show you a few tricks to maximize your score. Help you climb up the ranks."

"To join you at the top?"

"Miracles do happen," he teased.

"So, explain this to me. Do you have to approve each new member personally?"

"If you put as much time into hiking as you did questioning me, you wouldn't need my help."

"Is that a yes?"

He sighed. "I'm working to automate it, but for now, I do. But don't worry; all the data is secure. I use two-factor authentication. No one's trying to hack the site or manipulate the data."

"Except you."

He crossed his arms. "Funny."

"How competitive does it get?"

"You'd be surprised. And I was just kidding about fudging your score. I put procedures in place to stop people from cheating. They can watch what everyone else is doing but not even I could manipulate the numbers."

"So your profile is legit?"

He cocked his head, and his grin grew wider. "Checking me out, huh?"

"Yeah, and I noticed you were out the night Jackie died."

Rob's smile vanished. "I told you that."

"You didn't mention it was so close to where Jackie died."

He didn't say anything.

CHAPTER TWENTY-SEVEN

"Rob, your car was parked next to where she was killed."

He huffed and leaned back in his seat. "Eyewitnesses are notoriously wrong. You've heard that before, right?"

"I saw a photo of the area. Your car was there."

He shrugged. "Yeah, I guess. But I wasn't anywhere near the street when she died. I was out on the trail."

"You should be able to prove that with your app. Show where you were when Jackie died."

"I can't."

"Why not?"

"My watch ran out of power, okay? Noah thinks I shut it off so my movements couldn't be tracked. I was last clocked half a mile from where she was killed."

"Near the time of her death?"

He nodded. "I probably drove right by her body after my ride."

A shiver ran through me. So, Rob was in *exactly* the wrong place at *exactly* the wrong time?

A boisterous group of local cyclists bounded into the café. Rob bolted upright and forced out a smile. He shot them a jocular salute. Had deception always come easy to him?

When he turned back, he leaned forward so our conversation couldn't be overheard. He was so close I couldn't help but notice his hairline was a little further back than it had been a few years earlier.

"Why are you asking me about this?" It was more of a complaint than a question.

"Because I want to know. I'm a curious monkey, remember?"

My joke fell flat. Rob knew where I was going. Our history together was rocky, and trustworthiness was never his strong point. *Or mine.* "Maybe you saw something or heard something that you don't realize could help."

"I don't know. Honestly, I don't remember anything unusual. Other than the moon being extra bright. Everything else was status quo."

"It's a pretty big coincidence. You being there at the same time Jackie was killed."

He shook his head. "You didn't pay this much attention to me when we were dating. I'd be flattered if you weren't implying that I may have murdered my other ex-girlfriend."

"I'm not going to apologize for asking questions, Rob."

"Why are you even getting involved in all this? You and Jackie were like oil and water. Now that she's dead, you want to play the concerned friend? Give me a break."

I couldn't argue his point. Jackie wasn't my pal; Becka had called me off, and I knew Noah was perfectly capable of running his own investigation.

Yet I couldn't let it go. I felt too involved. I was fully invested. "I want to know what happened. Don't you?"

"You're not the same Emily Dalle I remember, you know that?" His voice was flat, abandoning his attempts to charm me.

He'd hear no argument from me. And he was right. I wasn't the same person. My shell had hardened. It wasn't the end of the world if people didn't like me. Including him. When we'd dated, he'd always had the final say because I was insecure and wanted his approval. It was like comparing a hollow molding to a solid rock.

"You might not like my questions, but you'd better prepare some answers. I won't be the only one asking."

We hit a standstill. There was nothing left to say. The gaggle of girls who'd been chatting with Fitz were now waving goodbye, giggling all the way out, elbowing each other as he thanked them for their visit. I watched the scene, glad to have something to look at besides Rob. Fitz turned and met my gaze, then glanced at Rob, his expression turning frosty.

Rob stood up. "I guess I'll see you around."

Fitz approached the table as he exited the booth.

"Don't leave on my account. I wasn't going to kick you out for at least another ten seconds."

Rob didn't bother to respond.

"See ya," was all we got.

Chapter Twenty-Eight

When Rob was out the door, Fitz sat down and looked at me sympathetically.

"Want to fill me in?"

My shoulders slumped. I wasn't even sure where to begin. "All I was doing was asking questions."

"Like why he didn't mention his car was in the vicinity of Jackie's murder? His exact location when she was killed?"

"I made no accusations."

He tilted his head to the side, his expression morphing into concern. "Em…"

"The thing is, I don't think he did it. So why is he so defensive?"

"Hold that thought," Fitz said. "I'll get the big guns."

Fitz gave a wave to a nearby barista and requested two double shot almond milk cappuccinos with extra whip and chocolate sprinkles. "Now," he said, turning back to me. "Before we get into the dirty details, have you talked to Noah? There were a few things he wanted to ask you."

"I went by the station. He wanted some insight into what Rob is like as a boyfriend."

"From you? I've heard of background checks, but that's more like ancient history."

I grinned. "It's uncomfortable thinking back to that time in my life. I was so young and insecure. My entire world revolved around Rob. Like, why?"

"He was your first love," Fitz said. "You went all in."

"I was so into him I lost myself."

"Maybe. But the experience made you who you are today. Remember that."

"I hate thinking back to that time, that place. Memory Lane is my least favorite destination."

Fitz didn't look surprised. "We all have regrets, Em. What did you tell him?"

I shrugged. "Nothing juicy. Run-of-the-mill dude."

Fitz frowned.

I sat back. "What? Obviously, the end was a colossal disaster. I can hardly blame him for that."

"Em," he said in a tone that set my teeth on edge.

"Fitz," I said with more aggression than I intended. "I'm not saying the guy's a catch. But he was cornered by Jackie. She pressed him relentlessly. And the truth was our relationship wasn't the picture-perfect one we'd been sharing on social media. Did I appreciate being dumped on live TV? No. But it was Jackie who took it too far."

Fitz began to shake his head. "No."

"No? No, what?" I said, feeling indignant. "What are you trying to say?"

He watched me carefully. "Rob knew it was coming."

My mouth dropped open. "What are you talking about?" I said with a shake of my head. "No, no, no. Rob was caught off-guard. Just like me. Didn't you see his face? Jackie must've realized our expressions weren't as sincere or inspired as they once were. She beat him down, pressured him into something he hadn't been ready for –hadn't even recognized inside."

He took a deep breath. "You don't know the real story. That's the one they decided to tell."

A feeling of dread washed over me. The old ignorance-is-bliss thing wafted through my mind. "What do you know?"

"Rob cheated on you with Jackie—before the show. Apparently, they hooked up during the pre-show interviews."

I stared at him. My thoughts were spinning.

"Remember you were so busy with exams, so he did the prep work for the show?"

I frowned. "It was only supposed to be one or two brief chats but he said they needed more material, that she'd wanted to ensure she got our story right."

Fitz shook his head. "Nope. That was a big fat lie. They said that to make sure they got *their* story right."

"How do you know this?"

"One of my regulars who worked at the station told me—*after* the fact. Obviously, I would've warned you if I'd known. Sort of like what Rob should've done."

"Are you sure?"

"I confronted Rob. Went to the bike shop. He admitted it. Begged me not to tell you because it was too late. Said he felt guilty. Wasn't going to go through with it, but Jackie pressured him on air. That expression you see as she pestering him isn't surprise; it's guilt, Em. He said Jackie thought it would make for great TV and that we were doing you a favor since there'd be no more pretending...I almost clocked him. But I knew he wasn't worth it."

"Why didn't you tell me?"

"I'm sorry." He rubbed his hands over his face. "I thought I was protecting you. It was a mistake. I'm sorry."

The barista came by and dropped off our drinks. I devoured a big spoonful of whipped cream while I glared at Fitz. "Wow."

I thought I'd made peace with what happened. How could the darkest time in my life still bring fresh pain? I felt like an utter fool, the sting of fresh humiliation washing over me like a cold shower without the dopamine spike.

"This pushes Rob beyond goofball status." It was cruel and heartless. If he'd been able to hurt someone he'd claimed to love in front of a live audience, what was he capable of doing when no one else was watching?

Fitz watched me closely. "If this is enough to change your opinion about Rob, we need to tell Noah." There was something comforting in his use of the word 'we.' Was I upset with Fitz? A little. But his intention was to protect me. Just the opposite of what Rob's had been.

169

"There was one incident I held back from him; maybe I shouldn't have."

He stiffened. "Why?"

I held up my hand. "He didn't hit me. But he lost control, and I was scared. Remember that time when Rob put a hole in my parents' wall, and he had to fix it in a panic?"

His face went white. "You said he'd been practicing baseball. How could I have been so clueless?" He pulled his phone out, fingers set to speed dial Noah.

"Wait!" I put my hand over his. "Do you think it really matters?"

He slid his hand out from under mine. "Don't you?"

My stomach twisted. "I don't know."

Fitz leaned in. "If Rob wanted to get back at Jackie for dumping him maybe he decided to go further than just a hole in a wall." He dialed the number and put his phone to his ear.

I suddenly wanted to be anywhere but here.

He pulled the phone away from his ear. "You going to be okay?"

I waved my hand dismissively. "Yeah. Fine. I'm going to hide under my covers for an hour." I left the café before Noah picked up.

He'd be upset with me. Again. *Oh well. Too late now.* Noah knew where to find me if he wanted to yell. There was nothing more I could do. I dragged myself up the stairs. Murray barked at my approach. My heart lifted a fraction. At least he still loved me.

Chapter Twenty-Nine

Once in the comfort of my own space, exhaustion set in. I collapsed onto the couch. Murray sat at my feet and gave my socks a bath. When was this nightmare going to end? "That's it. We're locking the door and not talking to anyone else today. What do you say?" Murray barked, settling in happily beside me. Other than two quick trips out to let Murray relieve himself, we kept to our plan. Nachos, a little online scrolling, and we hit the sack. Too tired to let my worries take over, I was out quickly and slept through the night.

I woke to my phone pinging. I ignored it. It pinged again. And again. I checked the screen. Somehow, I'd managed to sleep in again. That wouldn't have been so bad if it hadn't been Mom on the phone. She was on her way and wanted to make sure she wouldn't be interrupting anything. I wasn't sure exactly what she thought I got up to, and I was too drained to ask.

I texted back, asking her to pick up a coffee for me. In case she was close, that would stall her for a few minutes at least. I couldn't let her see me like this. I was a mess. I had to shower and ply myself with make-up before she coaxed the truth out of me and went on the warpath.

I snatched a towel off the floor and lunged into the bathroom. I wouldn't put it past her to have texted from the other side of my door. She'd done it before, hoping to catch me with some nonexistent boyfriend she'd attempted to manifest.

It was time to wash the past right out of my brain. A fast, hot shower was just what I needed. What was done was done. Maybe Fitz and I were looking too much into the selfish choices Rob had made in the past.

I was ready to think about something and someone else. From everything I'd seen, Jackie had as many issues at work as she had personally. The killer could just as easily be a staff member who'd been upset by something she'd said or done. There'd been a few things bothering me since I'd attended the WKRZ meeting, announcing Becka as Jackie's successor. One of Mom's best friends might be able to shed some light on my questions. Marilyn Myers, AKA Aunt Marilyn, was the wife of WKRZ president Mitch Myers. As Mom and Marilyn were both members of the Ladies Lunch Club, maybe even Mom would have some insight into the goings-on of *The Morning Dish*.

What did I want to know? Maybe a list of who'd been on the receiving end of Jackie's wrath most recently and why. There hadn't been any tears in the staff room, from what I saw. Did anyone stand out?

A knock on the bathroom door interrupted my thoughts. "Yoo-hoo, Emily?"

"Hi, Mom."

"You alone in there?"

I groaned, refusing to dignify her question with an answer.

"You never know, honey. Your father and I—"

"Mom!"

"Touchy, touchy. Well, c'mon out now. I haven't got all day. Fitz was busy so I didn't want to trouble him for coffee. I'll start the kettle instead."

Within five minutes, I stood in a fog of steam, unknotting tangles out of my hair as ringlets spiraled around my fingers. "Mom, why don't you throw a tea bag in the pot?" I called through the door.

After a pause, she responded. "I can see English Breakfast and Chai Cinnamon."

I fought a comb through my hair. "Your choice," I called back.

"Do you have Earl Gray?"

I glared at the door. "I meant to choose between the two I have."

"English Breakfast is perfect."

When I opened the door, Mom had already made herself at home. She sat on the couch, Murray's mammoth paws draped across her, breathing happily into her ear. He wore a tight pink sweater with "I Love My Grandma" in a sparkly heart splayed across the back.

The sight warmed my heart. I hugged her from behind. "You two are ridiculous."

"Good to see you, hon. I'd get up, but my attention is needed here first."

"I know the pecking order. Murray has been waiting for his Nanabear."

At the mention of the name, Murray leaned in and gave Mom a slobbery kiss.

"My little Murrbear," she cooed, scratching behind his ears. "Nanabear missed you, too."

"Are you hungry? I can whip up something quickly if you like."

"Bite your tongue," she said.

"Eggs might be tastier."

She shook her head, unimpressed. "We're going downstairs."

"Kind of early, isn't it?"

"Why do you think Murray is wearing his new sweater? He likes to look good when he has lunch with the LLC."

"Murray's invited?"

"Of course." She eyed my outfit. "You might want to change, too. Be a shame to be shown up by your dog." She nuzzled her nose into Murray's fur. "No offense, my big lug."

I looked down at what I was wearing, frowning. Dark wash jeans with a black knit cardigan. "What's wrong with what I'm wearing?"

"No sparkle. Why don't you wear the diamond studs Dad gave you for Christmas, at the very least?"

"Will do."

"Maybe throw on that cute pink floral scarf I got you for your birthday, as well."

I knew better than to argue. An easy fix worked better than digging in my heels, especially since I didn't feel like wearing any. "Will Marilyn be there?"

"Absolutely," Mom said. "Aside from me, she's the only member in town. Everyone else is still away. But it's the first meeting in months, so we're having it anyway."

"Makes sense. It'll be nice to see her." And ask if there'd been any recent dustups between Jackie and any of *The Morning Dish* staff. If there'd been any complaints, she'd be in the know.

When Mom finally separated herself from Murray, she got up and gave me a big hug. I couldn't deny having my mom nearby always made me feel better. My body relaxed as I breathed in Chanel No.5. Picture perfect in her coral, fitted jacket over black tapered pants with kitten heels, Mom oozed sophistication and style. Her hair sat motionless atop her head, but I couldn't deny the gently feathered bob suited her. When she finally let go, we sat down and sipped tea before leashing up Murray and heading downstairs to meet the gang. Mom could be a lot, but I loved every teeny tiny ounce of her.

As we entered the café, the front door swung open, and Marilyn Myers stepped inside. Fitz had a booth set up for us by the window with a large pot of sweet tea waiting. He approached the table as we settled in and gave a warm smile to the group.

He opened his arms wide. "Welcome back, Snowbirds."

Mom and Marilyn beamed at him, noting that he got more handsome with each passing day. He winked at me, and I rolled my eyes. He escaped quickly, and after a flurry of air kisses and hugs, plus a little fussing over Murray, we all sat down. Marilyn donned a sleek purple wrap dress that highlighted her full figure and complimented her rose-gold hair. She always wore the highest heels, and today was no exception, her Gucci logoed pumps on full display.

Fitz returned with a basket of buttermilk biscuits, complete with strawberry jam & butter on the side. The LLC had a standing order, and he had it prepped in time for whenever they were in the mood.

It didn't take long for Mom and Marilyn to get each other up to speed with how they spent their winters. I listened happily as they filled each other in. My parents and Fitz's parents spent a lot of the winter together in Florida. Marilyn and Mitch had gone to Europe for a few weeks, but with him still running the station and Marilyn almost as involved, neither could afford to be gone for too long.

I didn't have much to say since I hadn't been anywhere, and they all followed me on social media. Of course, I knew going in they would have something to say about my recent postings on Jackie's death and requests for information. It was the reason for my invitation today. But I didn't mind. This crew knew a lot, and I intended to ask as many questions as I answered.

Mom kicked off the fun.

"Honey, Marilyn tells me you joined the staff meeting on Sunday at the studio. We all wondered why."

Aunt Marilyn smiled at me. Obviously, her husband had mentioned my presence. Aunt Marilyn and Uncle Mitch weren't blood relations. But Mom had worked at WKRZ since its inception decades earlier, and our families had remained close. My mom had been the original singing weather girl, a popular draw for the new station, and she helped it become the success it was today.

"Becka invited me to the meeting," I explained. "I think she was nervous about her big announcement and wanted support."

"How's the poor girl handling everything?" Mom asked in between bites.

"She's doing great as far as I can tell," I said. "At the meeting, you'd think she'd had weeks to prepare her speech."

Mom didn't seem surprised. "Becka knows the business. After all, she was the go-to whenever Jackie was unavailable."

She was right.

Marilyn set her fork down and dabbed at the corners of her mouth. "It's not quite that simple. There were some changes taking place even before Jackie died."

Someone had mentioned that earlier though I couldn't remember who it had been. "Like what?" I asked.

Marilyn continued. "Jackie's base had been dwindling over the last few years. It was the reason we first brought in the outside consultant, Grant Henshaw. See if he had any suggestions for softening her image, as well as cutting costs. It helped, but not enough. Mitch thought it might be time to replace her. Go with someone who is less divisive."

My stomach twisted in knots. I had a million questions about Grant, like if that was why he was leaving his position, or if that was even true. But none of that mattered right now. Becka was my focus now. Was she in the know? And why did it make me feel sick to ask?

"Having a host like Jackie had become too much of a risk for WKRZ," Mom said. "We never knew what she was going to say, often going off-script."

Irritation rose up inside me. "Wait. Mom, you knew?"

I tried not to look hurt. Either I succeeded, or she didn't notice, focused too much on her friend. "Not the best-kept secret, was it?"

My stomach flip-flopped. "Did Jackie know?"

Marilyn nodded. "She did. So did Becka. We could've rivaled a *Real Housewives* episode with all the drama it created."

So Jackie's death expedited the process, but it was already in the works. "Huh," was all I could manage to get out, although, inside my head, alarm bells were ringing. I had a really bad feeling about this.

Marilyn reached her hand across the table and squeezed my hand. "TV is a tough business right now, kiddo. I know it sounds rough but Jackie had countless opportunities to make nice and change her attitude. She chose not to listen. And, once she and Grant became an item, he took her side, tried to argue she needed more time to grow a younger audience. So we parted ways with him, too. Not that he cared. He's very in demand. Apparently has a new job already cross country somewhere."

"Remember, Honey," Mom said. "Marilyn's telling you this because we're in a circle of trust."

Marilyn smiled at me. "There's a confidentiality agreement in place."

I could see how well that worked. If the LLC knew, my guess was that others did, too. Now I understood why no one else at the station seemed surprised when Uncle Mitch made the announcement. No one, except me.

Marilyn continued. "The announcement was originally set to take place this week."

"Wow." My head swirled. A confidentiality agreement might explain why Becka hadn't told me, at least that's what she'd say. "Aunt Marilyn, when did Jackie find out?"

Marilyn looked around, then leaned in. "Recently. And trust me, it wasn't an easy decision. We went back and forth a lot. But, in the end, Mitch decided to go with his gut. Jackie's time was up."

How right he had been.

Chapter Thirty

"I've been thinking about Becka," Mom said to me when we got back to my apartment. She'd kicked her heels off and was stretched out on the couch, Murray by her side. "Everyone knows she and Jackie had a tense relationship. It was old news in town."

"Sure."

"Don't act all casual, Honey. I saw the look in your eye. I want to make sure you don't go jumping to any conclusions."

"I said I'd stay out of it."

"Yes, the same way your father told me he didn't eat the last scoop of my marshmallow-flavored ice cream last Tuesday."

"Translation?"

"You both told a big fat lie. That clear enough?"

I passed her a plate of chocolate chip cookies. "Here, chew on these, Mom."

She sat up and took a bite of a cookie, then set the plate down on the coffee table. Murray grumbled and slid off the couch. "Think about it, Honey. If Becka was going to take over Jackie's show, then Jackie would've had a motive for murder. Not the other way around."

I dropped back into the armchair next to Mom. *Dang.* She was right. Becka was the winner. No reason to murder her sister, then. I'm not sure how Mom knew it, but the thought had crossed my mind while we'd been downstairs catching up. I just wasn't ready to admit it.

Mom was way ahead of me. Becka murdering Jackie would be literal overkill. A mixture of relief and guilt passed through me. "I agree."

Mom took a bite of her cookie. "Good. Any other theories?"

"Not at the moment. Nothing I'd put money on." I thought of Billy, Rob, and Grant. But the thought of unpacking all that right now was way more than my brain could do.

"Keep me posted," she said. "I have some pretty good resources of my own."

"The LLC?"

"Darntootin."

"I'll keep that in mind."

We decided to keep things light for the rest of the afternoon. Mom wanted to do some shopping. We took our time going to all her favorite local shops, including the pet shop where Murray was treated to two new collars and a bright blue spring coat. Next, we went to the grocery store to stock up on a few essentials since Mom hadn't even been home yet.

For dinner we picked up some take-out, choosing spicy Thai noodles and a green curry that we brought back to my place to share. We ate quickly then took Murray out with his new sweater on. After getting lots of attention and pets from passerby, all three of us were ready to finally chill out.

"Movie time?" I asked, flopping onto the sofa.

"Definitely." She poured two tall glasses of water and settled in next to me. "I have two requirements. Hot men on the TV and buttery popcorn within reach."

"I think I can handle that."

I made the popcorn while Mom pulled up the recent releases on Netflix. We settled on a cheesy action movie, complete with the required hot male lead. He rode a motorcycle, which didn't impress me, but Mom loved it, so I kept my opinion to myself.

"Don't you just love when he revves that engine? Mm-mm. He should've won an Oscar with that performance."

"Sure Mom. Spielberg's taking notes."

She looked closer at the screen and pointed. "Is that the one with all the chest hair?"

My phone pinged during the movie, but I turned it to silent without taking a peek. It was Mom time.

179

When the movie ended, she let out a big yawn. "Should I bring over some fresh strawberries tomorrow?"

I stretched my arms over my head. "For breakfast?"

She clicked her tongue. "Your sallow complexion needs serious treatment time before filming."

I steered her towards the door. "I'm suddenly feeling exhausted. I'll just meet you at the studio tomorrow."

"Book me some time on the weekend. I'll bring an entire cucumber and send those bags packing."

"Bye, Mom."

She swatted at me before putting her heels on and air-kissing me goodbye. "I'm going to drive in with Marilyn. Don't stay up watching too much reality TV."

"Love you, too."

I watched her drive away before shutting off the TV, deciding to take her advice. I got ready to crash, then plugged my phone in for the night.

It blinked. One unread message. Should I bother? *Absolutely not.* It blinked again. Who was I kidding? I turned it over to check the message.

My breath caught. It was sent an hour ago from an unknown number.

Emily, it's Billy. If you want to know what happened to Jackie, come by my shop at midnight. Alone.

Crap. Without thinking it through, I texted back. **Why?**

The texts disappeared off my phone as if they'd never existed. Billy must've deleted the messages. I looked at the time. It was nearly midnight now.

My heart raced. What should I do? If I called Noah, Billy would deny he sent it. Noah would believe me, but I'd lose the opportunity to find out what the biker knew.

Fitz. He'd come, no questions asked. That's what Ride & Die friends were all about. There was no time to mull it over. My gut told me to go. Logic might've disagreed, but it was too late. I had to find out. I put Murray's leash on and ran out the door.

Murray and I peeled out of the parking lot in under a minute. I slid my fingers across the keyboard of my phone to alert Fitz, then dropped it on the seat next to me. A pingback told me he'd replied. No need to read it. He'd be there.

I flew by Milligan's Pub. The last bar with the latest hours and the roughest crowd. Still packed. The place Billy would most likely be if he wasn't waiting to unload his guilty conscience.

A small voice inside me asked what I hoped to achieve by meeting a man who was in the most-likely-to-have-murdered-Jackie category. No idea. Yet, as Traitor Rob (as I now referred to him) pointed out, curiosity was my weakness. Billy wanted to see me, and I wanted to know why.

Besides, Becka trusted him. And I trusted her. Didn't I?

Glancing at Murray soothed my nerves. "I'm glad you're with me. My burly bodyguard." He leaned over and licked my face. A bark would've seemed more appropriate for a guard dog, but I'd take what I could get.

Before I knew it, we'd arrived. Fitz hadn't. *Should I wait?* I glanced at my watch. Twelve-oh-two. No time. He'd be here soon enough.

I scanned the area. The lights were off. I parked by the gas pump, as if I needed to fill up. If anyone saw me, I could say I hadn't realized it was closed. Even though it was dark. And silent. And terrifying. *And illogical.*

I shut off the engine and tiptoed out of the Jeep. I snatched my phone and shoved it into my pocket. Murray hopped down beside me and stuck close, sensing my hesitation. The place looked different at night. More run down than I'd noticed before. Shingles were missing from the siding, the roofline was crooked, and large patches of weeds grew where there once was a garden.

Silence surrounded me. This doesn't feel right. *Am I in danger?* I tried to swallow my fear. I couldn't swallow. That was it. Time to bail. Fitz wasn't here, and I wasn't safe. I turned to go.

Then I heard a sound. I froze. My eyes shifted to Murray. He'd heard it, too. His ears were pricked up at full attention as if on guard for what was next. My mouth went dry.

Another sound. It was louder this time. A faint muffle, coming from behind a row of parked cars. Murray bolted toward the noise. Hadn't anticipated that. I suddenly felt very alone.

"Murray," I hissed. "Get back here."

My attempts were futile. He was too busy barking his head off to follow a command. If we survived this, he was going right back to dog school.

Frustration pushed past my fear. *This is ridiculous. I'm standing here like clickbait for a killer.* With clenched fists, I cut my losses and stomped toward the building ahead. Enough games.

It was narrow and long and doubled as both a gas station and a service center. A closed sign was posted right above the handle, yet, when I turned it, the door was unlocked. I opened it a crack and peered in. A sliver of light emerged from under the closed door of the back office.

"Hello?" I whispered. "Billy?"

There was no response. Decades-old stale cigarette smoke lingered in the air. The front entrance was small, furnished with a worn vinyl chair and a dark linoleum countertop supporting an ancient cash register and a box of candy bars for sale.

I waited for a minute, then raised my voice. "It's Emily. You messaged me?"

No response. I drew a breath and entered. There was a hinged section of the beat-up countertop that served as an entrance to the back. I lifted it up and slipped through.

I broke the silence with a swift knock on the door. Nothing. I tried again. Zippo. What kind of game was Billy playing with me? I'd had it. *One...Two...Three.* With a quick inhale of breath, I turned the handle and ushered the door open.

A rush of cold air hit me. A back door to the parking lot stood ajar. Had he gone outside? I scanned the room. An old wood lamp with a warm amber glow sat on top of a big desk, with scattered papers strewn across it.

My focus snagged on a black leather office chair faced away from me. The crown of someone's head chaffed the top. Alarm bells drilled in my head.

Run! I didn't. *Run!* I couldn't.

"Billy?" I whispered.

He didn't move. *Maybe he fell asleep.*

My heart pounded. A little louder. "Billy?"

Nothing.

I moved to the side of the desk and peered around the chair.

That's when I saw his face. I couldn't move. Neither could he. His eyes were open. But in between them was a hole. Billy Bones had been shot in the head.

Chapter Thirty-One

Shockwaves of panic zinged through my body. I grabbed his wrist to check for a pulse, just in case. He was still warm, but there was no sign of life. Fear gripped me as I reached into my pocket and pulled out my phone. Should've done this as soon as I got the first text. Too late now. Noah would understand, or he wouldn't. All I cared about now was hearing his voice, whether he was angry at me or not.

I was about to dial when my phone rang. I almost leapt through the ceiling. *Fitz.*

"Where are you?" *I hissed.*

"At the bike shop," he shot back. "Where are you?"

I turned away from Billy and frowned. Uh-oh. "What are you doing there?" The righteousness in my voice had eased.

"You said to meet you here. I thought you were in trouble. I ran. Like, all the way. And now my lungs are on fire, and you're not even here." It was his turn to sound put out.

I glanced down at my phone and scrolled back to my last text. It read: *meet me at bikes.*

Fitz huffed impatiently. "Where are you?"

"Billy's. It was supposed to say Billy's."

There was a pause. "You're at the gas station?"

I squeezed my eyes shut. "Yeah, but I can't talk, Fitz."

"Why?"

I swallowed. "Billy's dead."

"What! Are you okay?"

"Yes, I mean no, but I'm not hurt. I'll call you back. I have to call Noah." I hung up without waiting for his reply. He'd forgive me.

I edged away from the desk and moved closer to the back exit to call Noah. He picked up on the second ring. "Emily?" His voice was gruff.

"Noah…" I swallowed. "It's Billy Bones. He's…" I couldn't bring myself to say it a second time.

"Where are you?" His voice now alert.

I willed myself to keep breathing. "At the G&R gas station, in the office."

"Are you hurt?"

"No, I'm fine. But Billy's dead."

There was clatter in the background. He switched me to speakerphone. "Are you there alone?"

"I think so—" my voice cracked, "I hope so—except Murray. He's with me."

"Okay," he said. "Hang up and call 9-1-1. Tell them where you are and that someone has died. They will dispatch a team of people who will be there within minutes to help. Then call me back. I will stay on the phone with you until I arrive in person. Do you understand?"

"Yes."

"Good. Hang up now and make the call. I'll be there soon."

"Okay. Bye."

I pressed end, then dialed 9-1-1. The operator answered, and I turned to look at Billy to give the most accurate information I could about his condition. His eyes haunted me. The sound of screeching tires pulled back. I lunged out the back door to see who'd arrived. My breath caught. Noah was here.

I blocked the beams of his headlights with one hand and waved with the other. He flew out of his car and hustled toward me, eyes darting left and right as he moved. I fought the urge to meet him halfway.

I swallowed a lump as he approached. "Hey."

"You okay?" His expression softened as he met my gaze.

I nodded. Murray appeared beside me. He sat at my feet and barked a greeting.

"Where's Billy?"

"Back here. Follow me."

I led him inside and pointed. Billy was still there, upright in his chair.

Noah showed no visible reaction. "What happened?"

Deep breath. "Billy messaged me, asked me to come by here. He said he had something to tell me about Jackie's death."

Noah frowned but said nothing.

I continued. "When I arrived, it was quiet. I went through the customer entrance, but no one was there, so I carried on to the back. That's when I found him and phoned you."

"Did you touch him?"

"On his wrist. There was no pulse, but he was still warm."

His eyes probed mine. "Did you see anyone else?"

"No."

"How did you get blood on your pants?"

I looked down. My white leggings had a smear across the thigh. My mind raced back. I stared at Murray. He sat calmly by my side. I gently brushed my hand across Murray's nose. When I turned it over, there was blood. I stared at it for a second as the reality sunk in. My mouth went dry.

"Emily?"

I held my hand up to show him.

He met my gaze. "It's okay." He reached over and squeezed my arm, then reached into his jacket. "Give me a second here. I'm going to take a sample, then we'll get you cleaned up, okay?"

I nodded as the sound of sirens grew louder in the distance. Noah put a glove on and swabbed my pants, then wiped the blood from my hand on a white tissue. He put the sample in a plastic bag he'd pulled out of his jacket.

I'd never wanted to undress so badly. I refrained. This was not the way I'd envisioned taking my pants off in front of Noah for the first time.

He led me back outside as the rest of the EMS team arrived. A squad car came first, followed by an ambulance.

Noah led me to a nearby picnic table, most likely where gas station employees took their breaks. We sat next to each other on the tabletop.

It was time to officially go over what happened. I detailed everything I could remember, starting with the disappearing text.

"How did you know it was Billy?" Noah asked. I didn't have Billy's phone number stored on my phone and I couldn't remember the number it had come in from.

"He identified himself on the message."

"So it could've been from anyone."

A shiver went up my spine. Why hadn't I thought of that?

"There's something you should know," Noah said. The solemn tone in his voice told me it wasn't good news.

"What is it?" I asked.

"Billy gave me permission to swab his bumper."

"You had it tested?"

He nodded.

"Did they find traces of blood?"

"Yes." I froze, unable to breathe. "But it wasn't Jackie's," he added.

"What do you mean? Whose was it then?"

"It's not a who, it's a what." He waited a beat. "Emily, the sample tested positive for raccoon blood. That means…"

I shook my head. "He didn't kill Jackie after all. You were right."

"It was good to clear his name, so there was no doubt."

"That means either Billy sent me that text and the real killer found out, or it wasn't Billy, and I was lured here by the real killer."

"There's a third possibility."

I frowned. "What's that?"

"I wasn't going to tell you, but at this point, I think you need to know."

I searched his face. "What is it?"

He sniffed. "Billy was a police informant."

I drew back. "Since when?"

"He felt abandoned by the club when they encouraged him to take the rap for something he didn't do. He started working with us after his release. It's possible the bike club found out and killed him because of it." Noah said.

My mind was spinning. "So his death could be a coincidence?" I didn't know what to think anymore.

"Given the text sent to you, biker involvement is unlikely," Noah said. "But I'm not ready to dismiss the possibility. Working with us had its risks."

"But what about his car? It was right next to where Jackie was killed."

"Billy knew more than he was letting on about Jackie's death," he said. "He'd been avoiding me. As soon as I saw that photo with his car, I figured it was that. I tested his bumper to make sure he wasn't lying to me."

"So, if he didn't kill her, whoever did wasn't keen on him sharing his knowledge."

Noah stood up. "The last time I saw Billy alive, I pressed him hard. Maybe he was ready to talk."

I stopped short of asking my final question. If it was Billy who had texted, why would he tell me and not him?

There was no point in asking. If Noah had an answer, he wasn't going to share it. After going through everything again in an official statement, I was beat. Fitz arrived just in time. Noah updated him on the night's events, then said he could escort me home once they dusted my hands for gunpowder residue. Fitz said he'd drive me to the station and then take me home. I wasn't about to argue the point. I didn't want to be alone. He followed me home. I parked the car and dropped Murray off before getting into Fitz's car and heading to the station.

It felt like we were there for days, but it was probably closer to an hour. A uniformed officer guided me through the procedure and took my clothes for analysis. When we were done, Fitz took me home again. I tried to assure him that I was fine, but he wasn't buying my tough act. He insisted on crashing for the night. We agreed to a quick snack before hitting the hay.

After settling on almond milk and a box of cookies I kept in the freezer for emergencies, we finally sat down. It was time for a session of Q & A, Fitz style. He didn't mince words when he had something to say.

"Something has been bothering me, and I haven't been able to shake it."

"What is it?" I asked through a mouthful of muffin.

"You hid something from me on your computer the other day, a message from someone. What was it?"

When Fitz and I were looking at the photo I'd been sent earlier, I skimmed over a nasty message I received to spare him some from worry. There had been a few of them. With everything going on, I'd forgotten. I let my head drop against the cushion and looked at him. "Why are you asking me about that? It's just another troll."

"Someone lured you into a dangerous situation tonight. With a message."

"Totally different." Internet trolls didn't have much effect on me anymore. I shrugged. "One has nothing to do with the other."

"Indulge me. You're doing your amateur sleuth thing. Let me do mine."

"Fair enough." I didn't move, instead making grabby hands toward my laptop sitting up on my island. Fitz picked it up and passed it to me. I pulled up the direct messages in my account.

Fuzz buckets. Three similar messages, all from the same sender. They were signed *Anonymouse*. Although I'd read them before, I hadn't paid any attention. It never occurred to me that threshold could be crossed.

"This isn't good, Em."

"Let's not jump to conclusions. Coincidences happen."

Fitz grabbed my computer. He began typing away like a mad scientist. Full of focus and intensity. When he finished, a grim expression crossed his face. "I think this is a legitimate threat."

I got up from my chair and sank beside him on the couch to see what he was looking at on my laptop. "What makes you so sure?"

He'd gone into the admin section of my website, where I posted my blog. "Let me show you." Fitz was a techie. Although never having done it professionally, he designed and managed all of my web stuff as well as the cafés.

"See here?" he pointed to the screen. "When I set up your website, I encoded it with software to track online visitors' IP addresses when they leave a message."

"Why?"

"My dad and brother are cops. Cyber protection seemed important. With a public persona, I thought you should have some knowledge of who's visiting your site."

"Okay, I get it. So what did you find out?"

He ran a hand through his hair. "The messages came mostly from one IP address."

"And that's important?"

"In this case, it is."

"Okay, so we'll ask Noah to track where they were sent from."

"We don't need Noah's help to find out where they originated. I can tell you that right now."

"How?"

"Because it's mine. I recognize the IP number. Whoever sent those threats sent them from the café."

Chapter Thirty-Two

L ess than twenty-four hours after finding out someone might really want to hurt me, I knocked at the familiar studio doors of WKRZ. The security guard opened the door with a yawn, looking like she may have just awoken from a nap. *If someone comes after me, can I rely on her to protect me?*

Now wasn't the time to think about it. All my worries about safety and murder and everything else that had gone wrong in the last few days had to be packed into pretty little boxes and shoved into the back of my mind.

It was time to focus on the upcoming show, *Friday Night Nostalgia.* Luckily, I'd already written up a number of ideas and questions last week that I wanted to talk about in our pre-production meeting today. While most movies were accessible online or, at the very minimum, on a streaming service, WKRZ had made a deal with a big production company of light mysteries and romantic comedies. They had exclusive rights to the content shown on their channel.

Mom and Marilyn Myers came up with the idea of having a Friday night movie show featuring the two of us. They agreed viewers would like the idea of Mom and me introducing each film with a recipe segment shown halfway through the movie. The recipe would be available on my Instagram feed beforehand in case eager viewers wanted to prepare the goodies to enjoy with the show. It was a good tie-in with my social media, which I appreciated.

While I hesitated at the idea of doing any sort of TV show at first, part of me worried that it could actually hurt my reputation as an influencer since few people under the age of forty even had cable TV. However, Mom convinced me that it would be a good bonding experience for us, it could expand my audience, and it would be a lot of fun. I'd agreed to it after approaching the idea with my clothing sponsor. They'd welcomed the idea with enthusiasm, even offering to sponsor the show. They'd launched a new cruise-line wear and thought Mom would be a perfect fit for the branding, aimed at a slightly older market.

I exited the elevator and entered the studio space. The receptionist directed me to a nearby room. It looked as if the meeting had already begun. I was five minutes early, so there must've been a meeting prior to my arrival. The producer, Simone Murray, stood up as I entered the room.

With all the big stuff sorted out, today was the day to discuss last-minute details for the show. Although we wouldn't be filming until next week, the last minute still allowed for a week in case we hit any snags. The script, hair & makeup, recipe, and camera shots were all on the list of things to go over. The episodes would be filmed in my apartment, so it would feel like an authentic Girls-Night-In. A simple but tight shoot. Three segments, two minutes each.

"There she is," Simone said. "Good to see you, Emily."

Simone was sitting at a conference table with my hiking buddy/producer, Vera Hansen, make-up artist and stylist extraordinaire, Alexa Kelly, and co-host of the show, Mom.

I smiled. "It's good to be seen. How's everyone doing?"

Vera beamed at me, both hands waving. "Hi! This is going to be so fun."

Alexa was the next to pipe in. We'd often collaborated on our social media platforms, our strengths complementing each other. "I've got a vision board you'll love," she gushed.

"Remember, we're not going glam on this one. It's a girls' night *in*."

She saluted me. "Ay ay, Captain. We're swapping the glitter for glimmer."

"Sounds perfect."

The last one to speak was Mom.

I sat down next to her and patted her knee. "Hiya."

She smiled at me. "Hi, hon."

"Emily," Simone said, "We have a good handle on how we're going to do the show. We're just here to flesh out a few details. Filming at your apartment comes with a few added complexities."

It was nice to see Simone was as organized as she appeared. A former producer on Jackie's show, Simone was one of many staff members who'd transferred to other projects within the last six months.

"How's the mood around here?" I asked. Jackie took up a lot of space. No doubt her absence would be felt.

"Honestly? We're all doing just fine," Simone said.

Alexa nodded. "Jackie was awful to work with."

"Leaving her show was the best gift I could've given myself," Simone added. "The woman was a nightmare. The stuff I had to deal with was ridiculous."

"I've heard it was pretty bad."

"Cattiness, tantrums, personal vendettas," Simone said. "You name it, she did it."

"Anything in particular stand out?" I hadn't planned on getting into this, but here we were. Why not see where it goes?

"So many stories, so little time."

"Just one?"

"Sure," she said. "My favorite features a pretty young production assistant and a spoonful of sugar."

My eyebrows shot up. "I'm almost scared to ask."

"The kid was late for work. Jackie was so mad she grabbed a packet of sugar from the coffee room and poured it in the gas pipe of her car."

My eyes widened. "No."

"Yup. Nothing happened. The next time she was late, Jackie tried again. That time, she dumped a lot more—apparently close to a whole bag. By the time the mechanic figured what the problem was, she'd run out of funds and had to sell the car."

"That's outrageous," I said.

"Uh-huh," Simone said. "I wouldn't have believed it if Jackie hadn't bragged about it. Then she fired the poor girl after her bus was delayed."

"Seriously?!" I said. "How could she get away with it?"

"No one ratted her out," Alexa said. "Fear of Jackie's wrath kept mouths shut."

"Very true. Now, let's get back to your show," Simone said. "A show we're all excited about."

Everyone agreed, and we moved on. Simone suggested we start with the styling element so I brought out my phone to share photos of the outfit sent by my sponsor. It was a pair of high-waisted jeans with a soft-pink button-up shirt. Mom loved the dress picked out for her, a floral shift dress that complimented her rosy glow. From there, it was easy to come up with a consensus on hair and makeup that would match the mood. I'd already told my online followers we were making my no-bake almond butter chocolate cookies. The final detail was conversation topics. Brainstorming ensued, with no shortage of topics to discuss. We agreed to a few pop culture faves and called it a day.

We were saying our goodbyes when the door opened, and camera operator Merle Fisher walked in. Jackie's former henchman. I wasn't happy to see him. No one else looked happy either, including Merle himself. He looked more disheveled today with a longer beard and a t-shirt with red food stains down the front, resembling splotches from a ketchup bottle.

"Looks like I'll be your camera dude on this project." He gave an unconvincing smile and sunk into an empty seat at the far end of the room.

I exchanged a look with Vera. "I thought Owen was assigned to the show."

Owen Taylor was a camera operator and one of the café regulars who kept Fitz up to date on studio gossip.

He shrugged. "There's been a last-minute change. It came from the suits upstairs."

"Any reason why?" Simone asked.

"You'd have to ask them. I just say yes, sir, and do what I'm told."

I had a guess. Becka probably didn't like or trust the guy so she passed him off onto us.

Simone offered Merle a copy of her notes. "This might help you to get a feel for *Friday Night Nostalgia*."

He waved them away. "Email them to me. I'll take a look at home. I've done shots like this before. I'll kill it."

His tone was condescending, but not quite rude.

"I'll send them to you first thing tomorrow," Simone said.

"Great." He slapped his knees and heaved himself out of the seat. "We done here?"

Simone nodded. "It's been a long day for everyone."

He grumbled something under his breath about payback. Should I be paying more attention? Considering his relationship with Jackie, he may have insight into who'd want her dead.

"I'm sorry for your loss," I offered. "I meant to say that last time I saw you. I know you and Jackie were close."

He scoffed. "Whoever told you that is way behind the times."

I looked to the others for confirmation. Wide eyes and subtle nods all around. "Sorry, I brought it up," I told Merle.

He grunted in response, sauntering out of the room. He slammed the door behind him.

I turned to the others. "Was it something I said?"

Simone cleared her throat. "She and Merle had a falling out."

Vera nodded. "Last week, I walked into a heated argument between them."

"About what?" I asked.

Vera shrugged.

"Jackie tried to have him fired," Simone informed us.

My eyebrows shot up. "Why?"

Simone and Alexa exchanged a look.

"I was under the impression they were thick as thieves," I said.

Simone shook her head. "Not after she turned down his son for a job."

"An unpaid internship, if you can believe it," Alexa said.

"Ouch," I said. "That must've stung."

"I bet," Alexa said. "Merle asked Jackie if his son could intern with the production team so he could get a feel for the industry. Jackie refused, telling Merle that she was never given a handout and he should be ashamed of himself for even asking. Merle was offended. He'd stood by her side for years, assuming loyalty went both ways. He was wrong."

"Went so far as to threaten Jackie," Simone said. "Said she'd reap what she sowed."

I looked at Vera to verify the story. She nodded. "Don't worry about him, Em. He's a little rough around the edges but always gets the job done."

"I'll take your word for it."

My only question was whether his last job was ending Jackie's life.

Chapter Thirty-Three

The meeting left me with more questions than answers. For example, did Merle murder Jackie? And how would Billy fit in if Merle was the killer?

Once Merle left, we wrapped it up quickly, agreeing to meet on the day of the shoot at my apartment two hours before we were going on air. Simone and Alexa were needed on other projects, and Vera left to go find Becka.

"Ready to go, Mom?"

"I better visit the ladies' room before being shaken around like a ragdoll in that jeep of yours."

I'd long ago given up defending my vehicle of choice, recognizing Mom and I would never see eye-to-eye on the issue.

"Okey dokey. I'll wait right here."

As she exited the room, an engine revved loudly outside. Curiosity drew me to the window. I had a soft spot for anything that would automatically drive my mother nuts. Ah-ha. Down below, a Harley Davidson purred loudly. More interesting than that was its driver, Merle Fisher.

There was the tie between Billy and Merle. Motorcycles.

Mom returned, and she and I left together. She'd driven to the station with Marilyn, but now Marilyn was tied up in meetings. All the way back, Mom talked excitedly about the show. I sat quietly and tried to listen. But all I could think about was going home to call Noah. I wanted to update him on what I'd learned.

* * *

Half an hour later, I lay on my couch and dialed Noah's number. He was prompt at returning calls, so I decided to close my eyes and wait. It might be the perfect time to sneak in a cat nap.

My nose woke up first. It twitched at the smell of pancakes. When I sat up, I found Fitz in the kitchen, cooking. He must've stopped by to check on me and decided I was in need of a hot meal.

He passed me a perfect latte. "Good afternoon, sleepyhead."

"Waking up to a hot guy making me food? Good doesn't begin to cut it."

"Too bad this hot guy has an ulterior motive," he said, gesturing toward himself with both thumbs.

"No, no, no. You can't bring me up just to tear me down."

He ignored my plea. "You need a babysitter because you meddled in a murder, and now someone is threatening to kill you."

I opened my mouth to argue, then shut it. Was that really true?

Fitz turned back to the stove. He flipped a pancake on the grill. "I only started cooking because I couldn't stand listening to your snoring any longer."

"I don't snore, Fitz. I'm a lady."

He grinned at me. "A lady that could cut down a forest the way she saws logs."

"You're a dream killer, you know that? If you weren't such a great cook, I'd ask you to leave. Lucky for you, my pride is on a downward trajectory, and my morals are consistently weak."

Another flip. "Judging by the crap in your fridge, I'd say you've hit rock bottom. Luckily for you, I have all the key ingredients nearby."

I wiped the corner of my mouth to stop a line of drool from slipping out as I took in the scent of vanilla with a hint of bananas and maple syrup. Murray barked, assuming he'd be getting some, too. A puddle of drool sat beneath his lolling tongue. Were we twinsies?

"Good thing you two are cute," Fitz said. Confirmation I didn't need.

Within a few minutes, he'd doled out the food. I munched every last morsel, using a knife and fork in a very well-mannered fashion. Unlike Murray. Downed a whole pancake in one big gulp.

Fitz headed back to work, and I lay back down with Murray at my feet.

Before I'd even digested the first morsel, my phone rang. It was a blocked number. *No.* It continued to ring, refusing to be ignored.

Eventually, I groaned and reached over to pick it up. "Hello?"

"Em, it's me." Becka. Her voice was strained.

"Are you okay?" There was a lot of background noise so it was hard to hear her. I pushed the phone closer to my ear in an effort to hear her better.

Her voice cracked. "Billy's dead. I don't know what to do."

I rubbed a hand over my face. *What a nightmare.* "Why don't I come over?"

"I'm at the police station," she said, her breathing shallow. "Noah came to get me at the studio earlier, and now I'm stuck."

I leapt to my feet. "I'll pick you up."

"You sure?"

"Of course. Give me five minutes."

She agreed and hung up. Guess that explained Noah not calling me back right away. I shoved a last bite of a leftover pancake into my mouth as I got my shoes on, then grabbed my phone and rushed out the door.

Fitz was sitting at our booth with his laptop out, looking very boss-like, when I entered the café. "Crunching numbers?"

He looked surprised to see me. "Whoa, whoa, whoa. Where are you off to in such a rush? I thought you'd be in a carb-induced coma for at least another hour."

"Becka called. I'm going to get her at the police station."

"Poor thing," Fitz said. "She must be a wreck right now. First her sister and now Billy."

He was right. Everyone closest to her was suddenly gone. I wondered how she'd react when she learned I'd been the one who found Billy, too. Maybe she already knew, and that's why she called me instead of Vera to pick her up.

Fitz closed his laptop and pushed a cup of steaming tea aside. "I'll come with you."

I shook my head. "Any chance you could take Murray out for a walk instead?"

"Of course. My legs could use a good stretch." He got up and studied my face. "You going to be okay?"

"Yeah," I said with a nod. "I just feel bad for Becka."

He squeezed my shoulder. "Good luck."

"Thanks."

I had the feeling I was going to need it.

Chapter Thirty-Four

Billy's death wasn't common knowledge yet in town, evident by the fact I hadn't yet heard his name whispered inside the cafe as I passed through. But it wouldn't be long before word was out. Rumors in Eliot Hill spread faster than a California wildfire.

I pulled up in front of the police station to pick up Becka within fifteen minutes, but it still felt like I'd taken too long. Anxiety filled me as I exited the Jeep and caught sight of Becka sitting on the steps outside the building, looking tense. Shoulders hunched, eyes cast down, and fists clenched; there was no doubt she was feeling overwhelmed.

She looked up as I called her name.

"Hey," I said, rushing up to meet her. "Sorry to keep you waiting."

Dark circles hung low under her eyes. "Didn't notice. I'm a little out of it."

"Want me to take you home?"

She nodded. "Noah offered me a ride but I couldn't face being alone right now. You can stay for a while, right?"

"Of course." Poor thing. "I'm glad you called."

It was a five-minute drive back to her house. She lived in a cozy bungalow once shared with her mom and sister. It was a modest place with white siding and a small wooden porch.

Becka led the way past the porch swing and pulled open the creaky screen door. She put her key in the door and ushered me inside, flipping on the lights as she followed. Becka had recently renovated the kitchen and taken out a few walls, so the space was mostly open concept, with two bedrooms and one bathroom down the hall. While she got us each a glass of water, I took a look at the photos she'd hung on the wall. There were some classics. She and Jackie as kids on top of the Eiffel Tower, her and Vera, standing in front of a castle, and one of Billy on a big motorcycle with her straddling him on the back. That had to be the Grand Canyon. My eyes lingered on it. She looked so happy and relaxed.

Becka set the glasses down on the coffee table, then slumped onto the oversized gray corduroy couch, rubbing her face with her hands. I joined her, waiting quietly until she was ready to talk.

She finally leaned back and looked at me. "What am I going to do?"

I sighed. "You're going to take one day at a time. You've been through a terrible ordeal."

"I feel so all alone now."

"You and Billy had grown pretty close, huh?"

"Yeah, I thought he was my person. He'd practically moved in." I didn't see any of his stuff lying around. Maybe he was a clean freak.

"You must be feeling overwhelmed right now."

"It's bizarre. It was late. We were watching TV when he got an alert. Something at the shop set off the security alarm."

So Billy wasn't the one who texted me. Had he interrupted the murderers' plan? A rush of cold went through me. He may have saved my life. "Why didn't he call the police?"

"Billy?" She huffed. "He didn't trust cops."

If she and Billy were so close, why wouldn't he have told her he'd begun to work with Noah?

"It wasn't the first time it had been set off," she added, as if sensing my skepticism.

I frowned. Bikers might've killed Billy after finding out he'd been working with the cops. There might even be multiple murderers at play. Was the timing of his and Jackie's deaths a mere coincidence? If Billy's alarm had gone off before, maybe this wasn't the first time his former club associates had made a play for his life.

Becka waved her hand in front of my face, snapping me out of a spiral. "Nothing sinister, Em." She must've sensed my alarm and confusion. She

202

leaned forward. "There was a rodent issue."

"Did he have a hidden stash of cheese?"

"Mice set off the alarm by chewing on the wires," she explained with a raised eyebrow. "Happened three times over the last few weeks. He'd assumed it was just that again."

Ahhh, right. That made sense, too. I was starting to understand how a seasoned biker might've ended up dead. "Billy was totally unprepared."

"He hadn't even bothered to put his beer in the fridge. Left it half drunk on the coffee table."

If what Becka said was true, Billy Bones never stood a chance. He was ambushed.

"I called him a few times. He didn't answer. I figured he was chasing mice or got caught up in paperwork. Then I fell asleep. Next thing I knew there was a knock at my door. It was Noah. He told me Billy was dead and asked me to come in for questioning."

If I'd had any doubt before, I didn't now. Becka didn't know Billy was an informant. Was it a trust issue? Did she trust him more than he trusted her? And why did Noah ask her to come in for questioning first thing? Was Becka on Noah's radar?

"What can I do to help?" I asked.

"Nothing." She dropped her head back on the couch. "I don't even know why I called you."

"You needed a friend? You had questions for me? I can help with both."

She looked confused. "Why would I have questions for you?"

"Because I'm the one who found him."

A deep flush filled her face, and she glared at me. "What do you mean?" Guess Noah hadn't mentioned that detail. Her tone was icy.

"Uh…"

"It was almost midnight. What were you doing at his shop?"

"I got a message. It was from Billy, or from someone pretending to be him. The message said he had information about Jackie's death."

She bolted upright. "Are you kidding me? You're still running around like some sort of amateur detective?" Her eyes narrowed. "Or is there more to it? Maybe Noah should start looking into *your* alibi. We all know Fitz would cover for you no matter what. Then again, Noah probably would, too."

A flash of anger surged inside me. "Stop it, Becka. You know I was only trying to help."

"What gives you the right? You should've stayed out of it!" With a shaky finger, she pointed to the door. "Get out."

I got to my feet. "I'm sorry."

Rage shone in her eyes; fists balled up at her side. "Get out," she repeated.

Heart racing, I scrambled outside. A shadow neared the window, and I knew her eyes were on me. A shiver went up my spine as I drove away without looking back.

Feelings of shame and regret coursed through me as I sped down the street, having no idea where I was headed. *Is she right? Did I take things too far?* I was too ashamed to go home and face Fitz. He had warned me to take a step back.

Was it my fault Billy was dead? If I'd called Noah when the message originally came in, could he have intercepted the intruder and saved Billy? Or would Noah be dead now, too?

I drove north, up the mountain, as more questions filled my head. I had to know whether Billy had been lured to his shop. If so, did it mean I was a pawn in the killer's game. Had I been played, manipulated, strung along like a fool?

There was a rest stop up ahead. I pulled into it and parked, willing myself to simmer down.

It was time to change my strategy. I may not be a hero, but I was no villain either. I didn't deserve to feel shame and guilt and regret. No more apologies.

It was time to beat the killer at his own game.

My phone lay on the seat next to me. I grabbed it and dialed Fitz.

"Em? Where are you?" His voice sounded strained.

"Sorry, rough day."

"Are you still at Becka's?"

"No, I'm on my way home." I paused. "We need to talk."

CHAPTER THIRTY-FOUR

"Okay. You on your way back?"

I chewed on my thumbnail. "I don't think Billy surprised the killer. I think the whole thing was planned. Me going there, finding Billy like that…"

"Come home and fill me in. I've got to get my order done in the next fifteen minutes to meet the deadline for next week. I'll finish up and be all ears by the time you arrive."

"Great, thanks." I got back onto the road with a renewed sense of purpose. It hit me then that I had been a help, not a hindrance, to the investigation. The killer murdered Billy before I'd arrived. It was not my fault he was dead. I wasn't going to let guilt determine my actions going forward. Finding the truth was my goal and I would not stop because Becka or anyone else told me I should.

The phone rang as I approached home. Fitz was usually a cool cat. But he was concerned about me. I could hear it in his voice. "I'm two minutes away, you worry wart."

"Really?" A deep voice said. *That's not Fitz.*

I held the phone out. "Who is this?"

"It's me, Rob."

I hesitated to respond. He was the last person on earth I wanted to talk to now, or maybe ever.

"Please." His normal jocular tone had vanished; in its place was strain and stress. "You've got to help me. I'm in trouble. Can you come by the shop?"

I needed to think this through. Rob had duped me for years. He'd been a bad guy all along and I never saw it. Then again, his shop was literally one minute from my current position. And he sounded desperate. That vulnerability could lead to answers.

"Be right there," I said.

He hung up without saying goodbye.

Chapter Thirty-Five

L uck was on my side. A parking spot was available right in front of the bike shop. I pulled in and hopped out. Fitz was waiting for me across the street. Hopefully, he wouldn't notice I'd made a pitstop, especially here. If he did, he'd punish me with weak coffee for a month. *Better make this quick.* I approached the store and noticed the closed sign was hung, and the lights were dimmed. Weird. I knocked on the reflective window, then pressed my forehead against the glass to get a better look.

My breath caught in my throat. I drew back. Rob was peeking out as I was peeking in. A loud click made me jump. The door opened, and he pulled me in. He slammed it again, peering out the slats of the blinds. Another click. Did he just lock me in?

"Anyone see you come in here?" he demanded.

I forced a smile. Time to play it cool. "I have no idea. Worried about your reputation?"

He began to pace around the room but said nothing. I watched in silence until I couldn't take it. "Rob, what's going on?"

He paused to look at me. "The cops are coming to get me. Noah will be here any minute."

I narrowed my eyes. "Why?"

He moved closer. "They think it was me."

"Slow down." I swallowed.

He invaded my space, so close I could feel the warmth of his breath. "You've got to help me. I was set up. Whoever did this is playing us."

I blinked. *Us?* "I don't understand."

"Last night. I was there."

"Where?" I demanded.

"At Billy's shop. I saw you arrive. Your dog came and sniffed me out."

My heart stopped. "What are you saying?"

Our eyes locked.

I couldn't breathe. "Why were you hiding?"

"I wasn't hiding," he almost shouted.

I flinched.

"The thing is, I'd just seen Billy with a bullet in his head." He pressed his fingers to the bridge of his nose and shut his eyes. "When you got there, I was doubled over behind a car trying to stop myself from getting sick. I wasn't exactly in a position to socialize."

This wasn't a confession. Good. "What *were* you doing at Billy's shop that late?"

He shook his head. "Good question. Same one I went to ask Billy. Only I couldn't, could I?"

"I can't help you if you go on the defense every time I ask a question."

He dropped his head like a dog being scolded. "You're right. I'm sorry. Billy sent me a message, telling me to come by the shop. Said it was urgent. What choice did I have?"

None of this made sense. "Did you even know Billy?"

"Sort of. Jackie had a love/hate thing for the guy. And before you ask, I have absolutely no idea why, okay? The guy seemed sketchy to me. Anyway, I care about her so I brought my car into the shop and tried to chat him up, find out what was going on between them."

Between *them*? Rob wasn't making sense. Jackie hated bikers. And Becka was dating Billy, not Jackie. "You don't believe me, do you?" Rob said. Before I could respond, he slammed his fist into the wall. "This is bull—"

Anger bubbled up inside me. "Stop it." I didn't have the patience for one of his testosterone-fueled tantrums. "You need to calm down. We'll sort this out."

"I don't have time, Em. Don't you get it? Whoever killed Billy set me up. Set us both up."

Another 'us.' I braced myself. "Why are you including me in your theory?"

He whipped around to face me. "I'm going to guess that you didn't just happen to go to Billy's shop last night, either."

He had a point. "Okay."

"I think whoever wants me to go down for this murder must have killed Billy and then lured me there to set me up. Obviously, you were part of it, too. Noah called me half an hour ago and asked where I was around midnight. I wouldn't answer the question. But why did he come straight to me? He must've been tipped off. By the real killer, I'm guessing."

His theory seemed complicated and outlandish, yet I wasn't ready to dismiss it. Too much of what he was saying made sense. "So you think I was sent there to find you at the scene of the murder. When I didn't, someone sent Noah an anonymous tip this morning?"

"Exactly."

One big sticking point sprung to mind. "If you weren't involved, then why did you have blood on you?"

He looked away.

"Blood, Rob. When Murray sniffed you out, his nose came into contact with blood. How did he get it?"

His shoulders sagged. "I didn't even notice it on my pants until I got home. I must've come into contact with it when I leaned on Billy's desk to steady myself."

He'd always been woozy before over the sight of blood. When the Red Cross came to our high school during a donation blitz, he was the first to volunteer. Also, the first to pass out. He got teased about it for weeks. "That might help prove your innocence. Noah's going to find out you were there. Let him analyze your pants. My guess is it'll prove you didn't do it."

His face went beet red. "I knew I should've called you earlier."

"What did you do with the pants? You still have them, right?"

"I burned them in my backyard."

"Tell me you're kidding."

He looked like he was about to punch the wall again. I held my hand up to stop him. "Listen, it's not the end of the world. Think about it. If what you're saying is true, there's still a hole in the supposed mastermind's plan. Motive, Rob. You have no motive."

He groaned. "I guess Noah isn't keeping you in the loop."

My stomach dropped. "What do you mean?"

He took a deep breath. "Jackie and I had a fight the day she was killed. Noah latched onto that and is gunning for me."

If Rob was right, Noah had to have a reason. "What did you fight about?"

"Grant Henshaw and I both proposed. She chose him."

Rob had never been a gracious loser. Was jealousy at the heart of these murders? He could be playing me. Maybe Rob was the one who'd sent me the text last night from Billy's phone. If so, Rob would know what it had said. Was this all an elaborate scheme to create an alibi for himself? Maybe he thought he could manipulate me. That I'd back up his story and cause enough doubt to muddy the waters, making it impossible to arrest him.

"Em? Em! Did you hear me?"

I flushed. "Sorry, lost in my thoughts for a minute."

"It doesn't matter anymore. The point is that Noah is going to twist my words around and use them against me."

One thing I knew for certain: Rob always liked to play the good guy. The problem? He didn't always fit the part. "I don't know what to think, Rob. This is so out of control. Lots of people had a beef with Jackie. Tell me specifically why you think Noah is targeting you instead of anyone else."

He rubbed the back of his neck. "I was upset when Jackie chose that weasel old man. We hadn't been broken up that long, you know? I thought I could win her back. So I proposed. Then *he* proposed, too. Right after I did. Like, seriously, right after."

"I got that. What are you leaving out?"

"The day Jackie was killed is the day I found out about their engagement. Up until then, she didn't seem to know where her head was at. One day, I thought she wanted to be with me, the next day Grant; after that I thought she might chuck us both and take off with a biker." He shut his eyes and raked his hands through his hair before taking a breath and holding my gaze. "She posted a photo on her social media with the engagement ring on her hand. She didn't even tell me first."

Did he get the irony here? He was complaining about Jackie doing to him what he'd done to me. No courtesy call. No tough conversation. No respect. Of course, he'd done it to me on live TV, but the basics were the same.

Part of me wanted to call him out. That he'd finally understood how I'd felt.

For a brief moment, I reveled in the idea. Give props to karma. Then I saw the pain on his face. The dark circles, the red-rimmed eyes, the sadness.

There was nothing to celebrate here. In this case, actions led to murder. Had Jackie played with fire and gotten burned? I let go of the past for good and moved on.

I softened my tone. "Tell me what you did when you found out."

"After I saw the photo, I went to the studio and confronted her. We argued, and it got a little heated. Someone called security, and I was ejected."

I nodded. "That must've been a tough moment."

"It was humiliating. Some superstrength security lady literally threw me out the back door onto the parking lot."

"And then?"

He looked down at his shoes. "In a fit of anger, I slashed her back tires."

"You did *what?*"

"Good old Grant had bought her this flashy new car a week earlier, and it was the first thing I saw after peeling my face off the pavement. It was like a stab to the heart. I punctured holes in the back tires. It was supposed to be symbolic. I couldn't stand the thought of Jackie driving off into the sunset with that creep."

"That's pretty aggro."

"Not my best moment."

If Jackie had two flat tires, she would've had to get her car towed to the only repair shop in town owned by Billy. "What happened after that?"

"I took off back to the store, finished work, and drove up the mountain. I parked my car and went for a long bike ride from there. I never saw her again."

The bike ride that placed him near the scene of Jackie's murder. Means, motive, opportunity.

A firm knock on the door ended our conversation. Rob stalked over and peeked out.

"This is it." He swallowed. "Will you help me?"

Another knock. With no time to think, I nodded. "I'll try."

"Rob, open up," a muffled yet familiar voice stated.

Rob dropped his head back, closed his eyes, and said a little prayer. He then took a breath and swung open the door.

Standing before him was Noah in his uniform, a grim look on his face. "Hey. Can I come in?"

Rob fanned out his hand. Noah entered.

He was about to say something when my phone pinged. His head whipped around, and his eyes met mine. "Emily?"

Feeling caught, I tried to pass off a confident smile. "Hey." I waved. "I was just leaving."

Both men stood back as I approached the exit.

"I'll call you when I'm done," Rob said.

"Okay," I said. "See you later, Noah."

He turned away with a nod. "Sure."

I left the shop feeling more confused than ever. As I walked back to the jeep, my heart sank as I heard the first snippet of conversation between the men.

"Listen," Noah said to Rob. "I need you to come down to the station."

The door shut before I could hear Rob's response. But it didn't take a detective to read the room. Rob had been right. He was going to be arrested for murder.

Chapter Thirty-Six

Tourists and locals scooted around me as I stood in the middle of the sidewalk, processing what had happened. My phone pinged. I pulled it up to read the screen. A new text from Fitz.

Fitz: Where are you?

Me: Be there in thirty seconds.

I hopped back in the Jeep and pulled out of the parking spot. I waited for a break in traffic, then raced across the street. I pulled into the driveway and parked the Jeep in the back. I rested my forehead on the steering wheel while I gathered my thoughts.

If Fitz saw where I'd been, he'd have questions. I couldn't blame him. I had questions, too.

One repeated in my head. Could Rob be a cold-blooded killer? Even with all the recent revelations, I wasn't convinced. Slashing tires was an aggressive move, but he was humiliated and heartbroken. He'd lashed out. That was a far cry from murder.

Then again, he'd lied to me before, and I'd bought every word. I needed to go inside and talk this through with Fitz. In spite of the fact he didn't like or trust Rob, he was fair and logical. He would be the voice of reason.

I grabbed my phone and dashed inside. The air was electric. People were still buzzing with the news that Jackie's death had been ruled a homicide. For a second, I had the urge to run back to the Jeep and take off. Instead, I stuck close to the narrow hallway and peered inside the noisy café. So many people. Could I face a slew of gossip and rumors? Maybe I should run upstairs and send Fitz a text, asking him to join me there. *Shoot.* Fitz was sitting in our booth with Vera. She wore a red and white polka dot collared jacket with matching lipstick and glowing skin, and she was too perky to process right now. Ugh. A bad mood set in like a flash flood. That's it. I'd rather stick forks in my eyes than rally up the strength to chit-chat about the show, or dog photos, or why Becka had thrown me out of her house. Time to skulk upstairs and hide.

"Emily," Fitz called out with a wave. He must've been keeping an eye out for me. I hunched over and pointed upstairs, hoping he'd accept my weasel ways and let me go.

No such luck. Either he didn't pick up on my bad mood, or he chose to ignore it. He called my name again, louder this time. Vera cranked her head around to see me and waved.

I tried to smile back, but it may have come out as more of a grimace. She didn't seem to notice, leaning over the table to whisper something to Fitz.

Fitz nodded, listening intently to her words, ignoring the icy glare I was sending his way. As I approached the pair, he turned his gaze on me. "You're late. I was getting worried."

I dropped into the booth like a rock. "Hi, you two."

Vera smiled. Fitz raised an eyebrow. "Get lost on the way?"

I squirmed a little in my seat. "Sorry, I had a pit stop to make."

"Where?"

I'd hoped we could have a private conversation. But what choice did I have? "I popped over to the bike shop."

His expression tightened. "Rob's shop?"

"It's the only one in town."

"Last time we talked about this, I'm pretty sure we agreed that wasn't a friendship worth rekindling."

"He called me, okay? I wanted to hear him out."

Before Fitz could protest, Vera interrupted by putting up a hand. "Hold on, here. Are you talking about the same Rob who dated Jackie?"

I scoffed. "The one and only."

"Yikes." Her long, perfect hair fell over her shoulders. "That guy is the worst. I used to think he was pretty cute until the other day. He came by the studio and lost it on Jackie. By the time he left, she looked pretty shaken up."

Rob hadn't described the argument quite like that. He'd left out the fact that Jackie had been scared.

I rallied myself and sat up straighter. "What was he upset about?" I'd heard it from Rob but wanted to confirm his story.

"Their breakup? Grant Henshaw? I don't remember exactly what was said, but it was pretty clear he wasn't happy Jackie had chosen someone else."

Fitz frowned. "What day was that?"

"Friday, I think?" Her eyes widened. "Wait, that's the same day she…she… died." The last word came out in a whisper, her face going pale.

"Did you tell the police about it?" Fitz asked.

"I'd forgotten about it. But the police were at the studio this morning. I'm sure someone would've mentioned it. It wasn't exactly on the down low."

The implication made me uneasy. "Rob told me he wasn't a fan of Jackie's new romance or her choice of suitors."

Vera raised her eyebrows. "I get the impression you feel sorry for Rob. Or, you like Rob?"

"Yeah, I'm getting the same feeling," Fitz said with a biting tone. "C'mon Em. Don't let him manipulate you again."

Maybe Fitz was right. There were so many strikes against him. Why couldn't I accept the facts? Probably because under all that ego was a not-terrible person. Even in spite of what he'd done to me. There wasn't any malice. At least, I didn't think so.

I rested my palms on the table. "Listen, Rob is a selfish blockhead, and he can be a goof, but I can't see him planning out a murder."

Fitz looked angry. "Maybe that's because you didn't witness your best friend humiliated the way I did." He stood to ensure he wouldn't have to listen to my rebuttal. "Maybe this time he won't get away with it. Excuse me."

Fitz extricated himself from the booth and stomped off to the small private office he never used, locking the door behind him. I wasn't sure if I'd ever seen him that angry before, at least that angry at me.

Part of me wanted to go talk to him, but the other part—the sensible part—knew he needed time to cool off. It never occurred to me that what I went through would have had so much effect on him. Had our situations been reversed, however, I would have a hate on for Rob, too. Maybe I wasn't looking at things from the right perspective.

"Whoa," Vera said. "That was intense."

I sat back again and sighed. "Sorry about that. Sometimes, I'm a jerk without realizing it until it's too late."

Vera reached across and squeezed my wrist. "You hit a sore spot, that's all. He just needs a few minutes."

"Maybe."

She searched my face. "Not a fan?"

"He never forgave Rob for cheating on me with Jackie or humiliating me on live TV."

"I can see why. What a jerk."

"Pretty much," I agreed.

"Guess it's true what they say. Once a dog, always a dog. No offense to Murray."

She was right. What had Noah said? Behavior dictates character. Something like that. Dealing with this mess was starting to get to me.

It didn't seem to affect Vera. She looked as flawless as ever. "Can I ask you something?"

She raised an eyebrow. "Isn't that what you do? Ask questions?"

"Can't argue that," I said, feeling my cheeks warm. "How did you keep your cool on set when Jackie targeted you? It sounds like she was pretty awful."

"True. I'll admit she wasn't my favorite person. But there aren't a lot of options around here to work in television. If I allowed her to bait me, it could've been the end of my career. Remember, I'm from the pageant world, where cattiness reigns. And I dated her boyfriend, so I'm not completely innocent. Besides, I wasn't her only victim. There were lots of us."

"Had she been worse lately?"

Her cheeks expanded, and she blew out a breath. "Definitely. She knew the end was coming. She was out for blood."

215

"What do you mean?"

She closed her eyes for an extended second. "Shoot. I shouldn't have mentioned that."

"I know there was talk about replacing Jackie before she died."

She searched my face. "Becka told you about her plan?"

Ah-ha. Now we were getting somewhere. "The plan to take over as host?"

"Exactly. Audiences were beginning to turn on Jackie. I'm sure even Grant knew there was nothing she could do to save her job. The Larissa Banks thing was the final straw. Becka decided enough was enough, and no one disagreed."

"Right," I said.

Larissa Banks was the name of a struggling actress who'd been killed by an ex-boyfriend a few months earlier. He'd thrown her off a cliff. Jackie made an off-color joke about the manner in which she died, referencing a game show host she'd dated in the past who called down contestants from the audience with his signature line, *"Take a leap and join the fun."* It was insensitive and cruel by all accounts.

"Making light of domestic violence crossed a line," Vera said. "After that, Becka came up with a plan. The show was getting more complaints daily. Jackie wanted us to hide it from Mitch Myers. Even convinced Grant to help. It probably wasn't that hard to do at first since the email went straight to the show's inbox. But emails were flooding into the show demanding she get fired. Becka knew something had to be done. When she asked if I'd assist, I didn't hesitate. We put together a presentation for Mr. Myers on why Becka should replace Jackie as host."

"Did anyone else know?"

She nodded. "Everyone knew. The entire crew. Everyone but Grant. It might sound awful to an outsider, but if we didn't get rid of Jackie, we knew our jobs would be on the line. We all agreed to work together and save the show."

Collective mutiny. Huh. Jackie knew about Becka. Did she know the entire crew supported the idea? If so, what did she say?

My guess? Just one thing. Over my dead body.

Chapter Thirty-Seven

Vera's watch pinged. "That's work," she said. "I better go." With so many changes at the station, the whole staff was on call around the clock. We exited the booth and walked to the entrance. I turned to face her. "Thanks for filling me in about what's been going on. I hate being in the dark."

"Any time." She gave me a quick hug before she strode out the door. "Talk to you soon."

I marched back to the booth and picked up our dishes, returning them to the nearby counter. With Fitz still locked in his office, I decided to go home instead of sticking around. Now was not the time to argue over Rob. There were more important priorities I had to consider. Specifically, the implications of what Vera told me. Becka and Jackie ran hot and cold, but if what Vera said was true, it meant Becka betrayed Jackie.

Or was I being too harsh? If Becka planned to take over a show that might otherwise be canceled, was it fair to think of it as stealing? There were a lot of jobs on the line saved by a continuation of the show regardless of who was in front of the camera. Did that justify Becka's actions?

I stomped up the steps, Murray at my heels. "You'd never let me down, would you?"

With a wag of the tail, I knew the answer. I unlocked the door and grabbed the nearby bag of treats. I flung one in the air, and Murray leapt up to catch it. Satisfied, he padded inside toward his water dish. I took my shoes off and flopped onto the couch.

My mind drifted back to Becka. I couldn't get past her disloyalty to Jackie.

If Becka had planned to take over the show behind her sister's back, she wasn't the person I thought I knew. The bigger question was whether she was also capable of murder. It was a stretch, but I couldn't dismiss the possibility.

Then again, there was the simple logic of Mom's argument that it didn't make sense for Becka to kill Jackie. She'd accomplished her goal. The green light had been given. Becka would be the new host of *The Morning Dish*. That was her end game. Period. Hence, no motive to kill Jackie. She'd already won.

Unless there was more to it. Becka left out some key details when she told me about the show. Maybe there was more I didn't know.

Marilyn said the decision had been made to replace Jackie recently. Before her death, the original announcement had been planned for this week. If she thought it was inevitable, what would Jackie have done to even out the score? No way she'd have gone quietly. With nothing to lose, Jackie would've been out for blood. Sister vs. sister can get ugly. Who hasn't seen an epic fight between the Kardashians? But there's no coming back from murder. No follow-up episode that features love and forgiveness. Does the Jackie and Becka story end in tragedy?

Maybe...however, like Mom said, this was all backwards. The show meant everything to Jackie. And if Jackie had found out, I could absolutely envision her killing Becka. So could it have been turned around? What could push it further? The rev of a motorcycle broke through my thoughts, and it hit me. *Billy Bones.* Rob had made some offhand comment about Jackie hooking up with a biker. I thought it was a joke. Maybe not. Was there any better way for Jackie to even the score with Becka by sleeping with her boyfriend? I could envision Jackie saying to Becka, "You took my job, so I took your man." I rubbed my hands over my face. Had I been watching too much Bravo TV? Doing such a reckless act would sever her relationship with Becka for good and likely end her recent engagement to Grant Henshaw. Would Jackie have risked it all and sunk that low?

My heart began to race as I sat up. My hand flew to my phone, and I fired off a text.

Me: We need to talk
Noah: Important? I'm busy
Me: I hope not, but I think it might be
Noah: Should I come to the café?
Me: My place is better
Noah: See you soon

A few minutes later there was a knock at the door. The corner of my mouth tugged up. *Hope he's not that fast in all his pursuits.* Murray barked as if chiding me, and I felt my face flush. "Inappropriate. You're right."

"One sec," I yelled as I grabbed my phone and hopped off the stool. I paused to take a quick look in the mirror and brush back my curls.

"That was fast," I shouted through the door. As I turned the knob, I continued to talk. "You're not going to believe what I—"

I froze. *Fishnuggets.*

Standing in front of me was Becka. Murray approached with a wagging tail and a bark.

I forced a smile. "Hey." A flush filled my cheeks.

She bent down to give Murray a good rub before meeting my eyes. "Hi."

We stood there looking at each other for a few seconds.

She scratched her nose. "Can I come in?"

"Yeah, sure." I opened the door wider.

She shuffled inside. Murray sat at her feet. The smell of exhaust fumes hung in the air. Becka wore black leather pants and a light pink moto jacket hung from her left hand. She fidgeted with one of the buttons on the sleeve. The simple black turtleneck and Doc Marten boots she wore for hiking were the only familiar items I was used to seeing her in. This was a very different look for Becka.

I pretended not to notice. Mom's voice echoed in my head. *Stick to the weather, Honey.* "Cold out there?"

"Not bad."

"I've got a bottle of rosé in the fridge. Want a glass?"

"No, thanks. I'm driving…or riding, I guess."

When I frowned at her, she gazed at herself in the mirror and then at me.

"Isn't it obvious I've got motorcycle gear on?"

I shook my head. "I'm already in the doghouse. I thought I'd keep my thoughts to myself." *Especially those involving murder.*

She grinned. "The outfit was an early birthday present from Billy. He was teaching me to ride a motorcycle. Leather pants protect my legs from the exhaust pipe, and the jacket has a built-in spine protector."

My eyebrows shot up. "Wow. I had no idea such things existed."

"Neither did I." On any other day, I would've demanded to try the jacket on and marveled at the cuteness of the edgy fashion.

But not today. Instead, I grabbed out the wine and twisted off the screw cap.

She hunkered down on the stool. "I rode my bike here."

I poured myself a glass of wine and took a sip while I studied her. "A motorcycle?"

"It's a Harley Davidson Sportster. Billy chose it. But I'm not experienced enough to drive on a busy road, so I parked on a side street and walked."

"Makes sense." As long as it wasn't so, she could kill me and not be seen. I pushed away the wine. Better stay alert.

Murray barked and stood by his bowl. I shifted around the island to give him some food. Whether or not it was dinnertime, I could see he was going to win this argument. Murray's food was kept in the closet near the door. After filling his dish and putting the mega bag safely away, I turned back toward Becka. I noticed on the back of her new jacket was a local biker logo patch.

"Did you join a biker gang, too?" The words were out before I'd thought them through.

She stiffened and glanced over her shoulder. "It's a club. Big difference."

"I thought Billy was out."

"He was, but after he died, one of the members came by to pay their respects. When they saw I'd taken up riding, they offered me a spot in their club."

"I assumed there was bad blood between those guys and Billy."

"Just the opposite. It's no secret Billy went to prison. According to them, he respected their oath and kept his mouth shut. And before you ask, I don't know what that means, and I actually don't care."

Her tone told me that line of questioning was done. I entered the kitchen and faced her again. I forced a smile, no clue as to what to say next.

Becka drummed her fingers on the island. She seemed different than earlier. An awkward silence hung in the air. I pretended to tidy up while she fussed over Murray, who'd finished his food and sat nearby.

I stole a sideways glance at her. Did I really know her? I'd *known* her for years, but deep down, I couldn't say if she was a good person. I didn't even know if she was my friend.

Murray followed me into the living room. I invited her to sit down on the couch. We settled into seats across from each other. Fatigue began to set in, and my impatience grew. I couldn't wait any longer. I had to know. "Why are you here, Becka?"

She fidgeted with the zipper of her jacket. "After you left my place this morning, I swore I never wanted to see you again. It took me about twenty minutes to realize that wasn't fair. I shouldn't have lashed out at you. I came here to apologize. I'm sorry."

Had I not found out about her actions before Jackie died, I would've eaten up her words like they were a chocolate sundae with rainbow sprinkles. But I couldn't let go of her willingness to go behind her sister's back to steal her show, whether it was justified or not. I simply didn't trust her.

"Don't worry about it," I said. But it's not what I meant. I sat and wondered how long I could stand to stay silent before I asked if she killed her only sister.

Chapter Thirty-Eight

A slew of barks from the street caught Murray's attention. He shot up, bumped the coffee table, and raced out the balcony door. He stood on the balcony to check out the commotion below, then joined in the noise. In his haste, he knocked over a half-drunk tea from earlier. I sprung up and ran into the kitchen to grab a towel. As I mopped up the mess, I smiled. *Message received, Murray. It's time to spill the tea.* I couldn't agree more.

"Need help?" Becka asked.

"Nah, it's fine. If something isn't fastened down in this place, it's guaranteed to take a tumble. It's Murray's superpower."

She glanced toward the window. "What's got him so excited? Everything okay out front?"

"It's probably the local dog walker," I assured her. "She takes three out at a time. Chances are they ran into a furry friend, causing all four to start yapping. It becomes a contest. Who can bark the loudest and the proudest."

The corners of Becka's mouth turned up. "Sounds like Milligan's Tavern on a Saturday night."

I snorted. "Pretty close. Gets every pooch going in a two-block vicinity." I marched across the room and swung the patio door open. Murray didn't even look my way, too focused on the dogs below and getting his two cents in. "Murball," I said in a sharp tone. He turned to look at me. With an outstretched arm, I made a sweeping gesture with my hand. "Get inside."

Murray whined but followed instructions. Once inside, I latched the door behind him and pointed to his bed. "Go lie down."

Instead of listening to me, he skulked over to Becka and wormed his way under her feet.

Sad puppy dog eyes met mine as he lay his head down on the floor. I shook my head. "Alright, knock it off."

He knew I couldn't stay mad at him when he did that. I rolled my eyes at Becka. "The cheek."

She smiled. "He's good."

"Yeah, and he knows it."

I picked up the soiled cloth and the empty cup and brought them to the sink before I sat back down. Becka and I started to speak at exactly the same time. "You go ahead."

"Thanks." Becka straightened up. "I just wanted to apologize again. I guess I don't know what else to say."

With suspicions fresh in my mind, I was still skeptical about the sincerity of her words. Then again, maybe I was way off. She'd lost the two most important people in her life. The question was whether she was responsible for their deaths. I had to stay open-minded to find out.

"It's fine," I assured her. "Your emotions are raw. I get that. But I wish you had told me about the show."

"I know." She took a sip of tea. "The thing is, I wanted to tell you, but I couldn't. I signed a nondisclosure agreement."

It felt like a flimsy excuse, considering the entire crew knew, but she could hardly be blamed for the rumor mill.

"When did you decide to do it?" Vera had told me, but I wanted to see if Becka's story matched.

She shifted in her seat. "I thought about it a long time before I did anything. But audiences had turned on Jackie. People were sick of her cruelty. I'm sure you can understand."

I couldn't argue that.

She went on. "Someone on set said Mitch and Marilyn Myers might cancel the show. Grant had helped to streamline things, but it wasn't enough, and no one, including him, could reign her in. Jackie had gone too far and begun to jeopardize sponsorship deals. If advertisers pulled out, the station could be at risk."

"So you decided to step in."

Her jaw clenched. "I put my time in and deserved a shot."

I nodded. "But it was *your* idea?"

"Everything happened so organically. I don't remember."

"Didn't you just sign the nondisclosure agreement?"

"That was a few months ago. I called Marilyn first to feel it out. She and I had always gotten along. Mitch didn't do anything without Marilyn's knowledge or approval. It had to stay hush-hush, even before we knew if it would happen."

"Didn't you feel any loyalty to Jackie?"

"Do you want me to lie?" Becka laughed. "My sister lived in her own bubble. She didn't care about anyone else, not the targets of her cruel jokes, not the writers or the crew, and certainly not me."

A-ha. This is it. The heart, the key, the missing piece.

"Jackie was always self-involved."

She shifted her gaze to the window, her expression hardening. "It got worse."

"What happened?"

"Some L.A. bigwigs came by a few years ago on break from a local shoot. Rumors swirled that Jackie had a chance at national syndication. I never knew whether to believe it or not, but she sure did."

I didn't need to ask how Jackie felt about that. From local to national? It would've put her on the path to becoming an A-list celebrity, including all the glitz and glamour she loved. "That's a big opportunity."

"Yup." She pressed her lips together. "Which makes the disappointment all the more difficult to accept when it never happens."

"They didn't like the show?"

"From what I heard, they only came out of curiosity. I don't think they were ever really interested, but she always had stars in her eyes. There were no meetings, no calls to ask for a reel. Jackie was convinced her best shot to get their attention back was to push the envelope. Be louder, more outrageous. It was a mistake. She began alienating her guests, even celebrities, who she only got in the first place because they were filming nearby."

"That's not good."

Becka shrugged. "Jackie missed the mark. She read the room wrong. The offers to syndicate her show never came. She blamed everyone except herself."

How very Jackie-esque of her. "Is that why the crew started quitting?"

She nodded. "A few months ago, Mitch told her to smarten up. Ego surpassed sense. She became intolerable to deal with. No one could stand the working conditions and began to leave their jobs in a mass exodus."

Ah-ha. Things were beginning to make sense. "So you decided to step in."

"Something needed to be done. I called Marilyn, and we talked. She encouraged me to be the showrunner. 'Now's your chance,' she'd said."

It was no secret Marilyn Myers had never been a huge fan of Jackie's show, finding her mean-girl antics immature and distasteful. So it didn't surprise me she'd supported Becka's idea when the opportunity arose. And Marilyn was a strong ally. Smart play by Becka. "You proposed a switcheroo."

"Vera and I worked our butts off to put together some ideas for a better show. Marilyn set up a secret meeting that only included me, her, and Mitch."

"Did you play up the sister vs. sister angle?"

Her cheeks flushed as she nodded. "Audiences love a good catfight, especially when sibling rivalry comes into play."

"In the promos, they could highlight her mean streak and sell you as the angelic one. The good sister wins out, and people forget you stole her show."

"*Saved* the show. But you're right. It wouldn't be hard to spin it that way."

"Audiences would cheer you on," I said.

"All we had to do was let Jackie self-destruct."

I couldn't decide if I was more impressed or disappointed. It wasn't exactly heart-warming. Did one sister's bad behavior justify another's?

Becka continued. "Mitch liked the idea. But he wanted time to think about it. I signed a nondisclosure and gave him time to think it over. After some time, I found out it was going ahead."

"And when Jackie found out?"

"She was furious. But I'd become so used to her verbal abuse it barely fazed me."

"Had it become that bad?"

She huffed. "Oh yeah. My subpar work quality, my slutty best friend, my criminal boyfriend—"

She stopped when she saw my face, drawn back in horror. "That's awful, Becka. I'm sorry."

"When you're used to being pummeled every day, it becomes part of the routine."

I'd thought Jackie had moved past that. Since I'd agreed to become a semi-regular guest, Jackie had actually become almost civil. I'd assumed most of her on-air rantings were just part of the schtick. "What happened when you told her?"

She licked her lips. "She came at me like a shark, baring her teeth, ready to attack. When I asked what I'd done wrong this time, she actually lunged at me. That's when I knew she'd found out. Someone stepped between us. The last thing she said to me was that I'd be sorry."

"Were you worried?"

"Honestly? It was one of the best moments of my life."

I'd been taught to surround myself with people who brought out the best in me. Hearing the bitter tone in Becka's voice reminded me why. Obviously, Jackie brought out the worst in Becka. Exactly how low did she go?

Time to keep pushing. I had to know. "What happened after that?"

With a casual shrug, her dark demeanor lifted. "Nothing. Jackie saw I'd won. She was going to move on."

Hold the chocolate sauce. "Are you telling me she raised the white flag and handed you the reins?"

"Not quite that simple. Like I said, she was mad. But I'd learned to tune her out. The last I heard before her passing was she'd planned to move to L.A. with Grant Henshaw."

Not so fast. I'd never known Jackie to back down without a fight. To start with a battle over her career and her dignity? No flipping way.

Becka was lying. Part of me wanted to argue. Another part of me wanted to run. There was only one reason I could think of for her to lie. It didn't fit the nice girl narrative she wanted to sell.

That's when I knew. Becka Hunter murdered her sister.

Chapter Thirty-Nine

At that moment, I remembered why I'd kept most people at arm's length. Fitz. It was his idea to accept Becka's offer to join me on my hikes. He was glad I'd found a few people to walk with so I wouldn't be alone in the woods. I told him I didn't want to "expand my horizons" by forming more friendships in the real world. I already had him. A true blue bestie. Who else did I need? Besides, online friendships were much less troublesome. And now I had proof.

Well, now I *needed* proof. And then I'd tell him I told him so.

Becka had taken the only thing Jackie ever truly loved. Her show. What would she have done when she found out her own sister had betrayed her and stolen it? Could it have been enough to make Becka avenge her revenge? Had murder put an end to the rivalry for good? I'd bet my bottom dollar the answer was yes. No one can outshine you when they're dead.

Before I could figure out a plan of action, Becka stood up.

"I've got to go. We start filming the new show next week, and there's a ton that still needs to be sorted out. Are we okay?"

I stood up, too. "Yeah, of course." *Other than you may have killed your sister.*

We left the apartment and headed downstairs. Becka waved goodbye while I scanned the room for Fitz. He was sitting in our booth, focused on the screen in front of him.

I slipped in across from him and shut his laptop. "Do you still hate me?"

He looked at me and quirked an eyebrow. "That depends."

"On?"

"Whether I'll have to sit through another session of ra-ra Rob."

I lifted my hand. "I swear never to speak another good word about that ratbag."

"Fair enough, you're forgiven. Good thing, too. I'm dying for you to fill me in on what's going on with Becka. I saw her slip out."

I grinned. "You don't miss much, do you?"

He shook his head. "No."

I had to give him something. Telling him I suspected Becka of murder without somehow testing my theory didn't make sense. I stuck with something I knew would still pique his interest. "Becka joined Billy's old motorcycle club."

Fitz drew back, eyes wide. "Becka's a biker?"

"Why are you so surprised?"

"They only offer membership to people they trust completely. They've become more and more distrustful of outsiders. That means they didn't know Billy was working with Noah."

"Unless it's a front. They offered her membership to draw attention away from themselves."

"No way. They don't operate like that. Once you're in, you're in. We should let Noah know."

"He didn't seem to hold them high on the suspect list anyway."

"True... which reminds me, that grumpy camera guy, Merle Fisher. Did you say he and Jackie had a falling out?"

"Yeeeah, why?"

"He came in today for a coffee, and I noticed something on his jacket. Thought it might be important."

"What was it?"

"There was a cartoon mouse on the back riding a motorcycle. Pretty sure it was a biker logo, maybe a rival motorcycle club. I couldn't quite make out the name. The illustration made me think of the threats you've been getting."

"Anonymouse," I said. He was right. Merle didn't try to hide his animosity for Jackie.

"I don't really get the mouse thing," Fitz said.

"Me neither," I agreed. "Most mice aren't so mighty. What's wrong with a tiger or a bear?"

"Do you remember that old movie, *The Green Mile?*"

"The prison film?"

He nodded. "There was a mouse character in it. He was the only part of life that brought the prisoners joy."

"A little depressing. But you could be onto something. If the members see little joy in life, maybe they're prone to do things like try to scare an innocent influencer with some mean mouse threats."

"It's not funny. Someone murdered Jackie and doesn't like you poking around. Merle might be in a mouse club, but I doubt they're dealing in cheese."

"Okay, I understand. I'll be careful not to step on anyone's tail."

I thought about telling Fitz about my suspicions about Becka. But I didn't need to add to his list of concerns.

He glanced at his phone. "I sent Noah a note. He's going to look into Merle and the mouse connection."

"Thanks," I said. "That reminds me, he should be here soon. I texted him earlier asking him to come by."

"Good, maybe he'll have an update. In the meantime, I need to sort out my orders for next month. And I'm a little short-staffed today, so I have to stick around."

I stood up. "I'll leave you to it then."

"Good. Call me later."

"Of course."

I went back upstairs and threw a frozen pizza in the air fryer. While it cooked, I grabbed my laptop. No more messages. What a relief. A few minutes later, the scent of oozing cheese made my stomach rumble. I ate a few slices, then pulled up recent photos. With hundreds to choose from, it always took a while to pick the most suitable one for upcoming posts.

A knock on the door took me out of my zone. I opened it up and was glad to see Noah standing there. He handed me a small cardboard box. I opened it up and peeked inside. Hard to say whether the sight or scent of half a dozen mini cupcakes was more appealing.

"What's this for?" I asked, holding the sweet treats up to my nose.

"I've got a soft spot for them," Noah said. "I thought it might be rude to eat one in front of you."

"I'm not going to lie. It might've gotten ugly." I ushered him inside. He made himself at home, hunkering down on the closest stool.

"A tour bus just showed up downstairs, packed full of fans of some movie that shot here a few months back. Fitz's slammed, so I thought I'd wait a few minutes to grab us coffees."

Us. I liked the sound of that. Noah put his phone on the counter and popped an entire chocolate cupcake into his mouth. I shrugged and followed suit with a vanilla one.

"Don't worry about coffee," I told him, covering my mouth. The rush of sugar hit the spot. Why didn't I eat these more?

"There's a first." He brushed crumbs off his shirt. "Want to fill me in on why you called?"

I finished the cupcake and dabbed at the corners of my mouth to make sure there was no stray icing. "I found out a few things."

"I'm listening."

"First? Merle Fisher. Fitz said he talked to you, but I'm not sure if you knew he and Jackie had a fight not long before she died."

He looked impressed. "I heard the same thing. I'm working on it, but so far, I haven't learned much. He's not exactly the only staff member who didn't like her."

"Do any of them have a tattoo of a mouse on their forearm? It connects him to the threats I received from Anonymouse."

His eyes snapped up to meet mine. "Threats?" When I flushed, he pushed his plate away. "Emily, what threats?"

"I thought Fitz would've told you..."

"No," Noah said hoarsely. "He didn't mention it. Why hadn't you? And how many have there been?"

"I'm sorry. I didn't think they were serious." I filled him in. He listened intently, his jaw muscles flexing.

"At least I know now. Anonymous is not an easy word to spell. Let's not assume that's a clue. It may tell us no more than the killer is a poor speller."

He had a point. One I didn't like. Guess it was time to face the alternative. "What about Becka?"

His eyebrows shot up. "What about her?"

"I think she's lying to me."

He studied my face. "Tell me more."

I set my second cupcake down. My stomach was in knots. "Becka had been planning on taking over as host of *The Morning Dish* show for months. I think Jackie found out and did something to get her back."

"What did she do?"

"That part, I don't know. Yet. But whatever it was, I think Becka may have killed her for it." There. Done. I clasped my hands together and waited for his response.

"Sororicide is very rare. I don't see it in this case."

"Did you know she's recently joined Billy's old motorcycle club?"

"The club had no beef with Billy as far as I know. He was discreet, and they've kept their noses pretty clean, as of late. I'm not surprised they reached out to her, actually, and I'm pretty sure I saw her driving a motorcycle the other day, although she was a little wobbly. Hopefully, they'll help her improve her riding skills."

I opened my mouth to argue but shut it again. Obviously, he didn't agree with me. And I had no proof. There was nothing I could say.

"I'm close to making an arrest, Emily."

By the grim expression on his face, I knew who he meant. "Rob?"

"You know I can't tell you that. But we've come across some new evidence, and it only strengthens my theory."

"What evidence?"

Before he could answer, his phone pinged. It was Fitz.

He grabbed one more cupcake. "I'll be back."

I listened until his footsteps disappeared. A phone rang, making me jump. It had an unfamiliar tone. I reached for my mobile and looked at the screen. No incoming call. The ringing continued. My focus shifted. Another phone sat on the counter. Noah's mobile. He must've been distracted by the cupcakes and forgotten to take it with him. Easy mistake, but what if the call was important? After two more rings, I picked it up.

Before I could say hello, a deep voice spoke. "You were right, sir. Double lines mean pregnant."

Pregnant? Jesus Jones. I couldn't speak. In a panic, I pressed the *End Call* button. My heart raced, but I couldn't move. What had I just found out? The door swung open. It made me jump.

"Sorry," Noah said. "I should've knocked. I didn't mean to scare you."

"It's not that." My hands were shaking.

"What's wrong?"

His phone rang again. Eyebrows raised in surprise, he padded down his jacket. He must not have realized it wasn't with him. He bolted forward and reached across me to pick it up. "Warner here."

Noah nodded while he listened to the speaker. "No...wait—what?" He shot me a look. "Okay, thanks." He nodded into the phone. "Bye." He hung up and looked at me. "Deputy Johnson says he couldn't hear me last time he called, about a minute ago. Know anything about that?"

My face burned. "I'm sorry. I was going to identify myself, but he started talking before I could stop him."

He ran his hand through his hair. "Too late now."

I studied his face. "Was Jackie pregnant?"

He passed me my coffee and returned to his stool. "It'll be a while before we get the coroner's report."

"But you found a test—her test."

He took the lid off his cup and had a sip of coffee. Our eyes met. He didn't say a word. I knew the answer.

My stomach twisted. Things just felt a whole lot worse. Something wasn't making sense. What was it?

"Is Grant the father?"

"Listen, Emily—"

"Is this the new evidence? You think Rob killed Jackie because she was having Grant's baby?"

He cocked his head. "Jealousy is a strong motive."

I frowned. "And Billy? Why would Rob kill him?"

"You tell me," he said, taking a sip of coffee.

I took a deep breath. "Maybe Billy saw what happened, and it got him killed."

He shrugged. Yup. That was the theory.

Rob the Knob a double murderer? No. This didn't add up. I thought back to the visit with Grant. "Grant Henshaw didn't seem that broken up by Jackie's death. Understandable if they were on a rocky road. But if he lost an unborn child, wouldn't he be more emotional?"

Noah held up a hand as a signal for me to stop. "I don't disagree. Before you ask, I checked out his alibi. He was hosting a party, as you know. I have him on his home security video at 8:30 p.m. arguing with Jackie on his front porch as she stormed off."

"And that clears him?"

"Not necessarily. He disappeared from the party for the next twenty minutes or so by most accounts. He says he went into his bedroom to clear his head after the argument. I have multiple witnesses that back his alibi from then on."

"He could've done it."

"Technically, yes. But he'd have to be pretty cool-headed to kill his girlfriend and then host a party as if nothing was wrong."

"But not impossible."

"True. Though it does create reasonable doubt."

Anger bubbled up in me. "You're determined to arrest Rob then."

He pressed his lips together, causing a dimple to appear. He looked genuinely sorry. "I didn't want it to be true, either. But it's my job to follow facts."

"And ignore anything that doesn't fit into your theory."

He dropped his gaze to the floor and ran his hand through his hair. "I'm going to go now."

I marched to the door and flung it open. "Thanks for the dessert."

He strolled to the door. "Anytime." His eyes lingered on mine, then he left.

I threw the door closed, then flopped down on the couch. *Time to decompress.* I closed my eyes and pinched the bridge of my nose.

In the quiet, questions swirled around my mind. Was I wrong about Rob? Could he be a killer after all? Every time, I came to the same answer. *No, I don't think so.* There was still Merle and Grant. And especially Becka. I wasn't ready to give up on my theory about her. She was lying to me. There had to be a reason.

I needed to find out more about what went down between the sisters in the days leading up to the murder. There was only one person I could ask who might know the real story. It was time to give her a call.

Chapter Forty

Last time I saw Vera, she'd been called into work. I had to ensure she was alone when I asked her about Becka and Jackie's relationship. The only way to find out was to ask. I sent a text. She replied right away.

Me: Hey, you around?

Vera: Sure, what's up?

Me: Can you stop by? I have a question I need to ask you.

Vera: Can't now. Swamped.

I hesitated in my reply.

My phone rang. The sound made me jump. I glanced at the screen before answering. "Hey."

"Everything alright?" Vera said.

Was this a bad idea? I sighed. "Are you alone?"

"Yes." She sounded confused. "I left the studio. Fewer distractions at home. What's going on?"

It was risky to ask one best friend something about the other. But I didn't see any way around it. "Vera, I hate to ask, but I need this conversation to stay between us."

"Okay." She paused. "What is it? Is Becka okay?"

I closed my eyes. "I feel like she's not telling me the whole story about what happened between her and Jackie. I need to know what went down. If Noah finds out first, we can't protect her."

Vera was quiet for a minute. "Yeah, I got you. We need to help our friend. I also promised Becka I would take her secret to the grave."

So there was something. I knew it. "This is a matter of life and death, Vera. That counts, doesn't it?"

"Okay, look. It's been weighing on me anyway, so it'll be a relief to get it off my chest. But you didn't hear it from me."

"Deal," I said.

"Jackie found out months ago that Becka went behind her back to speak to Marilyn Myers. I think Merle found out and snitched. But Jackie didn't tell Becka she knew. Instead, she went after the one thing Becka couldn't control."

"What's that?"

"You mean, *who*? Jackie slept with Billy."

My stomach seized. *I knew it.* "That's awful."

"From what I understand, he turned her down at first, but…Jackie can be persuasive. When Becka was officially given *The Morning Dish* hosting gig, Jackie told Becka she'd been doing it with Billy every chance they got. Six ways to Sunday is the expression she used."

"No!"

"Yeah, exactly. Becka never saw it coming. She and Billy fought. Even broke up for a short time. Then he bought her a new motorcycle as an apology. I guess that was enough."

I was quiet.

"You still there?" Vera asked.

"Yeah. Did you know that Jackie was pregnant?"

"*What?!*" There was a shuffling in the background. My guess was Vera had dropped her phone. A second later, she was back. "Did I hear you right? Jackie was pregnant?"

"Noah found a pregnancy test at her place. It was positive. What if Billy was the father?"

"I don't know," she said quietly. "Maybe you should go see Grant. Ask him."

"You're right. He might be able to help sort this out." I was getting close. I could feel it.

"You better be quick," Vera said.

"Why?"

"Apparently, he's decided to speed up his plans. At least that's what Becka told me. He called her to let her know he was leaving for Los Angeles tomorrow in case she wanted any more of Jackie's stuff. If you want to talk to him, you better go right now."

She was right. It could be my only opportunity to find the truth. "Okay, I'll head over right away. Any chance you can come with me? Fitz is short-staffed right now."

"I wish I could. Sorry."

Would it be a mistake to confront him myself? No. I'd bring Murray. I'd be okay. "Okay, thanks, Vera. I better run."

"Let me know what happens."

"For sure." We said goodbye. I promised to call her after and let her know how it went.

Murray and I were out the door within minutes. I grabbed a hoodie and threw it on, then dialed Noah's mobile as I flew down the stairs. The call went straight to voicemail, so I left a clear message telling him where I was headed. No way I'd risk another mix-up. Downstairs, Fitz was swamped. I thought about filling him in, but there didn't seem to be time. Given that Grant Henshaw had made the decision to leave town so quickly, who was to say he wouldn't speed up the timeline? I couldn't risk missing the only person who might know the truth. Had he informed Noah of his hasty exit? Could it mean he was the real killer? So many questions, so little time. I waved at Fitz as I sailed through the crowded café. I'd have to fill him in once I returned.

It didn't take long to get to Mountaintop Lane. The sky was darkening, and a thin fog was moving over the dense tree line up the mountain. A waving hand drew my attention to the side of the road, where I saw a familiar figure standing by. Vera was next to her car, obviously relieved, as I pulled off the road to help. That's strange. Hadn't she told me she was swamped at work?

I pulled over and got out of the Jeep. "Hey, you okay?"

"Not exactly. I'm literally on empty. It didn't seem right to let you come out here alone. But I forgot how low I was on gas."

"Shoot. That's no good."

"Can you follow me to the dead end? I'll leave my car there and come with you to Grant's place. I'll come back for it after and coast down to the gas station on the remaining fumes."

"Sure, sounds good."

I returned to the Jeep and followed her to the dead end. I pulled in next to her and parked.

My watch said it was getting late, and a feeling of frustration rose up inside me. She exited her car, but instead of approaching mine, she waved me over. *What now?* I hopped out and marched over to her. I didn't bother to pause and zip up my hoodie despite the dropping temperature. Time trumped temperature in this case. "What's up?"

She glanced back at Murray. His ears perked up, and he barked. I waggled my finger. "Patience, Murr."

She jutted her chin out. "He locked in there?"

"No, I left the key on the seat. Why?"

"Windows shut?"

I shrugged. "Down an inch or so. It's a habit never to leave Murray without a little room to breathe. But these parts are known for rogue squirrels."

She ignored my joke, bent down, and reached into the side pocket of the driver seat.

Trying to tamper down my irritation, I took a deep breath. "Vera, we should really get moving."

When she stood back up, she had something tucked under her arm. "All set."

I frowned. "What did you forget?"

"You'll find out." That's when I saw a flash of shiny steel. The corners of her mouth slowly raised. Something about her expression turned me from chilly to ice cold. She brandished a big knife with serrated edges. "Say hello to my deadly friend."

I flinched. "What are you doing?"

Her lips curled up into a snarl. "Shut up. It's my turn to talk."

My gaze moved from her to the knife and back again. My throat went dry. Hers were the eyes of a killer. Cold, calculated, cruel. It was her. She'd killed Jackie, and Billy, and... Now me?

Chapter Forty-One

I twisted my head and locked eyes with Murray. My sight blurred as I thought about the possibility I'd never get to hug him again. I swallowed a lump in my throat and blinked back the tears. *I will not let that happen.* Then he began to bark. But it wasn't like his usual impatient, attention-seeking sound. It was fierce and angry and protective. He knew. And when I turned back to look at Vera, she grinned at the sound, unbothered by Murray's desperate need to help. "Useless mutt."

Rage filled me, and my hands balled up into fists. She pointed toward the bike path beyond the dead end, unlit and sinking into darkness. "Start walking."

I squared my shoulders, ready to fight. I knew from true crime podcasts and self-defense classes that allowing yourself to be moved to a second location was never good. "No."

"Get moving before I kill you right here, right now."

She drew the knife to my neck. With no other option, I dropped my head and started to move. Time to think this through. Should I run, or should I fight? No way she'd let me live. It was up to me to save myself.

Vera followed so close behind me I could smell the scent of her mango shampoo. "I should've taken care of you days ago, like I did Billy."

My heart pounded through my chest. This was a good start. If Vera was in the mood to talk, maybe she'd explain what happened and why. It might just give me enough time to formulate a plan. I kept my head down and my mouth shut.

She pressed the point of the knife into my back. "I thought with Rob's arrest, I'd be in the clear. Who knew you'd be so determined to save a guy who screwed you over? Bad move, Em. You should've let it go."

I glanced back at my Jeep. Murray stood at attention, his eyes on me.

"Vera, please."

She held the knife up. I turned away. He began to bark again. It was a message. Move, he was telling me. Run.

He's right. What am I waiting for? I was about to take off when there was a quick swoosh and a flash from behind. Heat swarmed my ankle. Then, searing pain.

Vera had made a nasty gash. I screamed in pain. There went that plan.

"Move," Vera commanded. "Or I'll shut you up for good."

I hobbled forward, heat, pain, blood, and fear pulsing through me. I shoved my hands in my pockets. My watch caught on the seam. *Of course.* There was an emergency feature. I could use it to call for help.

I slid my hand deeper into my pocket, trying to reach the other hand in without her noticing. Then it pinged. I scrambled to silence it. Too late. Vera jammed her hand into my pocket and pulled mine out. Effortlessly, she maneuvered the watch off my wrist.

"It's a notification. You got a message."

"I can put it on airplane mode." Fingers crossed, she didn't know the SOS feature can still be reached regardless of its status.

She shoved it back to me. "Read it. I don't need any more goody-goodies messing me up."

She held up the watch and punched in my code. I clicked on the tiny icon.

"Well?" she said.

"It's from Vince Castro."

"Who's that?" she hissed. The knife gleamed in the sun, making me squint.

"It's the photographer I contacted about his photos of the Supermoon."

"Read it."

"Vera, does it matter right now?"

"Read it!"

I did as instructed.

Hi Emily, Vince here. I still don't have any shots for you, but I do have a nugget that may help you find the other local photographer my wife and I met the other night. Her camera was much nicer than mine, so it would be worthwhile contacting her if it's still important to you. I had her name wrong. I said it was Carol or Cheryl. My wife saw my note to you. Called me a knucklehead. I've never been good with names. She corrected me. It was Vera. Hope that helps you find her.

Take good care, Vince.

I started to shake. *Holy guacamole.*

Vera seized the watch back and deleted the message. "I knew that blabbermouth might end up being a problem. Those two wouldn't leave me alone."

She tossed it into the trees. Off it went into the darkness.

"I'll deal with that later." A hard jab in the back. "Keep moving."

I risked turning one more time. Murray's paws were on the dashboard. He began to howl and whine. I tore my eyes off him and shut them briefly to stop the tears. A lump formed in my throat and it was becoming harder to stay calm. I chanced a question as I walked on. "Why did you do it?"

Her shallow breath hit my neck, giving me goosebumps. "That witch hated me. When I tried to work it out with her, she said she'd destroy my career and leave me with nothing. Didn't give a damn I was going to have Grant's kid. I knew then it was either me or her. And I'm a survivor."

Grant's kid? My head snapped sideways. "You're pregnant?"

She swore under her breath. "Guess it doesn't matter anymore. It was *my* pregnancy test the cops found. Not Jackie's. I was very willing to make a deal with her, too. All I asked for was some hush money. But she refused."

My hand flew to my mouth as alarm bells went off. "You thought Grant would leave her for you. Between your beauty and your pregnancy, you thought you'd get the guy. But he proposed to Jackie instead. He loved her."

She grabbed a handful of my hair and pulled my head back to whisper in my ear. "Aren't you quick?" She shoved me forward again, and I rubbed the spot, now ripe with pain. "He's got money, and I'm going to have his

243

child. He owes me, and she didn't like that. She tried to convince him to shut me out, give me nothing. She was going to go to Becka next and insist on having me fired. She wasn't going to stop until I was destitute and alone. Now move!"

My mind raced. Could I use that nugget of truth to save myself? Maybe I could convince Vera she'd have a sympathetic case worthy of little punishment, regardless if it was true or not. "What Jackie did was cruel. You can argue you were under extreme emotional strain. A pregnant woman fosters sympathy. You'll get a slap on the wrist. Maybe community service. At the very worst, temporary insanity."

She clicked the side of her mouth. "Guess I should've thought about that before killing Billy, too."

For a moment, I was speechless. My throat clamped shut, and I couldn't breathe. I met her gaze. Cool as fresh-fallen snow. Good grief. This woman was going to kill me and not even break a sweat.

Chapter Forty-Two

She shoved me hard, and I kept moving. Time to change tactics. *Do not talk about Billy.* If I was going to change her mind, I had to focus on what she wanted.

I swallowed my fear and perked up. "What if Grant was willing to listen now and support you? Maybe you could even plan a family together?"

She let out a hoarse, bitter laugh. "It's too late. Jackie got to him."

I paused. "There could still be a chance. The night she died they'd fought, she'd stormed off."

Another shove. "Friday night. She was probably upset he'd bought the wrong party favors, the diva. Do you want to know where I was? Taking photos of the Supermoon, trying to think about something other than my spiraling future. And what better than a natural wonder? Something to remind me that beauty still exists in the world. I went to the best spot in town to see it."

Overlook Point. "That's where you met..."

She huffed. "Yup, me, and Mr. & Mrs. Blabberface. Great view of the night sky, though. Worth the hassle. I wanted to capture how vast and huge the moon was compared to our little lives. That's why I included a photo with the cars. To capture the vastness of it."

I stopped again and frowned, then peered back at her. "Wait. You took those photos?"

One side of her mouth raised, and she stood taller. "Yeah, me. Smart, huh? I took the picture, not even realizing I was helping Future Me."

I seized the opportunity to stall my movement. I was also genuinely curious. "Did you put it online for me to find?"

She raised her chin. "Of course. Always one step ahead, Emily."

"So you took the photo and…" I trailed off.

"And I was about to leave when I saw *her*." Vera's nostrils flared, and her breathing became raspy and sharp. She pointed the knife at her own chest for the briefest of seconds before aiming it back at me. Her eyes narrowed into slits. "I was pregnant and alone while Jackie lived it up like some overindulged celebrity. She went outside, and I felt like it was a gift from the universe, an opportunity to confront her. I got in my car and sped down the mountain. I wanted to give her a piece of my mind."

I swallowed. "And then?"

"Jackie was there, all by herself. I pulled up next to her and tried to smooth things over. She called me pathetic for trying to steal her man. Said me and my unborn child were worthless."

A shot of sympathy went through me. "So you killed her."

"She thought I'd skulk away and cry myself to sleep." Her eyes flashed. "Instead? I reversed my car and floored it. She turned around just in time to see me plow her down. You should've seen her face. Shock. Fear. It was my turn to win, and she knew it."

I shut my eyes. I wanted to cry and scream and run. But I didn't. This was my opportunity. I had to appeal to the vulnerable part of Vera, the mother-to-be, if I wanted to survive. "Look, Vera, you made a mistake. I'll help you; tell the world that you were desperate and scared."

Vera studied me for a minute. Our eyes met. I held my breath. Then she blinked and shook her head. "Stop it."

My stomach flip-flopped. "Stop what?"

"You're trying to manipulate me." Her voice grew louder and raspier. Not good. "What would you tell people about Billy? Another mistake? Oops, one, and oops, two?"

"That can stay a mystery. He's a convicted felon, a biker. People will assume their deaths weren't connected."

"No, it won't work." She shoved me again and gestured for me to keep moving. "Besides, Billy had changed, and Noah knew it. He didn't believe the biker angle. He'd figure it out."

Probably true. And I should've let him. But for now, I needed her to keep talking, to stall her. I inched along, with her close behind, well aware that every second gave me more time to plan my escape. The sun was dropping. If I could get away from her, I could hide in the darkening forest. "How did Billy even get involved?"

She let out a deep sigh. "He was there. Parked down the road. Waiting for Becka. She was so angry at him over the affair she hadn't bothered to let him know she'd changed her mind about attending the party."

"Why did he help you?"

"I threatened to tell the cops we did it together. He knew they'd believe me, maybe not Noah, but others would, based on his past. He told me to drive to the shop, then followed me back. I left my car parked in the back among a dozen others and he took the damaged bumper off, replacing it with one he had in stock. That took care of the most obvious damage. It needed more work, so I left it there. Billy said he'd finish it the next day. He drove me home on his bike afterwards. That's when I got the burn. My leg touched the exhaust on his bike."

"He helped you," I said, turning to face her. "And you killed him." I wasn't sure which fact I found more troubling.

We'd reached a small clearing. She stopped moving. "The guy was no prize. He covered up a crime. It may sound like he was doing me a favor, but I think he was glad Jackie was dead. It made his life easier. It was true what I told you; he and Jackie slept together behind Becka's back."

Becka. She was innocent. Her only crime was to hide the fact that her boyfriend was a louse.

It made me think back to our first meeting at the café and the threatening note. "Why did you bother threatening Jackie on paper?"

"I have no idea what you're talking about."

Before I could say anything else, she kicked my ankle. The pain dropped me to the ground like a marionette without strings. *Ouch.* I pushed back my hair with shaking hands and looked up at her. Vera still held the knife up but, with her free hand, picked up a nearby rock. A big one, the kind that could do damage to a body if applied with force.

She grinned down at me. Her eyes had gone from void of emotion to wide and wild, like she'd had a shot of espresso delivered straight to her veins by an IV injection. Nausea hit me like a tsunami, coming out of nowhere, dragging me down, and making it hard to breathe. Heat rose inside me, and I could feel beads of sweat trickle down my neck. *This is it.* I could either give up now and die or fight to survive.

I jerked my foot, trying to move, but my ankle was too hurt. Not good. I looked up, a sense of desperation seizing me. "Vera, please."

She drew closer, her eyes fixated on mine. "Call me Minerva. We're not friends. Only my friends call me Vera."

A slow chill crept up my back. "Not Minnie?"

"Only my grandpa called me that. Like Minnie Mouse."

I felt like smacking my forehead. She was Anonymouse. I thought back to all her cute outfits, polka-dotted and pretty. "That's why you like red and white polka dots."

She pointed a shaking finger at me. "I told you to leave it alone. I sent you messages warning you to stop. But you wouldn't. So full of courage and conviction."

No sense in arguing. "You're right."

"Ironic you were the only one to doubt Rob's guilt. And after what he did to you. You kept digging, going over what happened. Once you found out about the pregnancy test, I knew you were too close."

I blinked. Of course. "That's why you didn't want me to see Grant. He might've told me the truth."

She glanced around the area. "I've been so good at staying off Noah's radar. But that would put me in the hot seat. He'd want to know what happened, start asking more questions. There were so many people who Jackie was awful to, I didn't even stand out. Unfortunately, you were determined to help your dirtbag ex-boyfriend and find the truth."

I swallowed. "Rob knows about the pregnancy, too."

She shook her head. "Not for sure. He didn't trust Jackie anymore."

I wracked my brain. I was running out of time. "What about Becka? She would tell the police Jackie couldn't have children. They would find out the test belonged to someone else. You'd be caught."

She began to circle me like a vulture. She gripped the rock tightly in her hand. She was getting ready to strike. "Becka has no reason to question Noah's decision. She's looking forward, not back."

"Then what about me?"

"You'll be an unfortunate accident. Out for a walk in the dark, a tumble over the cliff... oops."

I began to tremble. "You don't have to do this."

She huffed in irritation. "Wrong. Killing you may even help me. Everyone will be so busy grieving the loss of their precious Emily, Jackie will be old news. No one will even miss her."

Vera had everything worked out. There was nothing left to do but run. *I can ignore my ankle, the pain. There is no other choice. I don't want to die.* I turned to make an escape. It was dark now, especially in the forest. All I had to do was make it to a tree. If I could hide in the underbrush, I could slip away while she was looking somewhere else.

With a clipped breath, I took off. *Don't look back. You can do this.* I'd gone about ten paces before I felt a yank on my hair. My head snapped back, and I went tumbling.

The wind was knocked out of me. I scrambled to move. My fingers spread out, desperate to grip the ground and pull myself to safety. With shallow breaths, I dragged my body along the ground, hoping somehow I could find the strength to escape. My mind scrambled to think of a plan. What I could say. Promises I could make.

I'd only gone about two feet before I heard the snap of a branch right next to my ear. I froze. Vera was too close. I looked up in horror as she lifted a rock, preparing to bear down.

Then something happened. A mass of black fur flashed before me. Murray. Teeth bared, ready to attack. I barely recognized the gentle giant. He lunged at Vera and she went flying, landing with a hard whump against the rotting trunk of an old tree. The knife flung out of her hand. Murray began to bark and attack. A gurgling scream pierced my ears.

I lumbered away and yelled. "Murray! Get off!"

He turned and caught my gaze; his teeth bared like a shark's. "Stop," I commanded. He backed away but turned his focus back on Vera. He continued to bark and threaten, ready for more.

Fitz bounded out of the bushes, breathless. He bent forwards, resting his hands on his knees, then spotted me, still half in a heap. He jerked up. "Em!"

I shot my hand up, letting him know I wasn't hurt. "It's okay, Fitz, I'm good."

Fitz sprinted over and pulled me into a bear hug while Murray continued to guard Vera, not allowing her to move an inch without baring his teeth.

I drew back from Fitz's vice grip. "How did you know where to find me?"

Fitz pulled his phone out from the front pocket of his jeans. "We share our locations, remember? When I arrived and saw Murray in the Jeep going nuts, I knew something was wrong. I opened the door, and he shot out like a cannon."

Tears welled up. "Murball. My hero." I wanted to rush over and give him a hug, but I stopped myself. I didn't dare interrupt. He was at work. He'd get his hugs later.

Vera sat watching us in silent disgust.

I turned back to Fitz. "How did you even know I was in trouble?"

"You slunk out of the café, and my spidey senses told me something was up. I looked up your location on the map. I tried calling again, but you were MIA. When I saw your Jeep with Murray inside, I knew something was wrong."

Fitz's phone rang. It was Noah. From what I gathered, he was nearby with two deputies. Fitz bent down to examine my ankle. Murray was still on guard, happy to play the role of protector. A low but threatening growl emanated from his big, furry face. Vera dropped her head between her knees and folded her elbows across to block us out.

"Your ankle is swollen. I can't tell how badly it's hurt."

"It's tender, that's all."

"Are you injured anywhere else?" He started to examine me from head to foot.

I swatted him away. "Stop fussing. I'm fine. I have a super dog to protect me, remember?"

"Fair enough."

I pointed out the direction of where the knife had landed. Fitz soon found the weapon. He took off his button-down, long-sleeved flannel, leaving him in just a t-shirt. He picked the knife up, making sure to keep his hands tucked into the sleeve as he did to ensure none of his DNA or prints would be found. He wrapped it up and tucked it under one arm before pulling me close with the other. With Murray on guard, we waited in silence for the cavalry to arrive.

Chapter Forty-Three

Two hours later, Fitz and I were back at my apartment, Murray snoring by my feet. Once the police arrived on scene, Vera knew the gig was up. She confessed and switched tactics, leaning hard on her condition. Was pregnancy a viable defense? I'd heard that hormones were out of whack, but murder might be pushing the boundaries. Grant showed up at the station not long before we left. In a surprise move, he offered to pay for Vera's defense, citing she was the mother of his unborn child. He showed remarkable concern for her well-being and offered to bring her a proper meal from a local restaurant, so she and the baby wouldn't be subject to the stale cookies and coffee at the station while she underwent interviews.

"Why do you think Grant never mentioned Vera's pregnancy?" I said.

"Who knows?"

I thought about it. "Maybe the whole story of him fleeing town was just so that Vera could get me alone." I shuddered. "With Jackie gone and no one else to care for the baby, maybe Grant will step up and take responsibility."

"If his reaction to her arrest was any indication, I'd say there's a good chance."

I yawned. "Speaking of chances, I'm going to heat up the Tikka Masala in the fridge."

"If it's the one from last week, I'd scurry from that curry. Three to four days in the fridge max."

"Try and deny me of my spicy goodness, and I may have to sic Murray on you next."

We both peered down at Murray, whose tongue was half out of his mouth, drool puddling just underneath. "I think I'll take my chances."

Before I could argue, there was a soft knock on my door. Fitz and I exchanged a look. "If it's my mom, stall her while I jump out the window."

Fitz shook his head. "Couldn't be. Her knock is much more aggressive. When she's looking for you, I can hear her banging that door over the sound of grinding coffee."

He had a point. I hopped off the couch and opened the door. Noah stood there, a pizza box in hand. "Hey, wondered if you had a sec—" he paused when he spotted Fitz on the couch. "Hey, bro. Sorry, I didn't mean to interrupt. I just wanted to stop by and check-in."

Fitz stood up. "Everything okay?"

"Yeah. We're waiting on the arrival of a lawyer whose ETA is over an hour, so..." a sheepish look came over him as a pink hue filled his cheeks.

"Oh." Fitz's eyes widened, and he stood straighter. "Oh, yeah. Right."

I looked from one brother to the other. "Right, what?"

"Um," Fitz shot me a quizzical smile. "I need to go."

I frowned. "Where are you going?"

Fitz pointed from me to Noah. "Somewhere I don't have to witness this."

"Oh." I felt my face heat up as I noticed for the first time Noah wasn't in uniform. "Yup, okay then. See ya."

He gave an exaggerated shudder, then shot out the door.

I turned back to Noah. "Hey."

He gave his head a small shake. "Sorry, that was way more awkward than I'd anticipated."

I reached forward to grab the pizza box out of his hand. "When you arrive with food, all is forgiven."

"Good to know," he said with a grin. "I'll remember that."

I waved him inside and closed the door, gesturing toward the couch. I grabbed two plates from the cupboard and set them down with the pizza on the coffee table.

He opened the box and grabbed a slice before sitting down next to me.

I breathed in the mixture of musky, savory sauce, fresh dough, and cheesy goodness. "So…"

"So." He cleared his throat. "I wanted to come by and make sure you're okay."

"No need to worry," I said with a shake of my head. "I'm okay now. But…"

His eyebrows drew together. "What is it?"

Something had been niggling at me. "Can I ask one more question? It's been bothering me, and I can't figure it out."

"Go for it."

"I don't understand how that first note fits in. The one that Becka found at Jackie's place. What did it say? Something like, I will destroy you, I think. Vera didn't seem to know anything about it."

"Probably because it was written by Jackie."

I frowned. "Jackie? Why would she threaten herself?"

"She didn't. She posted it on the staff bulletin board in a fit of rage when she found out about Becka replacing her. A general threat to the staff she felt betrayed her."

My mouth dropped open. "You're kidding."

He shook his head. "Merle Fisher saw it first and took it down, assuming it was directed specifically at him. He hadn't yet learned about Becka's bid to take it over. He confronted Jackie with it and mid-argument, and ripped it in half, removing her name from the bottom portion of the note. She denied it was meant for him and snatched back the top half. My guess is she shoved it in her pocket and forgot about it until she got home from work when she emptied her pockets. Next to it was a pack of tissues and a lipstick tube. Becka jumped to conclusions, understandably, since she was upset and overwhelmed."

"That must've made things very confusing for your investigation."

"Sure did. The only DNA on the note belonged to Jackie, Becka, and Merle. Sent me down a rabbit hole. Once I got the story out of Merle, I switched my attention to Rob." He let out a long breath. "Vera was never even on my radar."

"Makes sense. Guess that's what happens when you have a habit of making enemies."

CHAPTER FORTY-THREE

He looked at me again. "I'm just glad to see you're not too shaken up."

"Knowing I have the best dog in the world goes a long way in lifting my mood. Plus, the whole killer-on-the-loose thing is over. My sense of relief far outweighs the drama of the day."

He nodded. "Good to hear."

I looked at him expectantly, waiting. I could see there was something else he wanted to say.

"Everything okay?" I asked.

He shifted in his seat. "Maybe this isn't the best time."

"For?"

He ran his hand through his hair. "I was just thinking that maybe next time, instead of coffee, we could have dinner."

I bit my lip to stop myself from smiling. "Oh yeah?"

"Yeah."

A warm feeling spread inside me as my heart flip-flopped. "Does that mean you've forgiven me for interfering in your case?"

"Not even close," he said with a shake of his head.

"Worth a try."

He raised an eyebrow. "You going to leave me hanging?"

"Nah. Maybe dinner's worth a try, too."

He nodded. "Alright then."

My phone pinged. "I better answer that."

He gave me a quizzical look.

"My Mom."

"Got it," he said with a laugh. "I'll leave you to it then." He stood up and strode to the door, then paused as he opened it. "I'll call you."

"Sounds good."

He saluted me, and I shut the door behind him, reaching for my phone with a grin.

Chapter Forty-Four

Friday, May 10th

Happy F.E.T.S. Day, all!

*What, you ask, is that? Forget Everything Tomorrow's Saturday!
Forget may be not the original word used, but my mom is home from
her Florida vacation and I'm not about to start dropping F-bombs now.*

Hi Mom.

*Besides, after a week of curse-free vocabulary, I'm beginning to come
around. Especially since all the drama of the day is behind us.*

*As you all know, there was an arrest in the murder of Jackie Hunter.
While I can't talk about the case, I'll tell you I'm feeling better now than
I have since the beginning of this nightmare. You've been my rock in a
hard place, and I can't thank you enough!*

*In the meantime, I also want to thank a few others who saved my life.
First of all, a huge thank you to Fitz Warner, who you all know as my
brother from another mother. He used his big brain and deductive skills
to figure out I was in trouble and needed help. Without him, I don't know
that I'd be here today or tomorrow unleashing my pearls of wisdom and
wit on the world (*Complaints can be mailed to the Longbourn Café in
Eliot Hill). Next is Superdog extraordinaire, Murray, who was almost
unrecognizable as the courageous canine who saved the day by taking
down the mortal enemy I didn't know I had. Finally, much gratitude
to Eliot Hill's Shining sheriff, Noah Warner, who took control of the*

situation and arrested the offender without a whisper of I-told-you-so about sticking my nose where it didn't belong.

LAST THING, don't forget to tune into WKRZ one week from today at 8 pm to watch me and my mom introduce a fun flick and demonstrate our no-bake almond butter chocolate cookies.

Talk soon, all!

Onward,
  Emily

Acknowledgements

There are so many people I'd like to thank who've helped me with this book. First, my amazing husband, Troy. I love you! His unwavering support and encouragement have allowed me to follow my dream and see it come to fruition. My children, Scarlett & Remy, whose love, laughter, and light fill me with joy and gratitude. I'm so lucky to be their mom. Also, to my mom and my aunt, who have read and reread this book with endless patience and eagle eyes.

To the team at Level Best Books, particularly Shawn Reilly Simmons, thank you for believing in me and giving this book a chance.

I'm thrilled to thank my awesome agent, Carolyn Forde. To have you in my corner is an endless source of confidence and inspiration.

To Hannah Mary McKinnon. I don't know how you do it all. You are a rockstar and I'm grateful for your insight, advice, and most-of-all, your friendship.

Vicki Delany, thank you for all your help and support. You are my cozy icon.

To my writing group, the Deadlies, (Melodie Campbell, Des Ryan, Cheryl Freedman, Joan O'Callaghan) thank you for listening and sharing your thoughts on all my WIPs.

Finally, to the readers. Thank you for spending time with Emily, Fitz, and the rest of the cast. This was such a fun book to write. I hope you enjoy their story.

About the Author

Sydney Leigh spent several years running a seasonal business, working in the summer so she could spend cold months in cool places. Now she writes mysteries and thinks about murder. She served on the board of Crime Writers of Canada from 2018-2021.

AUTHOR WEBSITE:
 www.sydneyleighbooks.com

SOCIAL MEDIA HANDLES:
 Instagram: @sydneyleighauthor
 Facebook: sydneyleighauthor
 X: @sydneyleighcozy
 Threads: sydneyleighauthor

Also by Sydney Leigh

Peril in Pink, Crooked Lane Books, 2024.

www.ingramcontent.com/pod-product-compliance
Lightning Source LLC
Chambersburg PA
CBHW020415110726
47899CB00006B/1992